Prom
EVER AFTER

Prom
EVER AFTER

Dona Sarkar
Caridad Ferrer
Deidre Berry

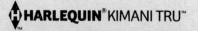

HARLEQUIN® KIMANI TRU™

Recycling programs
for this product may
not exist in your area.

PROM EVER AFTER

ISBN-13: 978-0-373-09147-8

Copyright © 2014 by Harlequin Books S.A.

The publisher acknowledges the copyright holders of the individual works as follows:

HAUTE DATE
Copyright © 2014 by Dona Sarkar

SAVE THE LAST DANCE
Copyright © 2014 by Barbara Caridad Pollak

PROM AND CIRCUMSTANCE
Copyright © 2014 by Deidre Berry

Printed in U.S.A.

CONTENTS

Dedication

To Bonnie Sarkar Grundtner: my baby sister and best friend,
for *unconditionally* and *always* being on my side. I can hardly believe the
loyal, beautiful woman you've become and I couldn't be prouder of you.

Acknowledgments

There are so many people I need to thank and there is such precious
little page space to do so! First and foremost, my amazing agent
Elaine Spencer. You've been the one who's always believed in me during
this crazy publishing journey. Thank you for reading and re-reading every
piece of every manuscript and contract like life depended on it. You're an
amazing woman. To Tara Gavin, Carly Silver and the Harlequin Kimani
team…you guys are miracle workers. Thank you for believing in me!

To my incredible plotting (and gossiping!) group: Kelli, Carolynn and
Lacey…you guys are the most talented and hilarious trio of women I've
ever met. Thank you for nursing me back to writing!

To my wonderful around-the-world family for being there for me
during the darkest and lightest days. I love you so much more than
you'll let me say. Thank you for embracing all the changes this year has
brought! Thank you for letting me liberally borrow your personalities for
my characters—you'll find yourselves in this book more than ever!

To my team at work: Told you you'd end up in my novels!
(Thank you for being the most wonderful group of people I could ever
ask to work with—jackassery, karaoke and all!)

To my fabulous Seattle-crew: you guys are my "Lean-In" circle, you guys
are my text-message-rant response team, you guys are what makes
every single day beautiful. I never knew how loved I was.
Thank you, thank you, thank you!

To Doug Watkins, I promise to make you fall in love with me every single
day and yet still, I can never repay you for what you've given me.

HAUTE DATE
Dona Sarkar

one

"NICE scooter!"

Ash Montague ignored the male voice as she dismounted her Vespa and removed her helmet. She glanced up at the storefront located on the side of the historic Fairmont hotel that held the key to her happiness: a prom dress so stunning and so unique that it would hopefully knock Armstrong Jones out of his disinterested hipster mode...for good.

A wolf whistle followed.

Ash tended to draw a lot of attention around town when she went anywhere on her burgundy Vespa. People apparently weren't used to seeing girls scooting around Seattle on little two-wheeled vehicles, especially while wearing dresses and ladybug-print helmets. "The expected was never memorable," Ash's glamorous globe-trotting grandmother, Glamma, had always said, and Ash stuck to that mantra as a tribute, even four years after her passing.

"Hey! I'm talking to you. Don't be a bitch." The voice was suddenly behind her.

Ash whirled around, startled. The voice had sounded like it was from across the street. She didn't like that someone had sneaked up on her so quickly.

The guy had to be in his *thirties*. Gross. He was standing in front of her, way too close, trying to look casual, jeans ripped down both thighs, thumbs tucked into his back pockets. Behind him were a group of men and women, all in the same skinny jeans, all seeming to be waiting for a bus. All of them stopped typing on their phones and were now watching her to see what she would do next. None of them looked as though they were in any hurry to help.

Jerks.

"Oh!" Ash forced herself to smile. If he thought he was going to intimidate her, he was about to be surprised. "You want to show off for your friends! Sorry, I didn't realize."

The guy's grin dropped for a millisecond, then the smirky expression returned. "Don't you know you're supposed to say 'thank you' when someone compliments you?"

Ash continued to smile sweetly as she reached into her purse and grabbed her cell phone. "I'm so sorry for my oversight. Let me give you my number."

The guy looked pleased at this and turned around to make sure his audience was still rapt with attention.

They were.

"Smile!" Before he could react, Ash snapped a picture with her phone. "For my 'pictures of pedophiles' collection. You know, for that show with the undercover cops. There's a bunch of them over there—" she head-gestured toward the Starbucks on the corner "—filming this right now. You're about to be famous!"

The guy's face changed in a second. Eyes widened, mouth dropped. In an instant, he was gone. She heard his footsteps as he skidded around the corner.

Ash blew out the breath she'd been holding—she hadn't realized how scared she'd been till just then. She did a little curtsy for the audience at the bus stop. Most of them looked shocked; a few pantomimed applause.

That guy was not going to be messing with her—or any other girl—for a while. She hoped, anyway.

Ash's apprehensive mood vanished as soon as she set foot inside Rebel Without a Dress. There was no longer a doubt in her mind that love at first sight was actually a thing. She reached out and paused, almost afraid to touch the most beautiful dress she'd ever seen. It was so perfect, it might simply disappear into thin air.

"Melanie, that is a customer who just came in. Don't stand there like a mannequin. Greet her. Make yourself useful," a sharp voice cut through the angels' choir in Ash's head.

Ash glanced over at the tall, basketball player–looking girl with a halo of frizz around her head who was the subject of the yelling. She looked familiar. Poor thing was now stumbling toward her after being dressed down by her boss, a pinched-nose, pale blonde woman who had a disgusted expression on her would-have-been-pretty face.

"Hi. Hi. Sorry I didn't come over earlier. Can I help you?" the lanky girl asked breathlessly.

Ash smiled at her, feeling sorry for the girl for having such a nasty manager. She recognized Melanie as a sophomore who frequently loped through the hallways like an antelope, always with a surprised expression on her face. She was a cute girl and would be enviably graceful and willowy once she grew into her long limbs. Ash was always envious of tall people—the one thing she would never be able to accomplish.

Melanie grinned back as she watched Ash lift the hanger off the rack and hug it close. "Would you like to try it on?"

"I would like to marry it." Ash twirled the orange silk dress around in the air. "God, it's beautiful."

"I'll open you a dressing room. We only got that one in

two sizes, the one you have there and...huge. I'll make sure no one else gets to see it before you."

Ash handed it over and made the rounds of the store, half-heartedly sorting through generic-looking dresses and accessories, occasionally stopping to make sure no one else was going into *her* dressing room. She was not letting the Dreamsicle, as she'd already deemed the dress, out of her sight.

"You're going with Armstrong Jones, right?" Melanie was back at her side in an instant. "God, you're so lucky. I love his blog. And his podcast. Is he really that funny?"

"Yes, he's amazing." Ash couldn't help but feel smug. Yes, yes, yes, she was going with Armstrong Jones, their school's star blogger and podcaster. His series on observations of society was so hilarious that local colleges had started asking him to blog for them, as well. Plus, he was incredibly hot in that skinny-on-purpose kind of way.

It had taken him four years to notice her. She was determined not to lose his interest on prom night, when his sensors would be in full gear looking for material for his blog. That gorgeous orange dress waiting for her in the dressing room would hopefully ensure that. She wanted the contents of his blog cynically recapping the prom to be vague because he hadn't been able to take his eyes off of her the whole evening.

"Melanie! Why are you just standing there like a statue in the garden of good and evil? Bring her other options!" The painfully thin voice of Melanie's boss barked more orders. "What is the matter with you? Move faster!"

Jeez, this manager was horrible. Plus, every time she screamed, Ash jumped as though she were committing a crime.

Before Melanie could start pushing things Ash didn't want to see anyway, Ash charged straight toward the dressing room, pausing at the checkout counter where Melanie's boss was poring over a catalog.

"I just wanted to say—" Ash gave the manager her sweetest smile "—I *love* that this store kind of just lets you shop. I hate when salespeople follow you around like you're about to steal something. Or trying to make you buy tie-dyed Ugg boots or something to drive up commission. That's so insulting."

The blonde supervisor didn't even look up from what she was reading.

"You should give Melanie a raise or something. She helped me find the best dress ever," Ash prodded.

Still nothing.

Wow. Poor Melanie. This job must pay well, at least.

Ash shot a sympathetic glance at Melanie and she ducked into her dressing room. She was so excited to try on the dress that she started to shed her '50s-style polka-dot dress into a ball even before fully closing the door behind her. She slipped the silky dreaminess of the Dreamsicle over her shoulders and watched it flutter to the ground.

It was lovely.

It made her look fun and regal at once—a difficult achievement when one was not quite five foot two inches, and in laceless Skechers at that. The color made her light olive skin glow. Her new Bettie Page bangs over her shoulder-length bob went elegantly with the dress's strapless neckline.

The dress had a dropped-waist bodice and a hem that stopped at mid-thigh in the front. In the back was a long, drapey train that fluttered every time Ash moved. The Dreamsicle was a glorious tangerine peacock.

The pièce de résistance was a series of boomerang-shaped cutouts all up and down both sides that showed off Ash's midsection, which she usually never thought much about. The ten years of tae kwon do her father had insisted on were *finally* paying off for something. Other than the defending of the small and nerdy, of course.

She couldn't believe she actually felt…pretty. Not just "kind of cute." But actually pretty. She almost squealed when she looked at her reflection again.

She quickly texted her neighbor and best friend, Sebastian, who'd accompanied Ash's mom to the bookstore down the street. Mission accomplished. Come see. Bring Mom.

Ash did a spin to the latest beat pulsating through the dressing room and stared at herself some more. She wanted Armstrong Jones to look at her as though he was looking at a vintage record from 1970. Would this dress do the trick? She was sure she'd be the only girl at the prom in it.

For weeks, Ash had worried she wouldn't find a dress that was cool, fun, unusual and most of all, unforgettable. All the things Armstrong was…and thought she was, too. She was not going to prove him wrong with some generic one-shoulder satin dress in an Easter-egg color.

Prom season was in full effect in Seattle, and every store in the city had its best selections out. Ash had purposely chosen Rebel Without a Dress, the most eclectic store in the downtown area, knowing most girls from her school didn't even know the store existed, much less remembered it during prom season. It was hidden away behind Luly Yang, Seattle's most famous couture dress boutique.

Armstrong hated mainstream things. And the Dreamsicle was the opposite of mainstream. She couldn't believe she'd snagged the only one in her size.

Fate. Destiny. Perfection.

Ash whipped out a matte red lipstick and sharpened her Cupid's bow.

Perfect. Her mother was going to be blown away.

Minutes later, Ash heard her mom's telltale high-pitched English accent.

"Ash! Ash are you in here? Where are you, darling? I don't see you!"

"Mom, in here!" Ash stuck her hand up in the air and waved, hoping Sebastian had come, too. This dress might need some convincing on the parental front due to the cutout situation. Sebastian was always good with her parents.

"Ashmitha!"

"Here!" She waved harder.

Ash heard peals of giggling from the dressing room next to her. Great. Witnesses. Embarrassment galore. At least the chances of their knowing her were slim.

"Mom! Seb! Seriously, you guys?" Ash stuck her head out from behind the door, wondering why this was so difficult. Her petite, dark-featured doppelgänger mother and tall, fauxhawked Sebastian stood right in front of the door, the complete odd couple. "Right here. I'm not deaf—you don't need to yell."

"Well, you don't answer, love. And no one can hear anything over this atrocious music."

Could she be any louder or more embarrassing? Ash hoped the girls who'd been giggling earlier couldn't hear the conversation over the music.

Ash saw Sebastian stifling a laugh.

"Sebastian said you found a dress."

"I did."

"Will you do us the grand honor of showing it to us then? Or are we to figure out what it is by means of osmosis?"

"Mom! This. Is. Amazing. You'll love it. Are you ready?"

Laila Montague did her own version of an eye roll. "Breathlessly."

"Okay, be amazed." Ash threw open the door with a hard bang.

Laila blinked as she looked over the dress top to bottom. Sebastian's eyes widened.

"That's...not good." Her mother was not known for tact.

"What? The fact that it doesn't already belong to me? You bet it's not good." Ash swirled the skirt around and around for effect, watching her reflection.

"No, the dress is horrid."

Ash's mouth dropped open. She couldn't be serious. The dress was amazing. She'd never seen anything like it before.

"*Mom!* You're being mainstream again. Seb, tell her not to be judgmental."

"Seb, tell Ash it's not judgmental to speak the truth. It's horrid. That color. Those...open parts." She gestured vigorously at the cutouts. "Why is it so short in the front? Did they run out of material? We can buy them some more at Nancy's Sewing Basket and fill in the rest."

"Seb!" Ash implored. Her mother was on one of her rants and only Seb could make her see reason.

"Mrs. M, the dress is really...unusual. And it does make Ash look very...tall."

"Sebastian, don't fall prey to my daughter's manipulation. You're smarter than that."

"Oh, Mrs. M. I'm staying neutral. Just showing a potential defense."

Ash's mother, a defense lawyer, raised an eyebrow at him.

He held up his hands in surrender. "Your dad. Smart man for staying home, that's all I'll say."

Ash exhaled, her blunt-cut bangs blowing straight up in the air. This was *not* going well.

"No matter," Laila continued. "I'm sure this shop is quite

expensive. How much is this dress?" She attempted to reach for the price tag.

"Does perfection really have a price?" Ash twirled around again, trying to keep her voice low and herself out of her mother's clutches. *Everyone* didn't need to know they couldn't afford anything. Plus, she hadn't had a chance to check, she'd been so blown away at its beauty. "Just look at how amazing it is. How one of a kind. No one else will have this."

"That's for sure. You couldn't pay me thirty-five dollars to wear that in public," her mother said. "How much is it?"

Ash grabbed the price tag. "Perfection at the low price of…$799."

Yikes. That was a lot more expensive than she'd thought it would be. This was about to get worse.

Her mother's eyes widened. "For *this* dress? This unfinished, cutout spectacle?"

Even Sebastian looked surprised, but thankfully said nothing.

"I'll help pay for it! I promise!" Though she had no idea how that was going to happen. The prom was less than a month away and she hadn't had the forethought of having a paying job during the school year. She *knew* she should have charged for her tae-kwon-do instruction to the younger students!

"Ash, you're not leaving this dressing room in this dress. It's…vulgar."

"Mumsie, please!" Ash tried the name she'd used to call her mother when she was younger. "I'll pay you back every cent of the dress by the time the prom arrives. I'll even put a down payment today!" She recalled having six dollars in her purse.

"Please change and let's go straightaway. We won't be able to afford anything in here. I've told you this before. Don't look at me with that hurt-puppy expression, love!" And with that,

Laila left the dressing room. Sebastian gave Ash a sorry look before trailing her mother out.

No. Ash stood hopelessly in the corridor. This was not happening.

"Harsh," said a familiar voice. The dressing-room door next to Ash's opened. Two girls from the soccer team came out, each with armloads of dresses.

There went the "no one knew about this store" theory.

"Wow." Jessica Moriarty, the taller but less-pretty one pointed at the Dreamsicle. "I'd love to try that on if you're not going to get it. That's amazing."

Ash's cheeks burned. "I *am* going to get it."

"Yeah, okay." Jessica shrugged and giggled in her friend's direction. "Maybe you can find something like it at a thrift shop or something. You know…*vintage.*"

Jessica didn't mean it in a helpful way. The Montague family's lifestyle had changed dramatically in the past year and, instead of shopping at Lululemon or Nordstrom like most of her friends, Ash had to resort to vintage scrounging at secondhand shops such as Crossroads Trading Co. and Red Light in Capitol Hill. She'd tried to do her best to make the full-skirted halter dresses, petticoats and sneakers look as deliberate as possible. At least they looked cute with her dad's vintage scooter when she pulled into the school's parking lot and always was able to park directly in front.

Though most people complimented her funky, offbeat style, Ash worried people were talking about her behind her back. Like Jessica, but actually discreetly.

Melanie appeared by Ash's side as the two girls left, still giggling between them. "I'll hide it for you. In the back. No one will know. Can you buy it by next weekend?" she whispered.

Ash shook her head and slammed the door before she started

crying in front of Melanie. The Dreamsicle was the last one in her size… There was no way it would be there past the weekend, even if Melanie did her damn best to keep it safe for her.

TWO

"Ash!"

Ash raised her head as she heard her mother's voice from downstairs.

"Your ladyship, please come down here."

She lay back down. She was never talking to Laila again. How could she have humiliated her in the store like that? In front of Jessica and that other girl. She was sure word of her mother yelling at her about being poor would get around school before lunchtime.

"Ashmitha, it's a surprise. You will like it. It's for your prom."

Ash was out of her bed in three seconds. Her mother had gone back to Rebel and bought the dress. She knew it. She knew her mother couldn't be so cruel as to deny her oldest daughter her only wish for her senior prom.

Ash flew down the stairs and came to a landing in the front hall, where her mother stood holding...not the Dreamsicle.

"What's this? Where's the dress?"

"This is."

Ash looked over the boxy, beaded two-piece tunic and skirt. It was about the furthest thing from the dress possible. "What are you talking about?"

"I'd like you to wear this to your prom."

Ash almost fell over. "What do you mean?"

"I told you you could go to the prom if you could keep within the hundred-dollar budget. Now you can. You will have extra money now for that nice dinner before." Laila genuinely looked pleased with herself.

"Mom, that's like some Indian costume. I can't wear that out of the house, much less to the prom!"

Laila's eyes narrowed. "This is not a costume. This is what I wore on the last day of my wedding. It was a gift from your Glamma."

Ash's heart hurt at the mention of her Glamma. She was the one who related to Ash the best and understood her desire for pretty, fun things. Ash still missed her every day.

"This *lehenga* is what you call a 'vintage' garment. It's better than anything you'll find at the store," Laila added.

Oh, God, her mother was going to get all 1950s Indian on her. "Mom, I'm pretty sure even girls in India don't wear these things to the prom."

"There is no prom in India. Or in England where I was a girl."

"No wonder you don't understand. You really do want me to be a freak," Ash muttered, hoping her mother wouldn't hear, but also hoping she would.

"I'm telling you, at this rate and with your remarks, you are not going to your prom, either." Her mother hung the dress on the coatrack in the front hallway and stalked past Ash. "I'm feeling quite regretful I'm even allowing you to spend money on a dress that you'll wear exactly once!"

Ash knew she'd hurt her mother's feelings, but she wasn't going to be the laughingstock at school with some garish costume. It was bad enough that she wore someone's old clothes every single day. Not for prom. She wouldn't be a hand-me-down girl for the prom, too.

She heard the faint sounds of the television and a keyboard clicking.

"Dad!" Ash spun around into the living room.

"I heard nothing. I saw nothing." Josh Montague was in his usual position, laptop on his lap, parked in front of the television, which played another rerun of *Project Runway*.

Her parents were polar opposites, and Ash thought it was a miracle that they'd even met, much less had been crazy-in-love married for twenty years. Ash loved telling her friends the story of charismatic Josh Montague, who had won a scholarship to study music abroad at the beautiful University of Granada in Spain. He had been in awe of his beautiful orientation leader on the first day: the no-nonsense Laila Ray.

Apparently, Laila had been a lifesaver for non-Spanish-speaking Josh, and he had promptly fallen in love with her and convinced her to take a train to Madrid with him for the weekend, and they had eloped before the semester was up. They'd spent a few years in London while Laila had gotten her law degree, and Josh had pursued computer science when he realized a music degree wasn't going to take him too far in supporting his new bride.

Ash still couldn't believe her practical lawyer of a mother had left England behind to follow Josh to Seattle so he could make his software dreams a reality. Till this day, he was the one who could charm her into anything.

"Dad, seriously. You need to talk to her. Where am I going to get a prom dress for a hundred dollars? And I'm not wearing that *lehenga* thingie."

"I think it's important for you to learn some negotiation strategies that don't involve yelling," a voice piped up knowingly from the corner of the room.

Ash shot a "get lost" look to Sonali, her little sister, who was in her usual position, hiding behind an easel that was bigger than her entire body. Ash caught a glimpse of Sonali's face.

"What did you do to your hair?" she demanded. Her sister had some sort of tangled bird's nest-looking hairdo on top of her head, very different from the satin sheet of black hair she'd left home with that morning.

Sona ducked back behind the easel out of Ash's line of sight.

"You better tell me, Sona. Right now."

Ash marched back to where Sona was hiding and grabbed her arm to make her stand. Gods. All of her hair was in a tangled, knotted mess. Ash couldn't even get her fingers through a lock of it. It was like someone had superglued it into a knot.

"Ow, stop!"

"Who did this to you?"

"Let go!" Sona pulled away her arm and sat back down. "I did it myself."

Ash glanced at her dad with an are-you-hearing-this look.

Josh shrugged. "She wouldn't tell me, either."

"Tell me what happened." Ash lowered her voice. "Did something happen at school?"

"I just wanted to do something different with my hair." Sona was the worst liar in the world. "That's not illegal."

Bad enough that the eleven-year-old was some sort of artistic genius, but was also in the progress of becoming a bully's target, apparently. The only person who was allowed to mess with her sister was her. Ash vowed to figure out who and why, and would resort to spying on her sister to do so.

"Let it go," Josh murmured. "She'll tell us when she's ready."

Ash disagreed. Sona was like a timid baby deer outside the

house… That was one of the main reasons their parents sent Sona to a very small private school for gifted artists.

"Why don't you come to the mall with me? You'll see what I'm talking about." Ash turned her attention back to her father. "Please? Please, please, please? I'll write the band's next song."

"Your mother's the decision maker on this one, love. I'm sorry."

"Next two songs."

"No."

"Daaaaaaaaaaaad."

"Some cheese with that whine?"

"Dad! Come on. Why don't we have a gig and charge cover this weekend? We can play the new stuff. I swear I'll learn it fast. We'll earn enough for the dress in a night."

The best thing about having Josh Montague home full-time was that there was more music in the house than ever before. He and Ash had started a band with a few other neighbors and were in the process of working on their first real set to play at the next neighborhood barbecue.

"I can pretty much assure you that giving people opportunities is more important than any dress. Ever." Josh had that stern note in his voice, signifying that he was no longer playing.

Ash sighed. Of course that was true. She'd even come up with the idea to donate any gig money they made to the inner-city school Josh had grown up in.

Josh always said he owed his life to the music program at his high school. Many of his friends had ended up in juvie… or worse. Josh had spent his teenage years learning every instrument from piano to guitar to the French horn. He vowed to always give back whatever he could, whether it was a little or a lot.

It had been very little the past year due to the family's financial situation. Josh had left his small tech company the previous year when it had started to go under. He'd been actively job hunting, but the opportunities were slim in an industry that was obsessed with kids out of college, not "people old enough to have kids in college."

He'd spent the last year writing apps for phones to earn some income, while her mother's law firm had been cutting out billable hours for the attorneys. Money had been tight on just her mother's salary, especially considering Ash's Seattle Academy tuition and Sonali's specialized art school. The family's lifestyle was far different from what Ash was used to… or from what all of her friends at school had.

Ash had heard her parents fighting—actually fighting—for the first time in her life over their financial worries. She understood their reasons for not wanting to spend a lot on the prom…but she knew she could find a way to pay her mother back for the dress if she only had a chance.

"Prom is a night when women are objectified. I think I'll boycott mine," the know-it-all piped up again, as if someone had asked for her opinion. "I'd rather give that money to an education program for young artists."

"Quiet, or I'll beat you, too," Ash ordered.

"Don't maul your sister. House rule number two," Josh said automatically, without looking up from his laptop screen.

"You actually went to the prom, Dad." Ash directed her tantrum at her father. "How much did your date's dress cost? I bet it was over a hundred dollars even in the '70s!"

"Hey, hey, hey. My prom was in the '80s, thank you very much. And Jeannie made her dress with her older sister's help. It was a big puffy yellow thing. Like one of those marshmallow–chicken things you get at Easter. Do you want me to call her and ask if you can borrow it?"

Ash shot eye daggers at her father.

"Just being helpful." Her father shrugged. "You've got to get with the program before the program gets you."

God, her parents were dorky.

"You people are seriously going to drive me crazy," Ash muttered as she grabbed her coat. "I'm going to Sebastian's!"

three

ASh glared at Sebastian in the middle of their drafting class the next day. He was still completely unconcerned about the prom situation, as he'd been the previous evening.

"I should just tell Armstrong I can't go with him. I mean, why drag it out? I should call it off now so he can find someone else. Someone with a dress instead of some belly dancer–looking costume."

Sebastian was focusing a little too hard on their drafting project still. No answer.

She knew she was being kind of a brat, but couldn't help herself.

"I should just call it off *right* now."

Still no answer.

"Like today."

She sighed loudly.

Sebastian finally glanced up from the giant sheet of paper he'd been leaning over.

"Oh, is it time for drama? Is it my turn? Noooo, Ash, you can't. You and Armie-boy belong together. Like forevvvvver."

Did no one have sympathy for her plight? Did no one understand that she was actually not going to be able to go to the prom this year—her senior year? She wouldn't have prom pictures, she wouldn't have the first dance, she wouldn't have that magical night she'd be talking about for years to come with her own kids and grandkids. And most importantly, she wouldn't have another chance with Armstrong.

"I don't like you," was all she could think of to say to Sebastian.

"You love me. Now, we need to do our assignment. What do you think? How many watchtowers, if any?"

"I don't care."

"Hey, you wanted the front of the school. You at least have to choose if you want a watchtower or not."

"I want a moat." Ash stuck out her lower lip. "And alligators. And that dress!"

Sebastian sighed. "Just have the tantrum and let me know when you're done."

Ash glared at him.

Sebastian ignored her and went back to sketching pointy roofs. He wrinkled his forehead and chomped down hard on the corner of his mouth as he worked expertly with the protractor. He looked cute today, in a dark blue University of Michigan T-shirt that clung well to his arms, a fact every girl, freshman through senior, had clearly noticed.

He was easily one of the cutest guys in the senior class. He knew it, but he also knew he was smart. He'd already gotten accepted into Michigan's honors program and amazingly, was still invested in keeping his GPA a 4.0.

"You can fail and repeat senior year and have another shot at the prom." Sebastian could tell she was not working without even looking up. "Get to work."

The small, twelve-person drafting class had a joint assignment. Each team of two was to choose a section of Seattle Academy to redesign into whatever style they wanted. The second part of class would be to take the flat sketches, make them into 3-D models and actually build a miniature version of the school redesign. The redesign would be displayed in the front entryway of the school to show off their skills.

Other teams had predictably chosen the gym or the cafeteria, which would've been much easier. Ash had insisted on choosing the front of the school—saying it needed to look majestic and haunting all at once. Plus she wanted her work to be the thing people saw first when they looked at the miniature. So far, Sebastian had done all the actual drawing work, while Ash had tossed out opinions every once in a while when things looked off. She was the creative force. Every team needed one.

When Sebastian still didn't respond to her threat of not going to the prom, Ash grabbed her pencil and within minutes had replicated the dress on the corner of their sheet of paper.

God, it was beautiful. She darkened the lines of the cutouts on the bodice. She didn't care what her mother said, the bodice was beautiful and it had looked great on her.

"How goes it?" Mr. Watkins's voice caused Ash to drop her pencil and let out a small scream. "Sorry, Ash, didn't mean to startle you."

"Uh…" Ash tried to cover up her dress sketch with her arm. The drafting teacher was very young and pretty cute, and generally gave interesting assignments, but he was also very detention-happy. If anyone was caught texting, tweeting, on Facebook, taking selfies, thinking about taking selfies or generally doing anything else but the assignment, he immediately gave them weekend detention, which meant cleaning the garage for auto shop, which he also taught. She did *not* want detention.

"What's this?" He turned the paper around to see what Ash had been working on.

"Oh. That." Sebastian cut in before Ash could make up a

lame excuse. "Ash and I were having a discussion. An argument, let's say."

Mr. Watkins's eyebrows rose. "About some ugly dress?"

"It's not ugly!" Ash's mouth dropped open. "You guys are mean!"

Sebastian grinned. "I was attempting to prove to my lab partner here that there are so many similarities between classic drafting professions such as architecture and…fashion."

"There are not." Ash rolled her eyes, not playing along, as she assumed Seb would want her to.

"Actually…" Mr. Watkins tilted his head. "I'd like to hear what Sebastian has to say on this one."

Ash looked to Sebastian. "Let's hear the crazy."

"Drawing flat sketches. Visualizing them in 3-D. Being able to put pieces together that fit and stay that way over a course of time. It's architecture," Seb insisted. "Look at the dress Ash is wearing for example."

Both of them looked. Ash self-consciously smoothed down the puffy skirt of the navy cap-sleeve dress with tiny white bicycles printed all over it.

"The flat sketch of the sleeves—" Sebastian pulled the sleeve away from Ash's arm "—would look something like this." He quickly sketched a triangle. "But when it was modeled in 3-D, it would look more like this." He made the triangle into a pyramid. "And the three pieces of fabric to make the sleeve would have to be sewed to make the pyramid. Fashion is an engineering problem."

"Mr. Diaz, I'm impressed by your knowledge of both fashion and architecture."

"Thank you."

"Carry on, you two. But please save your debates for when you're done with the assignment." He walked away.

Ash breathed a sigh. No scrubbing oil off the floor of the garage this weekend!

"Thanks for the save. Though the excuse was such BS. I can't believe he fell for that." Ash picked up her pencil again and started to actually work on the watchtower of their castle entranceway.

"It wasn't a save." Seb was being serious. "Your dad has *Project Runway* on 24/7 in your house, in case you haven't noticed."

Ash gave him a so-what look. Her dad had become oddly obsessed with any show where people gave up everything to pursue their life's dreams. She was pretty convinced he'd run off and audition for *The Apprentice* one of these days.

"I've been absorbing that show while I'm at your place. So much of it sounds like the stuff we learn in here."

Sebastian had been building a website for his family's church and had been working on it mostly out of Ash's house so he could get Josh's input on design. Apparently he'd been learning a thing or two, however wrong, about fashion, as well.

Ash leaned over and gave Sebastian a side-hug. "You're cute when you're wrong. But thanks anyway."

"I'm not wrong!" Sebastian looked insulted.

"I love having a guy as a best friend, but seriously Seb. Fashion…definitely not the same as some boring old building!"

"Hey." Ash tried to sound casual as she slipped into a seat behind Armstrong Jones in their Brit-lit class. Every time she got near him, she lost her nerve to say the fun, carefree line she'd come up with the night before. Every. Time.

"Cute dress. I like it with the Vans."

She'd worried that checkered Vans with a printed dress was too much, but apparently not. Before Ash could thank him, he was off on a tirade. "Don't you hate the reading list? God, it's so mainstream. Do we really all need to read *Emma* or *Wuthering Heights?* Why can't we find something a little more obscure... Something actually original? Like *The Doctor's Wife.* Or *East Lynne.* Or at least some Kipling everyone hasn't read a hundred times over. God."

"I know!" Ash nodded along. She had no idea what he was talking about. She loved all the Jane Austen readings they'd done, but didn't want to look *overly* mainstream.

Armstrong was unflappably awesome. She just loved the way he knew everything about literature. And even though she had no idea what he was talking about half the time, it had played to her advantage.

Ash had watched Armstrong from afar for years—commenting on the pieces he wrote for the school blog, sitting in the first row when he had the role of Jean Valjean in the previous year's *Les Misérables,* admiring the fact that he made being a scholarship kid look cool. He relished being a thrift-store junkie and the fact that his parents were frequently unemployed.

Ash had found out Armstrong was taking Brit lit that semester and had immediately registered for the class. She had made sure to grab the seat behind him on the first day, knowing the teacher considered those seats permanent.

She had also gladly accepted Armstrong's help when he'd offered to proofread her second paper on Jane Austen when the first one she'd written hadn't gone over so well. Laila had had a fit when she'd seen Ash come home with a B. "An English paper? A 'B'? You're half British for heaven's sake, you should be *teaching* the class!"

Ash had gotten an A on her second paper and despite this, had asked Armstrong to help proofread her third, as well. He didn't have too many changes to suggest, but she'd effervescently attributed the A-plus, the highest grade in the class, to his help. He'd asked her to the prom shortly after.

"Want to go thrifting this weekend?" Armstrong asked without looking up from his phone, where his fingers worked furiously to live-tweet whatever was on his mind.

Ash burst into a smile. "Absolutely!" She cursed herself for sounding so pathetically pleased.

"I could use a suit for the prom. Maybe. I don't know."

Ash's smile slowly faded. Here she was totally freaking out about what to wear and he hadn't even thought about it?

"So…the prom after-party. What are you thinking?" Ash asked casually, hoping he would ask her what *she* wanted to do. The senior class was planning an all-night "lock-in" at the school with dance contests, food, music and movies. Her parents had already agreed to let her go given that it was chaperoned and didn't cost anything extra. Ash was almost more excited about that than the prom.

"After-parties are so…I don't know, cliché. Don't you think? I mean the prom is such a cliché alone, right?" Armstrong turned back to face her. "I love that about you—you hate clichés."

"Hate them," Ash agreed, though she didn't understand what was so cliché about the after-party. This was the first year the school was having it.

"I'm sure every other girl is probably fixating on her dress right now. Trying to find something 'different' while getting the exact same thing as her six best friends. I love that you're not even stressed," Armstrong continued.

Ash was relieved she hadn't sent him the dress freak-out text she had almost hit Send on the night before.

"Why don't we go to Belltown after the prom and get into an open mic? You got a fake?"

Ash blinked, not realizing what he meant for a second. A fake ID? No, she didn't have one. Where was she going to get one?

Great, one more thing to worry about. She had no dress. She had no fake ID.

"Sure, I have one. I mean, who doesn't, right?" Ash smiled weakly. She'd just only gotten her *real* ID a few months ago.

"You'd be surprised. I gotta finish this blog. Text me later?" With that, and without waiting for a response, Armstrong turned around.

I guess we're done. She still hadn't gotten to deliver her fun, carefree line of the day. She'd gotten so light-headed being around him, she'd forgotten it anyhow.

Four

"what's that?"

Sebastian and Ash were spending the afternoon at Ash's house, each in their usual position around the kitchen table. Today, they were doing the work they hadn't finished in class. Both of them were rocking out to the music coming from the garage.

Josh Montague's band was playing a new song Josh had written the night before, he on drums, his former coworker on lead guitar, vocals and bass by their next-door neighbor. The only thing missing was Ash's role, keyboardist. She'd promised to join practice once she was done with her homework.

"What?" Ash looked up from the diagram of the moat she was surreptitiously adding to the front of the school. She knew as soon as Sebastian saw it, he wouldn't let her have any more suggestions in the project. "Be influenced by medieval times—don't be literal!" he'd already chided.

"That outfit." Sebastian was looking at Laila's *lehenga,* which was still hanging on the coatrack. "Is that yours?"

"Oh. That. You haven't heard?" Ash filled him in on Laila's master plan of Ash wearing the *lehenga* to the prom. Sebastian always knew the latest happenings in the Montague household through his mother, sometimes before Ash had a chance to tell him.

Laila and Sebastian's mother, Constance, had been close

friends since the Montagues had moved in across the street in the multicultural First Hill neighborhood. Constance had a babysitting business that she ran out of her home, and had watched both Ash and Sonali till they were old enough to stay home alone. Sebastian and Ash had grown up in each other's homes. Seb had no siblings and loved the constant chaos in the Montague household.

Sebastian shrugged. "I think it's nice of your mother to offer. You don't have too many other options."

"Can you not be my mom's fanboy for five seconds, please?" Ash was getting annoyed with Sebastian's taking Laila's side. He was supposed to be *her* best friend and support her despite his obvious and loyal admiration for Laila.

"I'm just saying."

"Just agree with me. That's your job as a best friend. And besides…" Ash was distracted by what she was seeing out of the kitchen window.

Sonali was cutting through the neighbor's yard, climbing over bushes and under hedges. Was she practicing to join the marines or something? Why wasn't she walking from the bus stop to home via the normal route of the sidewalk like all the other kids?

Ash rose from the table and went over to the window to see if there was someone on the side of the house she was avoiding.

No one.

Ash would bet anything this had something to do with whatever had caused the bird's nest in Sona's hair.

"I just don't think fighting with your mom over something as silly as a dress is worth it," Sebastian was saying. "Especially not since you're just trying to impress Armstrong. Do you really want to end up as the star of one of his podcasts that badly?"

Ash resented that remark.

"I'm not just trying to impress Armstrong."

"Then why were you not obsessed with going until he asked you?" Sebastian didn't look up from his sketch. "And you weren't stalking some expensive dress, either."

"Well, no one else asked me! He asked. I said 'yes.' What's wrong with that?" Ash clearly remembered texting Sebastian when Armstrong had *finally* asked her. He hadn't been as over-joyed as she'd expected.

"You never gave anyone the chance! It was always, 'I hope Armstrong asks me to the prom… Why hasn't he asked me yet… I hope he asks me out in his blog. Or like on Twitter. Twitter's so cool.'" He mimicked a voice that sounded nothing like her and more like Cartman from *South Park*.

"First, I do not sound like that."

Seb smirked.

"Second, it's not like there was a line of guys waiting to ask me."

"What if someone else had asked you? Someone nice. Would you have been this obsessed?"

"Like?" Ash raised an eyebrow. This was going to be good.

"Like…someone else. Say, Dave."

"Who the hell's Dave?"

"My friend Dave! The only Dave we know."

Ash furrowed her brow. "That guy you play *Monster Race Cars* with or whatever? Dave was going to ask me?"

Sebastian did an eye-roll. "*Portal* is not *Monster Race Cars*. He's one of my partners in app development—we don't just sit around playing games all day."

"Who's doing app development? Hi, Seb." Ash's father came into the kitchen to pour himself a glass of milk during the band's break. Sonali snuck in behind him and before Ash could say anything, sprinted up the stairs. That girl was acting weirder than usual, and her hair was still a mess. Ash made up her mind to figure out what was going on.

"Hey, Mr. M. I am. With two of my buddies for our AP Computer Science class. We already have BlueDog Studios interested in buying our first app!"

"Their IPO was amazing last year. That's huge, Seb. What's the concept?" Josh Montague sat down at the table and passed a glass of iced tea each to Ash and Sebastian.

"Thank you. Our app insta-catagorizes all the pictures you take with your cell phone. Like, Ash has taken 15,000 pictures of *that* dress." Sebastian pointed at the sketch she'd drawn in class. "Our app tags them all something like 'Orange_Dress'…"

"You mean 'The Dreamsicle,'" Ash interrupted.

Sebastian gave her an eye roll. "…so that she can search for that tag and find all of them in her Camera Roll rather than having to scroll through the year's worth of pictures she has on it."

"Now I remember us talking about this." Josh looked impressed. "Every company's asking for great apps and app development experience. I just submitted a multilayered tic-tac-toe game to the Windows Phone store. Sonali did the graphics for me."

"That's what our teacher said, too—app development is the best moneymaking strategy these days. With what BlueDog is willing to pay for the app, we'll be able to pay our first-year tuition at Michigan."

"You're a good kid, Seb." Josh smiled at him as though he wished Seb were actually his son.

Sebastian blushed.

"We have a lot of work to do. Maybe I can borrow Sona for the graphics, because none of us are that good at it."

Josh laughed. "She'd love that."

Ash felt a flare of jealousy. Her sister got a little goofy around Sebastian. She didn't like that one bit. Seb was *her* friend. Oddly, Sona hadn't come in to say hello today. She never missed out on a chance to talk to Sebastian and give him a dosage of the random factoids she'd learned that day.

"You guys have a name for your app?"

Sebastian grinned. "Still fighting over it, but Dave wants to call it Han Solo and the Chewbaccas."

"*This* is the guy you wanted me to go to the prom with?" Ash glanced at Sebastian. She was officially Seb's only non-weird friend.

"I assume my spawn has shared her dress woes with you?" Ash's dad slid his milk glass from one hand to the other.

"Oh, I was there to witness the showdown," Seb said, "in the Rebel store."

Ash's dad shook his head. "Try living with it."

"I'm not deaf you know, you guys."

"Let's ask your dad what he thinks about my dress drafting theory." Seb stood up.

Ash sighed. Great, more people needed to hear that her best friend was certifiably crazy.

"Mr. M, you're into fashion."

Josh looked doubtful. "I like watching stuff get made on *Runway*. I'm not really *into* fashion."

"Okay, but don't you think fashion is like architecture? I mean, look at this." Seb circled the *lehenga* and started plucking at the skirt. "We're doing a project where we are redrafting the front of the high school to look kind of medieval with as few changes as possible. We can easily do the same to this *lehenga*. The beading on this thing is nice—the shape is what's weird. If we redraw it as a flat sketch and change the outline

Dona Sarkar

of it, then figure out how it would look in 3-D, wouldn't that be pretty much how architecture is done?"

Ash watched her father, waiting for him to burst into laughter. He was an engineer. He was apparently a *Project Runway* addict. He would totally agree building *things* and dresses were two totally different things.

"Hand me those." Seb gestured toward a box of paper clips on the kitchen counter when no one answered.

Ash watched Seb tuck the hem of the *lehenga* up, flipping it out like a bell and securing it in place with a paper clip. "If we put some wire in here, we could make it stay like this."

Ash had to admit that the skirt looked infinitely better with the modifications Sebastian had made.

"We could do the same for the other side. And the top, we could change it, you know, make it like a thin strap thing or something. Draw a new sketch to get the lines right. Make it shorter like this." Sebastian clipped the pieces as he talked. "And suddenly…"

Suddenly, the *lehenga* was different.

"…and it's a whole new thing. With just a few tweaks."

Ash's mind spun. Something was coming together.

"And it's so unusual because of the original beadwork and construction, but now it's really modern and kind of cool. I haven't seen anything like it."

Unusual. Not mainstream.

"I see what you're saying," Josh agreed. "But do you really think making folds with paper clips is like sewing?"

Ash stopped listening.

Ash squinted at the *lehenga*. The color wasn't bad—the beautiful Tiffany blue looked good on her. The changes Sebastian had made were definitely an improvement to the boxy shape it had before. There was still a lot more that needed to be done. Could it be possible? Could she be looking at her prom dress?

"Seb. I think you might be a genius," Ash said slowly.

Josh was smirking. He knew exactly what she was thinking. Sebastian didn't.

"Wait, why? I don't like that look you've got going on."

"Remember how much you love me?"

Josh rose from the table, half smile still on his face. "I'm leaving before I get roped into something that's going to get me disowned by your mother."

FIVE

"HI." Jessica Moriarty dropped into Armstrong's seat in Brit lit.

Ash glanced up from her reading. "Yes?" She was hoping to have a chance to chat with Armstrong before class started—lately it felt like the only time they talked was online via Twitter or his blog comments. She certainly didn't want drama-queen Jessica hanging around eavesdropping on their conversation.

"What are you doing?" Jessica wanted to know.

Ash tried not to roll her eyes. "Reading, Jess. For our assignment today. Have you finished it?"

"Nope." Jessica continued to stare at her.

Ash tried to read another few lines of *The Tempest* and failed.

"Okay. What is it?" Ash closed her book. The staring was getting creepy.

"So...Sebastian Diaz."

"Ah." This was normal. A lot of girls liked Sebastian and most were afraid to talk to him. At least one or two girls asked Ash about him every week: whether he was single, liked them, et cetera. As if Ash were his keeper or something.

"Has he said anything about the prom?"

"Yep, he's said a lot about it." Ash was enjoying this now. Jess had never been particularly nice to her before. Ash was still annoyed at the "vintage" comment she'd made in the dressing room when Ash had been trying on the orange gown.

Jessica's eyes widened. "OhMyGod, are you guys going together? Did you dump Armstrong?"

"No!" Ash looked around, hoping no one had heard. This was how rumors got started. "I'm going with Armstrong."

"So…Sebastian doesn't have a date yet?"

Ash sighed heavily, as if divulging a huge secret, and lowered her voice. "He's still available."

Jess smiled as though she'd just heard that her grandmother's pecan pie was now available in the vending machines. She was from the South and was constantly lamenting the lack of good Southern food in Seattle.

"Do you think he'd go with me?"

"Um…" Ash pretended to think about it. Honestly, she had no idea if Sebastian even knew who Jessica was. That was probably for the best. Jessica wasn't the sharpest stick in the forest, and Sebastian tended to only hang out with the AP crowd. He'd only had one girlfriend during high school, the one girl in Computer Club who'd moved away their junior year.

"You'll have to ask him and see," Ash finally said.

Jessica's face fell. "Can you find out if he likes me?"

"I'll let you know." Ash picked up her book again when she saw Armstrong enter the room, exactly a second before the bell rang. "Go sit down before you get detention. Sebastian hates girls who get detention. His mother would disapprove."

Jessica hurried to her seat and was replaced by Armstrong a few seconds later.

"So…your Facebook page hinted at something very interesting about your prom attire. Along the lines of something no one at this school had ever seen before? 'Drafting class plus fashion unite'? Care to share a sound bite for my blog?"

Ash felt a rolling thrill down her back that Armstrong not only checked out her Facebook page, but also was curious about her cryptic status update from the previous night.

"You'll see on prom night," Ash said, she hoped, enigmatically.

"You tease." Armstrong shrugged. "I like it. I don't know what I'm wearing. It'll be good, though."

Lucky guy with that confidence. Despite her hopefulness about the idea she and Sebastian came up with last night, she didn't actually have a plan for what would happen next.

Neither of them was exactly Van Gogh. Nor was either of them Coco Chanel. They needed to make a drawing, make it into 3-D, then get it into a real garment. Were the modifications even going to be possible? Who was going to do them?

Ash barged into Sonali's room without knocking. Her sister barely glanced up from the huge book of oil paintings she was poring over.

"You're supposed to be offended that I'm invading your privacy, kid." Ash stood over her sister, who continued to sprawl across the carpet.

"Get out. You're invading my privacy," her sister said without looking up.

"Get ready. We need to go."

"We have fifteen minutes," Sonali mumbled. Ash and Sonali went to their weekly tae-kwon-do lesson on Wednesdays. Ash enthusiastically, since she loved punching and kicking out her aggressions for an hour. Sonali hated it, but Josh insisted both of his girls learn basic self-defense.

Ash reached over and tousled Sonali's still-knotted hair.

"Want to tell me who did this?"

Silence.

"Okay. Want to do me a favor?"

"Nope."

"Sure you do. Listen, so Sebastian and I came up with an idea to turn that *lehenga* of mom's into an actual dress that I can wear to the prom."

Sona said nothing.

"I need your awesome drawing skills to make a sketch for us that we can turn into 3-D."

Sona raised an eyebrow. "You want me to do fashion design? You told me I dress like Dora the Explorer."

"I don't need you to come up with something from scratch, genius. Just make a sketch of the *lehenga* we started to modify downstairs."

Sona shrugged. "I want a cut of the royalties if it becomes famous and Dolce & Gabbana wants to make it in bulk."

Ash had to laugh. "Do you even know what royalties are? Do you even know who Dolce & Gabbana are?"

"Dad was watching *Project Runway* reruns all afternoon."

Ash rolled her eyes. "Dad needs to get a job."

"Royalties?"

"How about, five laps around the gym if you're not ready in five minutes?"

"Let's not go today." Sona rolled over onto her back. "Let's just stay here. Let's make microwave s'mores instead."

Ash sighed, putting her hands on her hips. "Do you want to ever get your green belt?"

"I don't want to break a board in half."

"It's not that hard." Ash didn't understand how Sonali could be satisfied with her white belt after two years of training. Ash had sailed through the belts and now taught the more junior students with her brown belt.

"Why does no one understand that I'm a pacifist?" With a

huge sigh, Sonali rolled to her feet. She started grabbing her gloves, helmet and uniform out of the closet.

"It's about to become ten laps. And why do you know that word?"

Ash was assigned to lead three junior students in their sparring in class that evening. As a brown belt, she was allowed to use body contact in her sparring, though the white belts never were. Her job was mainly to make sure they used full force to throw their kicks and jabs, but always stopped short of actually killing each other.

Ash circled around Sonali, a timid, moppy eight-year-old named Jacob and a fiery little twelve-year-old girl with hair as bright as carrots, who was eyeing Sonali in a way Ash didn't like.

"Okay everyone, the next move all of you should do is the jumping front snap kick."

All three of them stood there and stared at her.

"That move sucks," complained the little red-haired one.

"Let's keep our opinions to ourselves and do the move," Ash suggested.

They still just stood there.

"I mean today. Now. Do it now."

All three halfheartedly hopped in the air, then threw out their right feet in the air in front of them.

"*At* someone. You're hardly ever going to have to fight thin air in the real world. Here, Jacob, you throw a kick at me. Sona, throw a kick at..." Ash gestured toward the red-haired girl.

"Angela, duh."

Ash resisted an eye roll. "At Angela Duh."

"It's just *regular* Angela. Duh."

"Sona, throw a kick at Regular Angela."

"That's not my name!"

Everyone got into their positions.

"Okay, let's circle."

The four of them circled one another in pairs, Jacob and Sona throwing out timid jabs toward their opponents. "Now, jump snap kick. Go!"

Jacob's little foot brushed the air near Ash's hip. "Good job, Jacob!"

Ash looked to see if Sona had done the move yet. She hadn't. She was still circling Angela.

"Come on!" Angela whined. "You're *so* lame!"

Sona tilted on her side and did a tentative kick.

"Wrong kick, Sona. Jump and kick. Come on, just one," Ash called out. Where was her sister's head today?

"God, you suck." Angela folded her arms. "Everyone is going to get their green belt before you, loser."

Jacob did another jumping front snap kick gleefully as if to prove Angela's point.

"Sona, the eight-year-old is doing better than you. Let's see a real kick," Ash said sternly. She was not going to let that bratty Angela get away with insulting her sister.

Sonali hopped back and forth, hands in a defensive posture, but staring at her feet.

What was Sonali's problem? Ash was going to make her do the kick before the night was over.

"God, why don't you just give up? Why are you even in here?" Angela dropped her defensive stance and stood with her hands on her hips. Ash could tell she was going to be a real pain in a few years.

"Sona, for the love of—" Ash started toward her sister.

Bam! Suddenly Angela went flying backward.

Sona stood there looking shocked. Jumping front snap kick success.

Ash didn't know whether to applaud or scold. Sona had never, *ever* initiated contact in class before. Now, Angela sat on her butt five feet away, her face crumbling.

"Uh, no contact, Sona," was all Ash could think of to say.

The head tae-kwon-do instructor blew the whistle. "No contact! Now back to circling."

Wow. Ash was stunned by her sister's sudden aggression for the rest of the hour.

After class, the sisters headed back to the locker room to change and wait for Josh to come pick them up. He didn't like them to walk home from the studio after dark, and he certainly didn't like for Ash to take Sona as a passenger on the Vespa.

"Did someone do something to you? Is that why you won't walk home the normal way?" Ash asked as she sat down on a bench and started running a comb through her hair.

"Are you spying on me?" Sona slammed her locker shut, piercing Ash with an accusatory stare.

"Clearly! Because I have nothing else to do," Ash snapped back. "I saw you come through the backyard. It's like you were dodging the other kids on your bus. Were you? Is that where all this aggression is coming from?"

Sona gave her a suspicious look and started shoveling her uniform into her gym bag. "No."

"God, I hope I sound more convincing when I lie."

"You don't."

"Who's messing with you?"

"I'm handling it, okay? In my own way. You don't need to interfere in my life."

"I never interfere!"

Sonali snorted.

"Yeah right. Like you never interfered when you beat the shit out of that Billy kid who was messing with Sebastian."

"Sona! Language!" Ash was hardly offended, but she knew if Sona used that kind of language around Laila, *she* would be in deep trouble and be blamed for being a bad influence.

"It's true, though. Remember how he used to trip Seb in the shower in gym class and call him a dirty—"

"Sona!"

"I wasn't going to say it."

Ash doubted it. "Why do you know all this, by the way? You were seven."

"Seb told me." Sonali went back to packing away her helmet and gloves. "He told me that somehow you just knew. He never said a word to you about Billy, but you just knew what was going on."

It had happened at the end of eighth grade. Sebastian had grown quieter and quieter the whole year, starting when Billy Walters had transferred to their school—and to Seb's gym class. Sebastian had always been shy, but that year he'd started to avoid even his nerd friends and hang out in the computer lab during lunch instead of going to the cafeteria.

Worst of all, he wouldn't tell Ash why and would snap at her when she pursued it too fervently. Ash started to think it was because they had started getting teased for being boyfriend-girlfriend because they were together so much of the time.

Hurt that he was so offended at being called her boyfriend, Ash had started to pull away from him and had hung out with some of the more popular kids...Billy Walters included.

She'd started to walk to Pacific Place mall after school with her new friends to people-watch and make comments at random strangers, rather than going home to watch TV and do homework, as she always did with Seb.

It had been awesome to finally feel like she belonged. A total thrill to have every day be a total unknown. She knew she was getting set up for a good place in the high-school food chain and it felt great.

On the last day of eighth grade, she was walking down the hall with some of her new friends when she overheard Billy Walters and his cronies start slamming closed all the open lockers while kids were still trying to empty them out. She'd never liked it when Billy harassed people who hadn't done anything to him, but up until then she'd never cared enough to stop him.

She'd looked down the hall and had seen Sebastian spot Billy and his gang as they started toward his locker. Sebastian hurriedly started emptying everything into his backpack. Ash heard Billy call out to him, by a very derogatory name.

Sebastian turned as white as Ash had ever seen him.

She'd looked from her former best friend to the group of guys who were now backing Billy as they stalked toward Sebastian.

She saw something she'd never seen before in Sebastian's eyes. Fear. In an instant, she realized what had been causing Sebastian's weird behavior that year. And she knew that she needed to do something to make sure Seb never felt that fear again.

She'd gone after the guys and stepped between them and Sebastian. She'd stood in front of Billy, half his size, and smiled sweetly. She'd whispered some nonsense under her breath. When he'd leaned down to hear what she was saying, she struck. She kneed him under the chin, punched him in the solar plexus, then flipped his entire body over her shoulder.

Just as she'd done to pass her green belt test for tae kwon do the week before.

After Billy's body hit the ground in front of his shocked

friends, she'd planted her left foot, clad in her first pair of high heels, in his chest and said quietly, "Bully someone again and see what happens."

Her father had been proud of and impressed by her.

Her mother had been convinced she'd go to jail.

Billy had never again looked her in the eye.

Her so-called new friends never spoke to her again.

Sebastian had grown six inches that summer and had never gotten picked on again…but had never stopped trying to make it up to Ash ever since.

"I am your hero, go ahead and admit it." Sebastian dropped a giant gizmo that looked like an old-school soda machine on the drafting table.

"I don't want a soda. They're bad for you, anyway. This is what you had to show me?"

When Ash had received a text from Sebastian asking her to skip lunch and meet in the drafting classroom, she'd been expecting... Well, she didn't know. But it certainly wasn't a soda machine.

"Do you even know what this is? Hint—not a soda machine."

"Slushees?"

"No."

"Frozen yogurt?"

"Stop thinking about food!"

"I'm supposed to be eating curly fries right now—just tell me."

"It's a 3-D printer!"

A 3-D printer. Ash's curiosity was piqued. "There's such a thing? What does it print?"

"Stuff in 3-D."

"Thank you, Wikipedia Brown. Like what stuff?"

"Like..." Sebastian paused for effect. "This sketch for example!"

He slapped down a gorgeous sketch of the *lehenga* modified and shown in a 3-D perspective using their CAD software. He'd spent the past three evenings working on it at Ash's place after school with Sonali.

It was even better than Ash had imagined it would be. And so much better than the schoolfront they were supposed to be working on. She'd taken over the school project so Sebastian could focus on the dress, and she had to admit she'd been having a lot of fun with designing a new entrance. Too much fun, probably, since none of the ideas she'd had were very practical.

Sebastian logged in to his PC and sent the sketch to the printer and pressed a series of buttons.

"How do you know how to do this?"

"The internet has all the answers," Seb replied as he made sure the printer was turned on. "We'll see if it knows the right answers anyway."

Ash watched in amazement as drops of some weird liquid started dropping, then accumulating and sticking together at the base of the strange machine.

"That's plastic and acrylic. It's going to shape the dress."

Ash continued to watch. She could see the hem of the dress taking its shape. "I see it!"

Even Sebastian looked surprised at his handiwork.

"Wow, I never thought this would work just like in the YouTube video."

"Where did you get it?" She squeezed Seb's arm. He flexed it tightly in response under her fingertips. She held on for an extra second, loving how he always wanted to protect her.

"The drafting department just got it from a donation. This local start-up sank and had to start giving up its stuff. I promised Mr. Watkins I'd clean the auto-shop garage if I could borrow it during lunch."

"Seb. No." There he went with the heroics again. She needed him to know she was willing to do her own bargaining punishments. "I'll do it. You've done enough for me."

"Too late. You're not the kind of girl who is ever going to clean a garage floor. Not while I'm around anyway."

Ash opened her mouth to protest.

"Anyway, he thinks we're printing our school sketch, so we need to do that, too. Why don't you work on making sure it looks kind of finished?"

For once, Ash didn't complain and started up the CAD software on her PC. She couldn't believe Seb was doing garage cleanup for her. He wasn't even getting anything out of this—it wasn't his dress, or his date's dress. Knowing Jessica, she'd chicken out and not ask and he would remain dateless. She still didn't understand why he hadn't asked anyone yet. Any girl would say yes.

Sebastian, however, didn't seem put out by it at all. Instead, he seemed really happy and sat with his hands folded under his chin, watching the dress get created, an intensely focused expression on this face.

Ash, in the meantime, deleted her more lame ideas, such as a moat and drawbridge, from the CAD drawing of the school and verified that all of Sebastian's great ideas were still in place.

She straightened out the pillars and archway and saved her work. It wasn't great, but at least they wouldn't fail. It was a hundred times better than the boring, boxy, '70s architecture the school was made with right then anyway. When she turned back to see how the 3-D dress printing was going, she gasped.

The *lehenga* bore no resemblance to what it had been. It was halter-style, came in at the waist, left a sliver of midsection visible, and then flowed into a mermaid-tail skirt that just erupted into a bouquet of sparkly ruffles at the bottom.

Somehow, it was better than even the orange dress she'd been lusting over.

"Oh, Seb," Ash gasped again as the last few drops of liquid solidified the neckline of the dress.

"Hit print." He gestured pointedly at her PC. "We need to get the schoolwork done so you're not doing garage cleanup with me. I want you to have a good weekend."

Ash did as he asked and then went over to admire the dress again. "Can I touch it?"

"Let me make sure it's not hot." Sebastian reached out and touched it first. "Yep, all yours."

Ash picked up the dress with two tentative fingers. It was much sturdier than she thought—like a little plastic toy. She was amazed by the printer gizmo.

"This is gorgeous!" She immediately threw her arms around Sebastian. "Did I mention I love you the most? How can I thank you for this? Let me take over your garage cleanup at least?"

When she didn't remove her arms from around his neck, he hesitantly put his arms around her waist and hugged her tightly in return.

"You can mention how awesome I am again." He was smiling as he pulled away. "That's all the thanks I need."

Though it was only two in the afternoon on a weekday, the line at Molly Moon's was around the corner, the for-sure sign that spring had arrived in Seattle. Ash insisted on buying cones for both of them, salted caramel and Earl Grey tea double scoops for her and balsamic strawberry for Sebastian. They had gotten the exact same order for so many years, Ash didn't even need to ask Sebastian if he wanted a drizzle of homemade caramel on his cone.

They wrapped napkins around their cones and walked across the street to wait for a unique Capitol Hill tradition: bicycle polo. Groups of eight people rode around on bicycles and tried to score goals on each other with polo sticks. The game was due to start any minute.

"I can't believe that 3-D printer thingie." Ash reached her head over and took a lick of Sebastian's cone without asking permission.

"It's cool, huh? I love technology." Sebastian held his cone out so Ash could have another bite without a struggle.

"I'm starting to love technology. I always thought it was just a bunch of nerdy guys making stuff no one understands…"

"But it's actually cool stuff that makes everyone's life easier." Sebastian finished her thought.

They'd always been that way. Ash would sometimes think of something to ask Sebastian and he would bring up the topic before she could. Laila had a scientific explanation for it, something along the lines of them being in sync because they had grown up together surrounded by the same environmental influences.

"What do you want to do?" Sebastian asked vaguely.

Ash took a few licks of her cone. "Figure out how to get that dress sewn to look like the figurine."

Sebastian smiled as Ash helped herself to more of his cone. She was liking going among the three flavor choices. "I mean more in the scope of life. What do you want to do?"

Ash considered this. "Be a lawyer like my mom?"

Sebastian raised an eyebrow. "That's a lot of research."

"Oh." Ash noticed a few polo-ists starting to arrive at the little basketball court they had the game in. At this point, even they had their lives figured out more than she did.

"So, you don't know," Seb said.

Ash shook her head. "I'll figure it out at U-Dub." She had gotten into the University of Washington along with half the senior class.

"I wish you were going to Michigan," Sebastian said, not in a nonchalant, casual kind of way

Ash was silent for a second as she took a few more bites of her ice cream and pretended to be watching the polo warm-up. *Where was this coming from?*

"It's going to be the first time in our lives we won't just be able to see each other whenever we want," Sebastian reminded her. "We won't be skipping last period to have ice cream and watch this spectacle." Sebastian gestured toward where an obviously beginner polo player rode his bike into the fence.

Ash swallowed. For some reason, she had not digested that information. Starting in about six months, she was going to be without Sebastian for the first time in her life.

"I promise to visit you," she said at last, after noticing Sebastian was waiting for an answer. "A lot. I hear Ann Arbor is gorgeous."

Sebastian shook his head sadly. "You'll be busy with school. I think we'll only see each other over vacations once or twice a year."

Once or twice a year?

They saw each other once or twice *an hour* right now.

This was not something she wanted to ponder. Having a teary meltdown while the polo players watched was not going to be how she was going to end this wonderful day.

"Wow. What on earth is that?" Laila Montague pointed at the 3D dress creation that was sitting on the counter. She was home early that evening as Sebastian and Ash sat in their usual places in the kitchen.

Ash was on her Surface, trying to make their school sketch look more school-like. Mr. Watkins hadn't been impressed by their work so far—he said it was too "literal" and needed to jibe with the rest of the students' work for their final project. Ash had promised to take over the project. Sebastian had done enough. She welcomed the distraction after their serious talk at Molly Moon's. She didn't want to even think of a time when she wouldn't see Sebastian every day.

Sebastian was searching sewing websites for ideas on how to make their dress sculpture a reality, with minimal sewing to the *lehenga* since neither of them knew how.

Sebastian glanced over at where Laila was pointing. "Oh, that's for my doll collection."

"Sebastian, really." Even stoic Laila looked amused.

Seb was grinning. He was one of the few people who could make Laila loosen up after her long workdays. "Actually, Ash said she would love to wear your *lehenga* to the prom."

Laila's smile was contagious. Ash suddenly realized how beautiful her mother was when her whole face opened up and relaxed. Those were the moments when she hoped everyone was right when they said she was a copy of Laila when her mother was her age.

"Really? I knew she'd change her mind."

"Again. People. I'm right here." Ash looked up from her work. "Talk at me, please."

"I knew you'd change your mind," Laila said smugly.

Ash did an eye roll. "I didn't. Seb came up with the idea of modifying the *lehenga* into something less...Mogul-esque, and that is what we, well he, came up with."

Laila picked up the tiny dress sculpture. "It's lovely."

"I love it," Ash said. "We just need to find instructions for how to modify the real one. It can't be that hard."

"What?" Laila almost dropped the sculpture. "You want to modify my dress? Into this?"

"Mom!" Ash could tell by the tone of her voice that she was about to quash their great idea. "Can you not be negative for once?"

"Ashmita Montague, *do not* 'Mom' me!"

"Seb, talk to her!"

"Here we go again…" Sebastian nearly flipped his chair over as he leaned back. He shook his head at the ceiling in despair. "The women in my life are going to drive me crazy."

"What's going on?" Josh Montague came in from the garage, where he'd just finished up with the band.

"Ash is eavesdropping," Sonali said helpfully, looking up from her chalk sketch of a lifelike tiger.

"Shh!" Ash shushed her father, who was talking loudly by the loud refrigerator. She was standing at the edge of the kitchen, trying to listen in on the hushed conversation in the living room.

He poured himself an iced tea. "What are we eavesdropping on?"

"Shh!"

"It's like I need a Twitter feed to keep up with what goes on in this house."

"Dad. Please. Let's play the quiet game." Ash strained to hear what her mother and Seb were saying. Of course, her mother chose this moment to speak quietly.

"Wow. I just got treated like a six-year-old by my kid. They say it happens to everyone."

"She told me the same thing," Sonali reassured him.

"Shh!"

"Shh!" Josh mimicked Ash with an exaggerated finger to his lips.

Ash waited for a break in conversation.

"Seb's talking to Mom," she explained. "We want to make this—" she pointed at the tiny dress sculpture "—out of that." She pointed at the real *lehenga,* which was still hanging in the kitchen.

"How're you going to do that?"

"They don't know," Sonali filled in. "It's a harebrained scheme with no execution plan."

"Have you been reading your mother's law journals again?" Josh laughed. "God, I love being at home with you guys."

"Have some faith. We'll figure it out." Ash waved her hand. "But first, Seb has to convince Mom."

"Is she really going to let a bunch of teenagers who know nothing about sewing hack apart one of her favorite dresses?"

"No," Sonali said.

"Does no one have faith in the system?" Ash gave them both a look.

"What system?" Josh asked.

"My system!" Ash whispered back loudly. They'd started talking again in the other room.

"Then, no."

Ash did an eye roll. "I know Mom doesn't. That's why Seb has to convince her."

And he was doing a fine job.

"Mrs. M, remember when you were, say, apprehensive about letting me build that computer for Ash? You were convinced it would overheat and burn the house down." Sebastian's voice wafted in from the living room. "She sulked for weeks and finally you gave in? Think of this project as that computer but not as useful."

Ash almost wanted to object, but knew better than to interrupt or let on that she was eavesdropping.

"And now look, that computer—" Ash could practically see him gesturing toward the den where the Franken-computer existed "—still stands. Safe and sound. Six years of abuse by that destructive daughter of yours and it hasn't exploded. You, yourself, have admitted you have used it for research for your cases on weekends."

Laila was quiet. The defense lawyer had no defense.

"…and I'm hardly an engineer, Mrs. M. But I was able to do the right research to build that computer. I would never let anything bad happen to something that belonged to you. Not your daughter. Not your dress."

Ash started to feel her hope returning.

"He's good," Ash's dad whispered. "He should be a lawyer. Taking down your mother is…"

"One condition, and I mean it, Sebastian."

Ash's fists squeezed together in excitement.

"Anything."

Ash could practically see Sebastian opening his hands in that way he did that got anyone to completely trust him. He just had a way of doing that.

"You find a professional to do the work. For the set budget of one hundred dollars. You do not try any stunts of your own. And I want to speak to whoever you find on the phone first to understand their credentials. And you stay in the budget."

"Mrs. M., I promise you that you will love the *lehenga* so much you'll steal it right back from your daughter and wear it to every holiday party this year."

"Sebastian?"

"Yes, ma'am?"

"Don't sell past the close."

"No, ma'am."

Both Ash and Josh Montague expelled sighs of relief.

"The defense rests," Josh murmured, hugging Ash close.

Sonali continued to not look convinced as she sketched in the tiger's whiskers.

seven

"Are you sure it's around here?" Sebastian glanced at the GPS on his phone and the surrounding buildings. "I don't see anything that looks big enough to be it."

Ash ignored him as she surveyed the line of eccentric windowed storefronts dotting Pike Street off Broadway.

"There! I've passed by it a hundred times." Ash gestured toward a familiar-looking window. "Park! Park!"

"Yes, ma'am." Sebastian expertly parallel parked his Mazda in front of the colorful doorway with a Some Like It Haute sign over it.

Ash had decided to act before her mother changed her mind. She remembered passing the cute little Capitol Hill storefront that boasted "Designer fabrics for those who can... Couture dressmaking for those who can't!" on the front window many times on her little scooter. She was sure that with the promises of couture dressmaking the storefront made, a little alteration to the *lehenga* would be easy-breezy.

Gathering up Sebastian's sketches, the tiny dress figurine and the garment bag containing the *lehenga*, Ash practically bounced out of the car, feeling very positive. Everything was going to work out fine. They'd come so far, it had to work out.

Ash giggled at the blush on Sebastian's cheeks as he noticed what was right next to Some Like It Haute: Babeland, a bright pink-and-white storefront boasting "women-friendly pleasure goods!"

Cap Hill was the artsy, eclectic and fun neighbor to First Hill, Ash's more subdued 'hood, and Some Like It Haute was no exception. It was practically bursting with bolts of beautiful embroidered fabric, ribbons, skeins of yarn and walls of sewing supplies, like a tiny, brightly colored dollhouse.

"Hello!" A familiar-looking girl about their age looked up as the entry bell dinged Ash and Sebastian's arrival. "Oh, my God, I love that dress. What a cool print!"

Ash smiled her thanks. The pale yellow dress with the pink skulls-and-roses was her latest vintage store find and was totally unique. She had bought it for the Day of the Dead celebration Sebastian's family had every year—where they honored those who had passed on.

"I want to steal this! God, look at this construction. Where was this made?" The girl leaned across the counter to get a closer look. "Not to be weird, but can I touch it?"

"Uh, sure."

The girl wasted no time reaching behind Ash and grabbing the tag from the back of the dress. "It's vintage! I knew it. No one makes good stuff anymore. We're going to get along so well!"

"Uh, thanks." Ash disentangled herself from the girl. Wow, she was enthusiastic. "I have a weird question," she said as she dropped her pile of stuff on the counter.

The girl picked up the tiny dress figurine. "This is so cute. Did you make this? I'm Lyra Matthew, by the way. This is my shop. Well, it's my mom's shop, but I work here more, so I guess it's more mine than hers."

Lyra Matthew. The name was so familiar... Ash suddenly

remembered where she knew Lyra from. "I know you! You were in *Les Misérables* last year. With Armstrong Jones?"

Lyra flashed a brilliant smile. She was *very* pretty. And wearing an amazing pale rose drop-waist dress with a feather fringe at the hem. Her eyes were done up all dark and smoky. She looked like a '20s movie star. "Yup, I'd just moved up from L.A. and was really surprised the part of Eponine was still open. Armstrong's cute, but kind of skinny, don't you think?"

Ash remembered how beautifully Lyra sang. When she finished "A Little Fall of Rain" with a whisper as Eponine had "died" in the middle of the final act, thunderous applause had rung through the school auditorium.

"I'm Ash and this is Sebastian Diaz." Ash gestured toward Seb, who looked uncomfortable.

Ash noticed Lyra flash her dazzling smile in his direction a second longer than normal, her giant dark eyes lighting up with recognition. *Of course* she knew Sebastian. Everyone did.

"We need some help." Ash opened the garment bag and pulled out the *lehenga*. "This is my mother's. We want to make modifications to this dress to make it look like this figurine."

Lyra's eyes widened. "That's some beadwork. Where was it made?"

"India somewhere, I'm not sure. It's my mom's."

"It's gorgeous. Why do you want to change it?"

"Because it's weird right now. Trust me." Ash pushed the sketch and the figurine toward her, ignoring Lyra's doubtful look. "I want to transform it and wear it to the prom."

"Wow. That's a great sketch!" A few moments of silence passed as the enthusiastic girl touched the fabric in various places, examining seams and sleeves and who knew what else. She glanced at the sketches and the figurine.

"This is complicated. Like, really complicated." She tossed

her waist-length curly black hair to one side and frowned. She turned the *lehenga* inside out and lay it flat. "Yes, this is very complex beadwork. See how each bead is hand-sewn to the fabric? If I cut into it, all the beads will scatter everywhere."

Ash and Sebastian glanced at each other. This was not a good sign. Ash had been hoping she'd look at it once and say, "Oh, that's straightforward. No problem. It'll be done in an hour."

"I think my mom and I can do it. She's a costume designer for stage plays and things so she does beadwork a lot. I can do the bodice part. When do you need it by?"

"Two weeks."

Lyra hesitated. Again, not a good sign.

"My mom's really busy, but I can make her do it. It's a good thing you came in today, though. We're about to go into bridal season and there is no way we could have done it if you'd come in any later."

Serendipity. It really was true.

Ash practically cried with relief. "Seriously, you have saved my life." She turned back to grin at Sebastian, who didn't look half as excited. She wondered why, but before she could ask, he stepped up to the counter.

"So…Lyra, how much is this going to cost? Because we do have a budget," Sebastian spoke up.

Lyra searched his face, as if gauging how he was going to react.

"Usually we would charge around two hundred dollars for this kind of work—total transformation…"

That wasn't bad! Ash thought. Surely she could talk Laila into two hundred dollars. That was just a little over the budget.

"…but because the beading is so complex and the fabric so complex, it's going to be at least five hundred." Lyra dished out the crushing blow.

Eight

I need to talk to you.

ASH hit Send on the text to Armstrong during English class. There was no point of dragging this on. He would be super-pissed at her if she canceled on him at the last second. Instead, she was going to tell him she got invited on a really great trip to Paris the weekend of the prom and just had to go. It was the only way to save face. There was no way she was going to show up to the prom with the coolest guy she'd ever known in some clearance-rack leftover.

What's up? Armstrong texted back immediately. Rare for him.

It's about the prom, Ash texted back after waiting a minute.

It's going to be great. My buddy is DJing. Which means the music will NOT suck. He's playing stuff no one's ever heard of, but wish they had.

Ash practically burst into tears. She was never, ever going to forgive her mother for doing this to her. Laila had tried to console her the previous night by telling her they could go bargain-basement dress-hunting that weekend. Ash had asked to leave the dinner table and go to bed early. She was done fighting for something that was not going to happen.

Her phone buzzed again and she quickly covered it with her hand, glancing up to see if the teacher had noticed. They were supposed to be writing an essay. The teacher, however, was sending a text message of her own. The formerly sporty Ms. Winter had recently gotten one of those Nordstrom make-overs and was sporting cherry-red lipstick and platform heels every day and had been texting nonstop, even during class. Ash was pretty sure she was actively doing the online dating thing. She'd caught Ms. Winter browsing Chemistry.com when she had claimed she was grading mid-terms.

Ash glanced down to see what other fun things Armstrong was planning for the prom where she would not be his date. Instead, a new text had arrived from Sebastian.

Awesome news. You're getting your dress. Meet me right after school at my car.

Ash almost dropped her phone. What was Sebastian talk-ing about now? He never, ever gave up, but even he had to be aware that there was no way in hell they were going to come up with five hundred dollars overnight.

"Where are we going?" Ash was being dragged down the hall by Sebastian the second she exited her last class of the day.

"We're about to make this happen." Sebastian tucked her hand firmly under his arm while he searched for his car keys in his messenger bag.

"Seb, tell me." Ash attempted to drag her feet so he would stop.

"Stop doing that or I'll fireman-carry you to the car."

Ash smiled. She had no doubt he would do exactly that. "Just tell me and I'll cooperate."

"You'll see. Trust me."

"I do, but…"

Seb stopped next to his car and opened the passenger-side door for her. "In."

"I need to tell Armstrong I can't go with him."

"You're going."

"But we don't have—" Ash reluctantly got in and pulled her feet to safety before Sebastian slammed the door shut on them "—five hundred dollars."

"Please fasten your seat belt before you fly out of the car and no longer need a prom dress for anything."

Sebastian was skidding out of the parking lot before Ash could say anything more. They took the familiar route to Capitol Hill again and parked right in front of Some Like It Haute.

"What are we doing? Negotiating isn't going to work. Lyra already told us how complicated the whole thing is."

"I got this." Sebastian grabbed all the stuff they needed for the dress project and was in the shop before Ash could protest further.

"Hi! Hey, Lyra, us again," Sebastian was saying by the time Ash made it in the door behind him. "I was thinking…"

"This is cute." Lyra was watching Sebastian with amusement. He did look cute trying to juggle a miniature toy dress and the giant garment bag at the same time. Ash felt a twinge of annoyance anyway. It was becoming quite clear that Lyra liked Sebastian.

"I was noticing you guys didn't have a website. I went to it last night to see if there were any other seamstress-type people who we could hire and you don't have anything resembling an online presence!" Sebastian neatly laid out all the stuff in front of Lyra.

Ash wondered what he was doing. Pointing out the little

shop's shortcomings was not going to work, no matter how much the owner's daughter liked Sebastian!

Lyra sighed. "We have one, but it's not a very good site. My dad made it and well, he's a doctor, not a computer person. We just don't have the money to hire a professional web designer right now. It costs over…"

"A thousand dollars. Or more," Sebastian finished. "I know."

"That's right." Lyra started to look suspicious.

Ash was, too. What was Sebastian up to? What did this have to do with anything at all?

"What if," Sebastian said, taking the *lehenga* out of the garment bag and laying it across the table again, "we cut a deal?"

"What kind of deal?" Lyra didn't look any less suspicious.

"The kind where you do this lovely girl's alterations and I build your website for you. For free. You save over five hundred dollars. At least."

Was he serious? Ash's eyes widened. Did he know how to build something as complex as a professional site for a store?

"You know how to build websites? Not just webpages, but with databases and things I don't totally understand?" Lyra echoed Ash's sentiments. "It has to be able to take customers' orders and list all the stock we have and stuff automatically. I need to be able to load info myself. My parents are going to make me be the main website administrator since they can barely figure out email."

Sebastian didn't look concerned.

"My credentials are here." Here Sebastian pulled up his phone and started showing her some pinned sites on his browser. "I made the school's website. I'm making my parents' church's website. I made my uncle's business's website. All have a database back end. All have search functionality as well as upload and download functionality. And I'm on-call tech support for all of them."

"Wow," Lyra and Ash said at once.

Ash was shocked at how lovely the sites were as she peeked over his shoulder. She'd known Sebastian had made the school's website, but she hadn't understood how complicated it must have been.

"I can make one for your store as my AP Computer Science class project. I'm in that class right now so I can start immediately."

Something was nagging at Ash's brain. She felt as though he already had a plan for that class and it did *not* involve making a website for Some Like It Haute. She made a note to ask him about it later. Right now, Lyra was looking very interested in the idea.

"I'll mock up a prototype and see if you like it. I kind of already started last night based on the personality of this store." Sebastian gestured toward the back. "Lively and fun. Fashionable. Young."

Lyra's eyes lit up at "young."

Ash glanced over at him again. Was he sure about this? This sounded like a *lot* of work. She knew he'd been working on the website for his parents' church for over two months.

"If you like the prototype, we're on our way and I'll make the website for you, with free updates whenever you need. It'll take about a month. In return, I'd love it if you would do the alterations for Ash's dress in the next two weeks. So she can be the most beautiful and *unforgettable* girl Seattle Academy has ever seen."

Lyra looked from Ash to Sebastian, Ash thought, a bit jealously. What girl wouldn't?

Ash held her breath and watched the cat-shaped clock on

the wall tick. Was this really going to work? She didn't want to get her hopes up again. She'd had her heart broken too many times over this whole fiasco.

Lyra broke into a smile. "Okay, I need to talk to my mom, but I can convince her. You can pick up the dress in two weeks. My mom will want to see a mock-up of the site by tomorrow though, before we start working on the dress. Can you do that?"

"You'll have it tonight. You have my word she'll like it. Or I'll change anything she wants. Or you want."

Ash couldn't believe it and discreetly snapped the hair tie she had around her wrist to make sure this was not a dream. The tiny pinch assured her it was not.

Sebastian turned to smile at her. "Told you."

Ash threw her arms around Sebastian and kissed him soundly on the cheek. "God, I love you!"

She felt his cheek grow hot under her mouth and pulled away. She'd never seen him blush so hard! For a second, she had the insane thought that she should have taken this opportunity to kiss him on the mouth. She'd always wondered what it would be like to press her lips against his perfect Cupid's bow. She easily could have blamed the moment.

Alas, she hadn't acted quickly enough and the moment passed.

Lyra continued to smile wistfully. "You guys are sooo cute. I wish my boyfriend was so sweet. Hell, I wish I even had a boyfriend!"

This didn't help Sebastian's blushing.

"You—" Lyra turned to Ash "—are very lucky to have a date who cares so much about her dress. Most guys have no idea what their girlfriend's wearing—and don't care much, either!"

Ash opened her mouth to thank her, but Sebastian got to the false statement first.

"Oh! I'm not her girlfriend. I mean, she's not mine. My girlfriend I mean. We're just friends."

Sebastian's words stung. Suddenly, Ash felt as if they were in eighth grade again and everyone was teasing them about "going together" and Sebastian was very insistent that they were friends and nothing more. He always made being mistaken for her boyfriend sound like the most horrific and unbelievable thing in the world.

And specifically now in front of Lyra.

"She's—going with someone else." Sebastian was still uncharacteristically fumbling for words. "I'm not going."

"You're not?" Both Lyra and Ash asked together. She *knew* it. Jessica had chickened out.

He shrugged. "I didn't have anyone special in mind to ask."

Ash noticed Lyra's eyes light up again as she said, "I'm not going to the prom, either. No one asked me. Plus, it's really expensive."

Sebastian nodded knowingly.

"Maybe you and I should hang out when everyone else is at the prom!" Lyra sounded like she was joking, but Ash suspected she was not. "Be losers together!"

On top of her hurt, Ash felt a sudden anger at Lyra for blatantly flirting with Sebastian right in front of her. Lyra had assumed he was taken thirteen seconds ago, for God's sake!

And Sebastian was just standing there smiling like an idiot at the idea of him and Lyra hanging out.

Ash bit her tongue before she could utter the rude thought that was in her head. Both of them were doing a lot to get the dress done for her, and she was grudgingly grateful to both.

"Okay, you'll hear from me tonight." Sebastian was suddenly in a big hurry to get out of there. "I'll call you."

Ash couldn't shake the irritability as they exchanged numbers. Somehow...this whole thing just felt wrong. Sebastian should be at the prom. He should not be out having some random date with a random girl from an alterations shop.

Sebastian was silent during the car ride home and didn't try to draw Ash into conversation. He probably had his mind on Lyra's invitation to hang out. Ash started to seethe with anger and stared out the window. The usually beautiful Seattle sunset looked like someone had dribbled a blob of purple paint in the middle of the sky and let it smear all over itself.

Laila had the day off and was talking quietly on the phone in the living room when Ash walked into the kitchen after school the following afternoon. Sebastian hadn't come home with her that day, saying he wanted to get the second iteration of the website prototype to Lyra that night. Apparently, Lyra's mother had feedback on the colors of the first prototype he'd made. Something about feng shui or something or other.

Sebastian had been oddly quiet the whole day at school, glancing down at his phone and texting furiously every chance he'd gotten. He'd been so distracted in drafting, he'd almost gotten them auto-shop detention. Ash had tried to catch him after class, but he was gone the second the bell rang.

She hadn't texted him the rest of the day and had been hurt when he hadn't texted her, either. She suspected this behavior was all due to Lyra.

"Connie, you wouldn't believe what a talented and responsible young woman this girl is!"

Ash set out her homework on the kitchen table and listened

halfheartedly. Laila was gossiping with Seb's mother again. Probably about some case she was on.

"She's Ash's age. It's astounding."

Ash opened her copy of *The Tempest*. She still wasn't done reading the book, and the essay on it was due in forty-eight hours. Maybe she would call Armstrong and see if he was done. Maybe they could get together for a late-evening date at the Elliot Bay Book Company to drink coffee and compare notes. Maybe she'd post a picture of their date on Facebook.

I'm not sitting at home alone, either, Seb.

"No, she called me just now to reassure me of her sewing credentials. She sent me photos. You must see them. Absolutely stunning work."

Ash stopped reading. Her mother was talking about Lyra! Apparently Lyra had wasted no time showing off her skills. Ash knew she should have been overjoyed, but she was getting annoyed at her mother for gushing so profusely. *Of course* Lyra would be good at sewing...that was her job for God's sake.

"She and her mother are going to work on the *lehenga* together. Her mother has a lot of experience in beadwork, but I truly believe Lyra is the talented one. She spoke to me about things I haven't heard since the days we had a family tailor!" Laila said. "Yes, boning, corsetry and French seams!"

Ash poured herself an iced tea and added guava syrup to it as she continued to eavesdrop on the conversation.

"Oh, goodness, no, I hadn't realized Sebastian's not going to the prom. That's a shame. Did he tell you why?"

Ash stopped what she was doing and listened harder.

Come on, Mom. Snoop more.

"He said that? That he'd like to go out with her if he could? Oh, how sweet!"

What the heck, now they were just gossiping. Ash's ears

burned. She had a sneaking suspicion it was Lyra that "he" would like to go out with.

"Oh, I'm glad! He's seeing her tonight, I'm sure? He should just tell her."

Ash gripped the glass so tightly, she felt the ice from her glass start to freeze her hands. Sebastian was going out with Lyra! That must be why he hadn't come home with her. And he'd felt the need to lie to her about it, too!

"Oh, she'd be a fool not to like him. He's a wonderful boy. No mother would worry if her daughter was out with a boy like Sebastian."

Ash couldn't just sit and listen to this. Why was Laila so desperate to set up Sebastian? What was wrong with leaving things the way they were, anyway?

She started to gather up her books and leave this conversation behind when a motion from the backyard caught her eye.

Like the other day, Sonali was sliding under bushes and climbing over hedges. Ash went to the kitchen door and watched from the little window.

This time, Sona wasn't alone in her weird maneuvers.

A plump, cherub-faced blonde was close at Sona's heels, doing the exact same thing. She struggled as she climbed over a hedge into their backyard. "You wait till I catch you!" she called out. Ash's hand reached for the doorknob. She was not going to let some kid harass her little sister.

Sona rolled under some questionable-looking bushes and was a few feet away from the kitchen door. The blonde girl was behind her by seconds.

Ash immediately threw open the back door. "Get in here!" she hissed.

For once, Sona didn't argue and ran for the door and

slammed it behind her. She threw her back against the closed back door. A smile broke across her face.

"What?" Ash was confused. She was pretty sure she'd just seen Sona get chased by a bully. A really clumsy, not-very-big bully at that.

"That girl's been bothering me for weeks."

Ash had an *aha* moment and was about to make an all-knowing statement.

"She put superglue in my hair on the bus."

"Sona, we need to tell Mom. She can't just—"

"I just led her through a bunch of poison ivy." Sona couldn't stop smiling. "I don't think she's going to mess with me again."

Ash's mouth dropped open.

"You, you… Evil little… How?"

"I told you. I'm a pacifist. But I'm not a pushover."

NINE

"Hey." Sebastian dropped into a seat next to Ash at lunch. She pulled off the headphones she'd been sharing with Armstrong, who was sitting on the other side of her.

They were previewing the music his friend was going to be debuting prom night. Well, Armstrong had been previewing with a serious face. To Ash, all of the tracks pretty much sounded the same. Apparently Armstrong's friend had played his stuff at Neighbours, the popular club in the neighborhood that had eighteen-and-over night on Fridays. Ash had pretended she'd been there the past Halloween eve and had appreciated the DJ's awesomeness, though the thought of being out at a club till 4:00 a.m. on a Friday was laughable. Laila would murder her for even asking.

"Hi." Frankly, Ash was surprised to see Sebastian. They had barely spoken for days outside of their drafting assignment. She'd chalked it up to his secret love affair with Lyra. "What's going on?"

Before Sebastian could answer, Armstrong noticed the latest addition.

"Hey, we don't know each other. I'm Armstrong," he said loudly, leaning over Ash to shake Sebastian's hand, not having removed his headphones. "You're James, right?"

"Sebastian Diaz actually," Seb replied back just as loudly. "You've known me for twelve years."

Ash gave Seb a look. Armstrong was just trying to be polite—what was Seb's problem?

Seb returned her look with a hurt one and averted his eyes. Armstrong went back to his music.

"What's wrong?" Ash asked quietly, so she wouldn't disturb Armstrong's music selection. He was painstakingly marking the tracks he liked the most.

Seb actually looked quite distressed. She wasn't used to seeing him anything less than totally on top of things. The meltdowns and tantrums were usually her department.

Sebastian shook his head and stole a few of her curly fries.

"Tell me."

"Just class stuff. Don't worry about it."

Ash reached up and brushed a fleck of salt off his chin. "You don't think I'm smart enough to share it with?" She was teasing. He had no problems talking about his computer stuff with her, though she usually had no idea what he was talking about.

"No!" Seb looked horrified. "I just got into it with Dave and Richard."

"About?" Ash had a hard time imagining the three of them fighting about anything.

"Just…stuff. It's dumb."

Ash doubted it. Seb never got upset over dumb stuff.

"Will you come over after school today?" she asked even more quietly. She didn't want Armstrong to hear it and think it was something it wasn't.

Sebastian hesitated and glanced over at Armstrong as if knowing what Ash had been thinking.

"You sure?" He shifted his focus back to her, looking into her eyes. His eyes were bright hazel that day, the color they got when he was especially troubled.

"I've missed you." It was hard for Ash to admit, knowing that he'd probably been with Lyra instead of her the past week. "Come over and we can go out somewhere. Let's go check out the window displays at Pretty Parlor and play with that cat. We can get Malaysian fried rice after." The vintage store was a favorite of Ash's, and Sebastian liked to sit on the fluffy white couch and play with a frisky gray tabby who liked to hunt human fingers while Ash tried on '50s-style dresses.

"I have stuff to do." Sebastian looked past Ash and suddenly got up. "I'll text you in the evening. Sorry for being a pain."

And he was gone.

Ash turned around and wondered what he'd seen. She spotted his two friends, Dave and Richard, leaving the lunch line with their trays.

"I'll be back," Ash said to Armstrong, who didn't appear to notice.

Ash intercepted Dave and Richard as they were leaving the cafeteria.

"Can I talk to you guys for a second?"

They looked at her warily. Sebastian had introduced them many times, but neither guy had been interested in talking to her for more than a few seconds. She knew Dave a little bit from their calculus class, but not Richard. He just always looked surly.

"Seb's really upset by something."

"Well, he should be!" Dave burst out. Ash was taken aback. The blond Harry Potter look-alike always was very polite, serious and quiet, even when he knew all the answers during calculus. If Ash had known half what he did, her hand would perpetually be in the air.

"He's such a jackass," Richard added. Ash was not surprised

to hear this. She'd never heard Richard say anything that didn't involve the word *jackass*.

"Can you believe this shit?" Dave continued to surprise Ash. He knew how to *swear*? "Did he tell you what he did?"

Ash held up her hands. "Wow. Okay." She hadn't expected them to actually tell her. She'd assumed they'd go away, find Seb and handle whatever software emergency they were having on their own. "What did he do?"

Dave crossed his arms and stewed. Richard stared at his feet. Oh, the guy code. If she didn't know, they weren't going to tell her. Great.

"Come on you guys. You can tell me," Ash cajoled. "I won't tell him we talked."

Richard glanced at Dave and broke. "We were building a phone app for our AP Computer Science class. It's really cool. A *really important* local company wanted to buy it. We already had all the paperwork ready to go based on the prototype. We can't tell you what it is, it's a secret."

Ash resisted an eye roll. This had to be that picture categorizing app thing Seb had been talking about with her dad. The one BlueDog company that was based in downtown Seattle wanted to buy.

"We've planned to do this together since we were freshmen," Dave added. "It was Sebastian's idea to use this app for our careers as legit app developers. He's our main developer."

Ash was slowly starting to recall. "Your app is like the Chewbaccas or something?"

Richard looked more surly than before. "He told *you*? Why doesn't he just post it on the internet? God."

"Hey!" Ash started to protest.

Dave raised an eyebrow. "Then you know he backed out,

right? Just yesterday. Told us he's doing his own thing. He's going to build—"

"A website," Ash finished. She knew something was wrong with Seb's offer to Lyra.

"You know about that?"

Ash nodded, the dread inside her stomach growing by the second.

"Why did he do it?"

"I don't know," Ash said honestly.

Both Dave and Richard stared at her, finally seeming to believe her.

"I just don't get it. He's acting so weird." Dave shook his head in disgust. "It's been his dream to build this app and he's the one who convinced *us* to start the project. We've worked so hard to come up with the business plan for how we'll make money off of this so we can all pay for college. The app was due in a month—there's no way we'll get it done now. That company will never buy anything from us again after this fiasco."

"Because the jackass just ditched us!" Richard spat out, completely in character.

Ash stared up at the ceiling. This was her fault.

"Ash, can you talk to him?" Dave asked. "Figure out why some store's website is more important than BlueDog? They're going to find someone else to do the app as soon as we tell them we won't do it, and we'll lose out. And we can't do this without Sebastian."

Ash nodded. "I'll fix this."

Richard stopped ranting. "Can you?"

Ash nodded and turned her back before she started crying in front of those two. She had to duck into the bathroom when her eyes got too watery to see what was in front of her. How had she not realized the kinds of sacrifices Sebastian had made for her? How did she not know this start-up was his dream? How could she not only have *not* helped, but actually *hindered* his goal?

Why was he doing this? He didn't need to build the website for Some Like It Haute. He didn't need to keep helping her. Not for some prom dress.

But he did. He kept helping her. Over and over again. Because that was how much he cared about her.

Ash slid down the wall of the bathroom—barely noticing how dirty the floor was—and wondered how she had never realized this. And what that said about her as a friend.

ten

"should I come with you?" Laila twisted her hands and asked for the fifth time.

"Mom, you'll just be judgmental." Ash grabbed a mirror out of her purse and checked her makeup to make sure her lipstick was still fresh and sharp. She was *not* going to see Lyra looking like a slob. It was dress pick-up day and Ash didn't know if she or Laila was more nervous.

"I will not! I'm never judgmental," Laila continued to argue.

"That's kind of your job, hon," Ash's dad reassured his wife gently, swinging an arm around her shoulders.

Laila gave him a dirty look.

"...and now I know where our daughter gets it. Ash, please take her with you."

"Seb's here." Ash ignored them both and ran out the front door.

It was the first time she'd seen him outside of class all week. Every day after school, he'd made an excuse for why he was busy. She was almost relieved. She didn't know what to do with the revelation she'd had the other day about the sacrifices he'd made for her. She'd wanted to talk him into doing the app with his friends, but she knew he would never back out of the commitment he'd made to Lyra and her website.

"Drive! Drive!" she practically yelled as she slid into the passenger side of the Mazda6.

"Did we rob a bank?" Sebastian obliged and stepped on the accelerator.

"Mom wanted to come."

"Aw." Alarmingly, Sebastian slowed down. "She should!"

"Why? Why would you say this? Stop saying crazy things. Drive!"

"But…"

"No. No but! Drive!"

"Ash, it's her dress. I think she's terrified we've destroyed it. Let's just give her the peace of mind."

Ash sighed. He was right, of course, but she didn't want Laila's two cents on everything for once.

"Oh, come on, it's already done. She can't exactly have *that much* to say about it," Sebastian said, as if counterarguing Ash's thoughts.

"This is where you brought my dress?" Laila looked more and more concerned as Sebastian parallel parked the Mazda outside Some Like It Haute for the third time. "Are you sure this is a professional establishment? Where are the alterations done? Inside the shop? I expected something like the Nordstrom's workroom."

Ash shot pointy looks at Sebastian. From her angle, it looked as though Laila had plenty to add.

"Mrs. M. Just trust us. Lyra and her mom know what they're doing. You talked to her on the phone, right? Let's go in. And please…let's be a little quiet, so Lyra's feelings aren't hurt."

That quieted Laila down.

Lyra glanced up as the door *ting*'ed a greeting. "Hey, you guys!" She was wearing a gorgeous champagne-colored silk dress with bugle beading at the bottom. She looked like she was headed out to a speakeasy or some other glitzy spot. Again,

Ash envied her sewing ability. The power to just make whatever beautiful thing she wanted must have been amazing.

They exchanged pleasantries and Ash introduced Laila. "This is my mom."

"Oh, my God, so nice to finally meet you!" Lyra abandoned the bolt of fabric she was rolling and came out from behind the counter. "Wow, you guys look exactly alike!"

As Laila and Lyra talked, Ash glanced back at Sebastian, who was busily examining a rack of zippers by the door. She didn't miss the surreptitious glances Lyra shot in his direction, almost as if she was waiting for him to get closer to her.

She really liked him.

"I have the dressing room all set up for Ash. Do you want to try it on and show us?" Lyra beamed her brilliant smile again. "I'm so excited."

Ash took a deep breath. And she was so nervous. This was it. If this didn't work, prom was officially off for her. Not to mention, Laila would kill her. She found herself not caring as much as she had in weeks prior. So much had happened.

She pulled closed the curtain of the tiny dressing room and admired the turquoise beaded dress hanging from the mirror. She snapped a quick picture of it with her phone.

"Your dress is stunning." Ash heard Lyra say to her mother. "My mom and I enjoyed working on it so much. She apologized she couldn't be here. She wanted me to ask where you got it."

"North India. It was part of the bridal trousseau when I was married to Josh. My grandmother gave it to me. She lived in India her whole life."

"It looks hand-embroidered."

"It is. By our family tailor."

Lyra sighed. "How romantic. Family tailors just aren't a

thing anymore. No one seems to wear handmade anything anymore."

"That's even more the reason I wanted to pass on this beautiful thing to my daughter."

"Or maybe to me if she doesn't want it," Lyra said.

That drew a laugh from Laila.

Ash listened to the conversation as she slipped the heavy skirt over her hips. No chance, Lyra. If the dress looked halfway as good on as it did on the hanger, Ash was planning to wear it out of the shop.

So far, it was looking good. The fit was perfect around the hips.

"Sebastian did a phenomenal job with the sketch and the 3-D sculpture. The alternations were really easy to understand. I still can't believe how cool that little sculpture you made with the 3-D printer is!"

Ash heard Lyra shuffling some things around.

"Thank you. I hope you'll like the website I make for you as much."

Ash strained to hear as she slipped the halter top over her head.

"The prototype you sent me was so awesome. Where did you get the graphics?"

"I made them."

"Amazing. Laila, you have to see."

Ash could practically hear him blush. He didn't do well with compliments.

Ash heard the clicking of the keyboard, presuming it was Lyra bringing up the website prototype.

"Wow." Ash heard a sharp intake of breath from Laila. "Sebastian, you are so talented. I wish my husband was in a place to find a good summer job for you. I wish there was something *I* could do."

"I'll be all right." Sebastian was his usual independent self, though Ash knew the truth. The two people he'd been planning his software dreams with were no longer speaking to him. She had to fix this somehow. "Right now I just want to make sure the website is what you expect. You're my first retail client."

Ash posed for the mirror. The dress was amazing, but she was even more interested in hearing the end of their conversation.

Sebastian said nothing more than, "I just want to make sure it's worthy of the work you did to make Ash her dress."

Ash took that as the cue to throw back the curtain.

In the big mirror outside the dressing room, the dress was even more stunning. It was cut perfectly at the hips and was fitted until it reached her knees, where it just exploded into S-shaped ribbons of chiffon fabric overlaid on top of the glittering *lehenga* fabric below.

The halter top was elegant. Beaded at the bodice sides and the straps, which tied behind her neck. Cut just to the top of her navel and showed off a discreet amount of midsection.

The room was silent as Ash twirled.

"You were right, Ash. I do want my dress back," Laila deadpanned. "It's just beautiful."

Lyra was practically jumping up and down. "Oh, please tell me you're nominated for prom queen. You deserve to be. God, that is gorgeous!"

Ash was watching Sebastian. "What do you think?" She did a curtsy in his direction.

He shrugged. "It's amazing, of course. But then you always

are. In this dress or anything else. You're always the most beautiful girl in the room."

Ash felt her heart speed up. He'd never told her that before. She believed that to him, that was true.

The room was again silent. Lyra gazed at Sebastian in adoration, but he didn't take his eyes off Ash.

How stupid I've been, was Ash's only thought.

This is crazy.

BANG!

He's your best friend.

CRASH!

It's just the emotions talking.

CLANG!

Don't get so carried away by the past few weeks.

"Honey?" Ash's dad smiled gently at her from the doorway to the garage. "When did you become a drummer?"

Ash shifted the drumsticks to her left hand and swigged more iced tea with her right. "Just giving it a shot."

"Your mother is asking for that shot to be over soon. Apparently this household is big enough for exactly one drummer and I've already claimed the 'most annoying' title."

Ash vacated the spot and handed off the drumsticks to her dad.

"So, what's really going on?"

Ash shrugged as she took a seat on the ratty old beanbag on the floor.

"You can tell me, I'm forgetful. I won't hold it against you when you're older." Josh started playing air-drum dramatically.

Ash smiled, despite her mood.

"It's the dress."

"What? This again? I thought you loved it." Josh paused

his drumming motion in midair. "Even your mother said it looks incredible."

"It does."

"Yeah, this sounds like the worst thing *ever*."

"It looks so good thanks to Seb."

"He's a great kid. And your best friend. I don't see the bad news anywhere."

Ash sighed and picked up a stray Nerf ball off the garage floor.

"He's not a great kid?"

"He did all this for me and he's not even going to the prom. He didn't want to ask any of the girls he knows. Any one of them would *die* to go with him."

Josh raised an eyebrow. "It's modern times. He can ask a guy."

"Daaaad." Ash sighed even more dramatically.

"Aaaaaash," he replied. "Tell me what's really bothering you."

Ash filled him in on the app fiasco, Seb's friends being ultrapissed at him and how she was at a loss for how to fix it.

"Now he has to spend the rest of the quarter making that website. All because of me."

Josh twirled his drumsticks. "Sounds like you're feeling guilty."

Ash considered this as she tossed the ball from hand to hand. "I feel like a lousy friend. What should I do?"

Josh stared at her for a minute. "If you could do anything for him, what would it be?"

Ash bit her lip. "Make that app for him with his friends. I wish I could just write the app for him. Is JavaScript really hard to learn?"

Josh laughed.

Ash took that to mean a "yes."

"And plan B is?"

Ash's shoulders dropped. "Don't know."

"There's the problem-solver I raised!"

Ash threw the Nerf ball at him.

"Prepare for amazement." Armstrong's voice floated over the dressing-room door.

Ash looked up from her phone. Sebastian hadn't texted her all day.

"I'm ready."

She was at the final fitting of Armstrong's suit for the prom and was trying to sound as excited as possible. This was what she wanted! This was what she'd been hoping for since freshman year. She and Armstrong together. Prom. Her in a gorgeous, unique gown no one had ever seen. Armstrong in a cool suit that was so him. She had to pull it together.

"Ready-ready? You'll never get a first glance again."

Ash tried not to sound annoyed. Was he always this dramatic? Was this how she sounded when she was in a dressing room? No wonder no one liked to shop with her. "Yeah, Armstrong. I really am."

Seconds ticked by and finally he threw back the curtain.

She blinked as Armstrong stepped out in front of her.

"So? Awesome, right?"

She nodded. "Yeah, really cool."

He looked...pretty much the same. Skinny pants. Nice shirt tucked into it. Only a slightly oversize jacket was different.

She smiled, she hoped, encouragingly.

"So...first thoughts. Tell me fast. I want quotes for my blog."

"Um…"

Ash's stomach sank as she realized what she'd been trying to bury all day. She had wanted nothing more than for Sebastian to be on the other side of that dressing-room door.

Eleven

Ash had never been so nervous. There was a huge chance this was not going to go well. She'd paced up and down her driveway for half an hour, wondering if today was the day to do this.

It was not going to get easier.

Shaking, she raised her hand and knocked. She hoped he would just answer so she didn't have to make chitchat with his mother. She almost got her wish when Connie, Sebastian's mother, opened the door with one hand, the other holding a cell phone to her ear.

"Yes, yes. We'll send that basket of peaches over right away," Connie said into the phone. She gestured for Ash to go on up to Sebastian's room. Ash wondered how much Connie knew about Sebastian's app development fiasco…and her role in it. She hoped very little.

Ash clutched the book she held in her hand tighter as she knocked on Seb's door. Everything was about to change. For the good or bad, she didn't know yet.

A muffled noise sounded like a "come in."

She pushed the door open.

He sat at his desk in front of his computer, staring at lines of code. "What's up?" He didn't seem surprised to have her in his room after almost a week of very little communication.

"I need to talk to you about something."

Seb didn't turn around as he typed a few words, then scrolled to the very top. "Sure."

"Can you stop that for a second?"

Seb turned around and noticed she was holding something. He didn't ask what it was.

"How's it going?"

Sebastian shrugged.

"I know it was a little…weird. At the shop the other day."

Sebastian didn't say anything, instead turning around to face his computer screen again.

This was not going the way she'd envisioned. Ash forced herself to launch into the speech she'd memorized on the driveway beforehand.

"So…since like the first day of high school, I've been making this book. It's kind of like a scrapbook, but not the crazy old-lady kind with cats and string, just the regular kind."

Ash paused to breathe, realizing she sounded an awful lot like Laila when she got nervous.

"You're a closet scrapbooker?" Sebastian said, not turning around. He pressed a few keys on the keyboard. It looked as though he was working on the website.

"No!" Ash laughed, tension broken. "Well, sometimes. Seb, can I sit down?"

"What next? Knitting and collecting cats?" Sebastian moved to the bed and motioned for her to take a seat on the chair he'd just vacated.

"I've been making this book for almost four years now. I wanted to show it to you."

Sebastian watched her expectantly.

Ash took another breath and handed it over. "Every page has some important thing."

Sebastian flipped open the cover and looked at the first two pages. "Orientation."

Ash smiled. "Oh, I remember how lost we were!"

"We didn't find the cafeteria in one shot for a week!" Sebastian recalled.

"Look at how cute we were." Ash gestured toward a picture of the two of them standing between their driveways on the first day of high school. They'd been terrified. Laila taking fifteen million pictures of them hadn't helped at all.

"Remember the time you didn't know if school ended at two or three or if you had another class after fifth period?" Sebastian broke into a smile as he flipped another page. "Freshman homecoming."

"God, the float we made was terrible!" Ash recalled. "A giant cake float?"

"You wanted a cake, you got a cake."

Ash stopped laughing. "You've always tried to make my harebrained schemes happen. Always."

Sebastian continued to smile ruefully. "It's my job."

"Remember when no one asked me to freshman year homecoming and you got everyone together in the limo to come pick me up? You wouldn't let anyone else have a date, either." Ash remembered how Seb had saved the day—yet again.

"Oh, God, the bagel shop!" Sebastian stopped flipping. "You worked there for what—a month?"

"Or less!" Ash peered over his shoulder. "You drove me every day since my mom wouldn't let me get my learner's permit till I was sixteen!"

"Remember the time your parents came in and you refused to acknowledge them?"

Ash shoved him. "I did acknowledge them!"

"You yelled at them for spying on you and made me get rid of them!"

Both were laughing so hard, it was getting difficult to breathe.

"This is really cool," Sebastian said as they started to reach the end. "You kind of made your own yearbook. Just your memories."

"Our memories." Ash touched the last filled page, which just had a picture of the finished dress, the picture she'd taken in Haute. "Just the final prom page left. And graduation. And summer."

Sebastian was quiet as he stared at the last blank page. "I can't believe it's almost over."

"You're on every page, Seb." Ash moved from the chair to the bed next to him.

Now was the time.

Sebastian glanced at her, his eyes full of love…and so much more.

"You've been a part of every single aspect of my life. You've always given everything possible to make my dreams happen."

"I love watching you shine," Seb said simply. "Nothing makes me happier. You know that."

That was what Ash had started to realize that week. He truly did love making her happy. He always had.

"I don't want my prom page to not have you in it. I want you standing next to me in that gorgeous dress we—you really—made."

Sebastian sighed and closed the book. "I'm not going, if that's what you're here to convince me of. You don't have to feel guilty! I just want you to have a good night."

Ash paused. "You won't go no matter what?"

Sebastian glanced away as he handed the book to her. "No. You'll be fine. You guys will have a good time."

"There is no 'you guys.' There's just me."

A flutter of confusion crossed Sebastian's brow, but he didn't say anything.

"What if I asked you to be my date?"

He didn't look up. "Stop."

Ash reached over and stroked his jaw, where he was getting the finest stubble. She'd realized recently how much she liked touching him. How natural and wonderful it felt.

"Sebastian, please?"

"Does Armstrong know you're inviting a third wheel?" Sebastian attempted to sound lighthearted as he pulled his face away from her hand.

"I broke it off with him. It wasn't right. It was never right." Ash bit her lip. "He's—he's not for me."

"Are you being serious?" He turned to her. "But you were so into him for like four years."

She shrugged. "I was into an idea of him. Not really him-him. Turns out I was looking at the wrong thing."

He took her hand, tracing her palm. "This isn't funny if you're messing with me. Tell me what's going on."

"I want to go with someone who means something to me. Someone who means everything to me." Ash paused, hoping he would catch on.

Sebastian kept his head lowered as he continued to tickle her palm with his tracing fingers. She realized he was tracing her heart line.

"Will you go with me, Seb? To our senior prom? Will you be my date?" Saying it out loud was so much simpler and easier than she'd expected.

He stopped tracing her hand.

"It would be such an honor if you were my date. Sebastian, please say you'll go with me. I won't go if you say no."

twelve

"Tell me again how this happened?" Sebastian put an arm around Ash as Laila took the hundredth picture of the two of them.

"You came to your senses and finally asked me to the prom."

"Me!" Sebastian hadn't stopped grinning since he'd arrived almost an hour ago for pre-prom pictures. "Crazy girl."

"You could have saved us months of angst by just asking me in the first place. God, Seb."

Seb twirled Ash in the living room for Laila's benefit so she could capture more pictures.

"Mom! We'll miss the prom."

"One more." Laila snapped at least six as Josh stood off to the side, looking as proud as could be. "Last one. That one wasn't good. Last-last one."

"Leaving now. Bye, Dad. Be good, Mom."

"One more photo of you two getting into the car."

She snapped two more before realizing they were truly leaving.

"Don't spill anything on the dress! Don't drink alcohol! Certainly don't spill alcohol on the dress!"

"Drive! Drive!" Ash yelled as Sebastian jumped into the driver's side of the Mazda6. "And this time she is not coming with us!"

She could see her mother snapping more pictures through the rearview mirror as they drove away.

"Our hero!" Dave, Sebastian's friend, practically picked Ash up in a bear hug as Ash and Sebastian made it out of the photo booth inside the Palace Ballroom in Belltown.

Even surly Richard managed a smile.

"Why are you guys here?" Sebastian looked confused as he looked from Dave to Richard. "You do know this is the prom, right?"

Dave shrugged. "Once-in-a-lifetime high school experience and such, right?"

"We're here to photobomb all these people," Richard explained.

Ash was not surprised by his goal.

"Who are you here with?" Ash asked, looking around for Dave's date.

Dave shrugged again, in Richard's direction.

"You're here. Together?" Sebastian looked questioningly at them. "Like, as in a date?"

The foursome squeezed together as another couple pushed past them in an effort to get into the photo booth.

"Not all of us have a computer-savvy chick show up in our bedroom and ask us to go, man." Dave held up his hands. "It was a mandated man-date. It's a thing."

Sebastian raised an eyebrow in Ash's direction. "Computer-savvy?"

Ash smiled, she was sure this time, enigmatically. "Maybe."

Sebastian looked among the three of them. "What are you guys talking about? I don't like this."

Dave nodded in Ash's direction. They'd agreed she was going to be the one to announce the news.

"Remember that app you guys were supposed to do?"

Sebastian frowned at Richard and Dave. "The one we agreed we were done talking about?"

Ash smugly smiled. "It's happening after all. With or without you."

Sebastian looked completely baffled. "But—"

"My mom, dad and I are going to help you guys to make it happen. This summer. That's the Montague family project for this summer. All of us."

Dave and Richard were now smiling smugly.

"Wait. Your dad. The professional software engineer. Is going to help us? Your mom. The lawyer."

"And me. Let's not forget me. I'm excellent at marketing good ideas."

Dave broke into a huge smile. "Ash's dad is going to help us formulate the codebase. Ash's mom is going to help us with the venture-cap paperwork. She already convinced BlueDog to give us an extension till the end of summer. Something about labor laws since Richard here is under eighteen. Ash's sister is going to help with graphics and story. Ash is going to help us with… Wait, what were you going to do again?"

"Market the good ideas!"

The three of them looked expectantly at Sebastian, who still looked dazed.

Seb's mouth dropped open, as if he just realized what they were saying. "You mean, we're…doing it? For real?"

"Don't be a jackass," Richard added helpfully. "Does it sound like we're kidding?"

Ash practically bounced from the excitement. "You have no idea how hard it's been to keep it from you! Before the summer is over, the app is going to go broad! We even named it! It's called Red-Eye Flight!"

"It's almost as good as Han Solo and the—" Dave started to say. It had been near impossible to convince him that was a stupid name for an app. *Laila* had had to do the work to tell him it was just not marketable.

"Why are you still talking?" Ash gave him a look.

"But…how? You guys said you were freelance web developing all summer!" Sebastian was still stuck on the first part of the conversation.

"We lied."

"We've been conspiring for weeks!" Ash gestured toward Richard and Dave and speaking for them. "We all love you so much. You do so much for us. Lying and deceiving you was the least we could do!"

Sebastian continued to look shocked as Ash led him deeper into the dance floor. "Now, let's make this an unforgettable night!"

"Thank you for this night," Sebastian whispered in Ash's ear.

"It's perfect." The last dance started and Ash was dizzy from dancing and happiness and whatever someone had put in the punch. It had been a perfect night. The comments on her dress had been in the hundreds, and Seb had blushed every time she had pointed at him when someone asked who the designer was.

A lifestyle reporter from a Seattle blog had even asked to take a picture of it for the headline the next morning.

Ash had barely even noticed when Armstrong Jones had swept by them, cell phone in hand, snapping pictures of little details around the ballroom. Jessica Moriarty was trailing him closely, looking desperate to not lose him in the crowd. He'd wasted no time finding another date.

Under the swirling lights of the ballroom, safely in Sebastian's grasp, Ash now looked shyly up at him, hardly able to believe things had worked out the way they had. Perfect.

"It's not a perfect night."

"No?" Ash asked quizzically.

He gazed back at her, slowing down his twirling. Slower, slower… He finally stopped and pulled her tightly into his arms.

He brushed her lips with his fingertips.

Then finally with his own lips.

"Now it's a perfect night."

And Ash finally realized what the word *unforgettable* meant.

★ ★ ★ ★ ★

Dedication

In memory of Charlie Savage Irwin, who will forever live on as every wish, every hope, and every dream.

Acknowledgments

First off, many, many thanks to my wonderful agent, Adrienne Rosado for being my cheerleader and champion and chief talker-off-the-ledge. To everyone at the Nancy Yost Literary Agency and Harlequin Kimani TRU, thank you, you guys are all rock stars in my book.

To my internet family, especially those of you on Twitter (*especially* my Psych-Os) and Facebook—you inspire and challenge and help when I ask. I'm eternally grateful that so many of you have transcended the realm of invisible friends in the box to become treasured real life friends. Thank you for making a very isolated job feel much less so.

To my Writer Girls, Serena, Erin, Cathy, & Shannon—I wouldn't know what to do without you guys. You make me laugh until I cry and make me laugh when I cry. You're the best ever.

To my twinling: Yeah…you. Thank you. For everything.

To Lewis and Nate and Abby—thank you for being proud of me and being my life and making all of this worth it. I love you.

SAVE THE
LAST DANCE

Caridad Ferrer

one

"Man, I'm gonna miss you, Peyton."

People hurried past, anxious to secure their place in the ever-massive security lines at Miami International Airport. Around us, the sounds of announcements and conversations conducted in at least a dozen languages hummed like a swarm of multicultural bees.

I gently butted my head into Eddie's chest—about as high up as I could reach without heels—and held tight to his hands.

"At least it won't be too long before we see each other again," I said. "Barely five weeks until Claudia and I come back for prom."

I glanced over to where my Warrington Prep roommate and Eddie's cousin, Claudia, was holding tight to *her* boyfriend—and Eddie's best friend—David, as they, too, said their goodbyes. The goodbyes we were saying after having come down to Miami for spring break because

1. it was Claudia's hometown;
2. the boys were here;
3. it was Miami, *duh;* and
4. *my* hometown of Boston? For spring break? In April? Wicked cool… *Not.*

Besides, with Dad off conducting business in London and Mom scouring Christie's and Sotheby's for treasures for the interior-design business she was starting "since, you know, darling, everyone just *loves* how I've been decorating our houses," it would just be all Ghosts of Christmas Past, when Mom and Dad had informed me they wouldn't be making it home from Hong Kong in time. They *had* been good enough to inform me I'd be taken care of because they'd made "arrangements." Or if I wanted actual human company, I was free to go hang out with Ancient Aunt Regina and her Ricola-and-brandy-scented breath.

Still not sure if it was the "arrangements" part or the thought of Ancient Aunt Regina that had set Claudia off but either way, it had offended every sense of Cuban family sensibility the girl possessed on a massively deep, personal level. She'd immediately invited me to come stay with her family for the holidays and while I'd tried to decline—polite WASP reserve and all that—it had really been halfhearted.

God, listening to her description of a typical family holiday, I'd felt a longing like I had never felt before in my life.

They made her crazy, she confessed, her nosy, interfering family with some old-school notions that made even the starchiest of my Boston Brahmin relatives look hip and modern by comparison, but she wouldn't miss holidays with them for the world. And she was inviting me into that world and WASP reserve be damned, I just couldn't resist the temptation.

So I'd gone and without an ounce of hyperbole or exaggeration, I could honestly say it had changed my life. I'd loved it. I'd loved everything about it. I'd fallen in deep, intense love with Miami. The colors, the language, the culture, the food. Claudia's family...

Eddie.

Who was as amazing as he was infuriating. And pretty hot to boot, but I had to keep declarations of such to a minimum.

He was a Cuban boy and had quite the well-developed ego and sense of self.

Thank goodness the inherent sweetness and the fact he could kiss like no one's business balanced the Cuban boy-ness out.

As if Boston for spring break *ever* stood a chance.

Of course there had been my parents' other option—to join them because, "Darling, we know how much you love England and it would be lovely to give Oxford another look before you make a final decision, no?"

Not happening, either.

I mean, it wasn't as if they'd be going out of their way to hang out with me or treat it like a vacation, and I *knew* they had no intention of going with me to Oxford to "give it another look." Work, you know. Meetings to be conducted. Lunches to have. Cocktail parties to attend. Three-hundred-year-old enameled snuffboxes to be purchased.

And there in a nutshell, my family—epitome of New England work ethic with a soupçon of elitist WASP privilege.

Besides, not that they knew it yet—or would care if they did, really—but Oxford was already off the table and another look wasn't going to change my mind. I'd made my decision.

Eddie's long sigh ruffled my hair and teased the rim of my ear—sweet caress combined with genuine longing. "It's gonna be a long-ass, miserable, craptastic five weeks."

I squeezed his hands as I lifted my head to meet his gaze. "Oh, come on. You're going to be so busy with school and baseball, you'll barely notice the time passing."

An odd shadow passed across Eddie's face. The same one I'd seen on more than a few occasions during the past ten days. It had taken just a couple of those odd expressions for me to realize they only occurred when baseball was mentioned. As

if…he had something on his mind. But he hadn't said anything about it and honestly, baseball was one of those things
I wasn't sure *how* to ask about. As a native Bostonian, I was
well aware of the history of the game—and my town's love-
hate relationship with the Red Sox. As a mathematician, I
understood the game and of course, statistically speaking, had
a deep appreciation for it—even more so since dating Eddie
and keeping track of his season numbers—but the intangibles
of what made the sport *magical* to him had escaped me until
fairly recently.

Until I'd started cooking, actually. That's when I'd begun to
appreciate the visceral sensations that came along with physi-
cal engagement. With creation.

The complete and utter satisfaction of knowing you'd
kicked ass.

How Eddie looked when he talked about baseball—how he
sounded—was a perfect reflection of how I felt about cooking.

But just because I now understood the intangibles didn't
mean I was ready to go asking my boyfriend questions. Comfortable as Eddie and I were together, things were still too
new and I was *way* too much a product of my reserved New
England upbringing.

Maybe Claudia would have some ideas. Even though she
was every bit as reserved as I was, she still had years of experience with her family poking their noses into everyone's business. Some of it had to have rubbed off. Besides, Eddie was
her cousin. And David was his best friend. Somebody had to
know *something,* right?

A second later his expression cleared and he gazed down at
me with those eyes—deep golden brown of the caramelized-
sugar syrup that was the basis for a flan—that had captivated

me from the first flirtatious glance he'd sent my way last Christmas.

Half "how *you* doin'?" half wondering, as though *I* was the fascinating one, and that *never* failed to make me just a little weak in the knees.

And here I'd thought myself impervious to knee weakness.

"Trust me, girl." He leaned down far enough for his lips to brush my ear. "I am definitely going to notice you not being here."

I smiled, part from the tickling sensation, part because of what I now knew I could say. "Hang in there, baby. Five weeks until prom, another four after that until graduation and then I'm back here in Miami *for good*."

And back with Eddie, since he'd be going to University of Miami while I'd be attending Johnson & Wales, one of the best cooking schools in the country.

I'd have cooking, Miami and Eddie—a win-win-win situation.

I tilted my head back far enough for a kiss, but froze.

The shadow was back on his face, darker than ever, and for the first time I could recall, there had been no mention of baseball involved. Just me. And coming to Miami.

Oh, God.

He wasn't *sorry* about all of this, was he?

But before I could ask, because New England reserve be damned, I had to *know*, I felt a hard tug on my arm.

"Holy shit, Peyton, we have got to *go* unless we want to flap our arms and fly our asses back to Warrington."

I felt myself caught between Claudia's impatient pull and Eddie's tight hold on my waist as he leaned down and kissed me—hard enough to leave me seeing stars behind my closed lids and for my knees to do that watery/weak thing.

"I'll call you tonight," he whispered. "I love you."

Thank God for Claudia. Without her hanging on to my arm the way she was, I might have just collapsed into an undignified puddle that would have shamed my ancestors right down to their Pilgrim skivvies.

It was the first time he'd ever said that to me.

Okay, then.

So the shadows weren't my fault.

I should have probably been embarrassed by how relieved that made me feel.

I wasn't.

I was just relieved.

TWO

"That one," Claudia said from behind me as we both stared into the dressing-room mirror.

"Are you crazy?"

"Nope."

"You *are* crazy."

"I believe that's exactly what I said to you when you talked me into that obscenely clingy red number at Christmas and did you listen to me? No, I believe you did not." Her smile was a thing of pure evil as she loomed over me—and I do mean loomed, since she stood five foot nine to my much shorter five-three. She thought it made her seem intimidating. *Pfft*. I'd known her too long for intimidating to factor into the equation any longer.

Besides, lower center of gravity. I could totally take her out at the knees.

"You're suggesting I wear white, Claudia. White chiffon, at that. I'm going to look like some damned sacrificial virgin, waiting to be flung off the cliff into the fiery depths of a volcano."

"You forgot to mention swallowed by the flowing lava." She crossed her arms and hit me with her best Cuban Mother stare. Which was *so* not effective since I'd been on the receiving end of the real thing, courtesy of both Claudia's mother and *abuelita*. Compared to them, Claudia was a mere neophyte.

"It was implied by fiery depths," I grumbled as I fidgeted with the dress some more, although no amount of fidgeting was going to change the color.

White. For a *prom*. Clearly her mind was addled. Had to be the lingering effects of inhaling too much mineral dust in her geology labs.

"Oh, for God's sake, would you stop, Peyton?" She slapped my hands away from the elaborate web of thin straps that began at the sweetheart bodice and worked their way over my shoulders, where they expanded into an even more intricate pattern across the back.

"First off," she continued, holding up one finger, "one would think you'd be getting used to the idea of the color, what with the chef's whites that are soon going to be your mandatory uniform, and second—" a second finger joined the first "—and perhaps more important, *not* white, ivory, which looks gorgeous on you and makes your hair take on those volcanic, lavalike hues."

A finger of my own shot up, to which she just laughed.

As I returned to fidgeting with the straps, I said, "You say lavalike like it's a good thing."

Because bright red hair and its accompanying pale lashes and freckles were just *so* much fun to deal with in a society far more geared toward the "blondes have more fun and bru-nettes are sultry and sexy" mind-set. On the upside, at least my freckles were confined to a sprinkling across my nose and cheeks with only a slightly heavier pattern across my chest and shoulders, as opposed to the blanket my strawberry-blonde cousin Jessica had been gifted with.

I'd feel bad for her, except, well…let's just say "sweet cousin Jessie" was a bitch of monumental proportions who'd once slathered me with sunscreen that she'd liberally cut with baby oil. I'd spent three days in the hospital recovering from a vicious case of photodermatitis—aka sun poisoning.

My insistences that it had been her fault fell on deaf ears—attributed to delirium and a long-held perception of me as absentminded. Clearly, I'd simply forgotten the sunscreen. Besides, what gains could "sweet cousin Jessie" possibly achieve by doing such a mean-spirited thing?

Well, according to her whispered aside when she'd visited me in the hospital with her parents, it had been an experiment run a little amok. She'd simply wanted to see if it was possible to match the hue of my skin to my hair. In the interests of science. Offered with a smile that gave her an uncomfortable resemblance to The Joker.

Please. Science experiment my *ass*. To say Jessica had any genuine interest in science was like saying Velveeta was real cheese.

"Oh, please, Peyton, I know you're not that disingenuous. Even if your looks aren't to someone's specific tastes, no one can deny you're classically pretty."

"I said nothing about not being pretty."

"But you were thinking it."

Busted.

And yet another one of those reasons to hate the fair skin and red hair? The blush I could *see* creeping its way up my chest, across my shoulders and over my face.

See? That's just how stupid Jessica was. If she'd really wanted to see if my skin tone could ever match my hair, all she needed to do was embarrass me. Easy enough to accomplish—no nefarious plan necessary.

"You have this great bone structure your relatives were kind enough to hand down to you, skin that hasn't seen a zit since sophomore year, you bitch, and lovely delicate eyebrows that require zero upkeep, also reason to consider you a bitch if I didn't love you so much."

"Gee, thanks," I muttered, but she was on a roll.

"Then let's talk about this hair of which you despair." Before I could say boo, she'd reached for the elastic at the end of my braid and had loosened the heavy mass.

"Just *look* at this."

"I generally do," I said in another mutter, not that she was paying attention. "At least once a day when I do my best to get it the hell out of my way."

"Do you have any idea what half the celebutantes who show up on TMZ pay to try to get these 'just fell out of bed' waves?" she demanded while I blushed again. Not at the description, but at the memory of Eddie, running his fingers through my hair, a look of wonder on his face the likes of which I'd never seen before from a boy. At least, not directed at *me*.

"And triple that amount for what they pay to even come close to the color you come by naturally." Dropping my hair, she crossed her arms and met my gaze in the mirror with a smirk. Hoo boy—I knew that smirk.

"Of course," she added, "you then also have to factor in the cost of the Brazilians to which they must subject themselves on a regular basis because we all know those carpets ain't matchin' the drapes, baby."

I shuddered, both at the imagery and the memory of the one and only waxing I'd ever submitted myself to. Never. Again. Thankfully, not really a necessity.

"Claudia?"

"Yeah?"

"Remember how you once asked me never to use the words *horndog* or *douche canoe* ever again?"

"Yeah."

"Don't ever use the words *carpet* and *drapes* in that context ever again. Please, I beg of you."

"Wuss."

"Absolutely." I resumed staring at my reflection, acknowledging that with my hair loose and swept mostly to one side, the dress did take on a bit of a sexier vibe. But still...

"You're really not digging it, are you?" Claudia's voice was soft and had completely lost the bossy tone.

I sighed as I adjusted the straps yet again, but with a bit less irritation and more consideration. It was...*okay*. But this was prom. A rite of passage I'd quite honestly never expected to be attending primarily because Warrington—small, elite and with its science and math focus—preferred having an all-grades, all-night, pizza-and-movies bash. I'd been perfectly fine with such a setup. Proms were a leftover from the Dark Ages. Stressful, what with the having to find the perfect dress and the perfect shoes and of course, the whole waiting to be asked, please God, let *someone* ask.

Then, during one of our late-night text exchanges, Eddie asked if I would be his date, and all of a sudden, I realized how much I *really* wanted to attend a prom.

Okay, hadn't realized until I met Eddie and completely fallen for him, how much I wanted to attend a prom *with him*. That I might actually *want* to stress over the dress and the shoes and the hair and the flowers, like a normal teenage girl.

I think it was maybe because my whole life, I'd always been just out of step with the rest of the world. Because of my intellect, who my family was and my own sense of not really caring whether or not I was in step with the rest of the world. But, you know, for just this one moment I wanted this *one* taste of normal.

And for this taste of normal I definitely wanted more than the *okay* of the dress I currently wore.

"As your reward for indulging my desire to see if my impulse about you and ivory was right—which it was," Claudia said with that blessedly familiar smirk, "I offer you this."

I gasped as she produced a hanger from which hung the Perfect Dress.

Snatching it from her hand, I rushed back into the stall and about thirty-two seconds later, I was back out. I grinned as Claudia's dropped-jaw expression reinforced what I'd garnered from the split-second glance I'd gotten in the small dressing-room mirror before emerging into the larger dressing area with its triple mirrors.

We looked at each other and said it at the same time:

"*That* one."

three

All in all, it had been a highly successful weekend. Taking the train into Boston from Worcester—hanging out at the family homestead, which was at our disposal, what with the parents in…Buenos Aires, I think? Maybe Brisbane. Somewhere in the Southern Hemisphere. Look, the details were on my computer's calendar if I absolutely needed them. In the meantime, we had the run of the house and the city, and the mercurial Boston spring weather had even cooperated, allowing us to comfortably wander Newbury Street until both Claudia and I had found the dresses, shoes and other various accoutrements that would ensure a perfect prom.

"Do I need to match my tie to your dress?" Eddie asked during our nightly Skype session on the following Tuesday. Claudia had tactfully taken herself off for a shower—a long one, she'd joked, easily dodging the pillow I threw at her—so Eddie and I could have a few minutes of relative privacy.

"Oh, good God, *no*." I laughed at the relief that was so obvious, it almost reached past the confines of computer screen. "Well, if you didn't want to do it in the first place, why'd you even ask?"

"Uh…it's a *thing?*" He lifted a shoulder. "David and I went past the tux shop the other day and they had all these pictures and displays of prom dresses and tuxes with matching ties and vests and what're the things that go around your pants?"

"Cummerbunds."

"Yeah. Those." He made a face. "I can never remember what they're called."

"They're kind of stupid, actually," I said as I reached for my ever-present can of Diet Coke. "I've never seen one that actually stays where it's supposed to." And the shirts would end up all wrinkled and puffing out beneath the strap if the man happened to shed his jacket. There was no precision to it whatsoever. "If you're going to go with one over the other, my vote's for the vest. But you do not have to match it to my dress at all."

He tilted his head and stared at me through the screen as if trying to figure me out. Not an uncommon expression from him, really. The irony was that he inherently understood me a lot better than most people.

"What?"

He was silent for a few seconds longer, then said, "You are so unbelievably low-key. All the other guys at school, their dates have gone completely batshit, I swear. Going with them to the tux store, telling them exactly what to wear and how to wear it up to and including the color-coordinated Trojans. But not you. You trust I have the sense to pick something appropriate and you're willing to leave it at that."

I tried to shove the horrifying visual image of color-coordinated condoms *way* to the back of my mind, hopefully never to be heard from again.

"Don't forget, I've seen you dressed for a formal event." New Year's—when he'd taken my breath away in his well-cut black tux. The night everything between us had changed.

"I'd never forget that."

"Me neither—" I touched the computer screen, wishing I

could touch him for real. "I don't care what you pick. I just can't wait to see you again."

He smiled, his hand rising into view of the camera. My cheek tingled as if feeling his caress.

"See? Low-key."

I laughed, recalling how by my family's standards I was downright neurotic. "Is it really that strange to you?"

"Considering the majority of women I'm surrounded by are Cuban?" His shudder was evident even through the screen. "Yes."

I laughed, midsip, bubbles going up my nose. "I'm so telling Claudia you said that."

"*Pfft*. She doesn't count." He rolled his eyes. "She's been away from Miami long enough, the Cuban high-maintenance has worn off."

"I'm sure she'll be relieved to hear that." I settled myself more comfortably against the pillows and adjusted my laptop's screen. "Seriously, whatever you want to wear, short of a baby blue tux or all-white tails, is fine by me."

A wicked grin curved one side of his mouth. "So the UM orange tux would be a go, then?"

"The what?"

An instant later a link popped up in the message window below the video. Cautiously, because I was all too familiar with Eddie's penchant for terrifying links—like the Prancer-cising lady in her tight white pants—I clicked.

Then couldn't click the window closed fast enough.

"Are you *trying* to blind me?"

He fell out of frame until all I could see onscreen were a pair of sock-clad size twelves, accompanied by hysterical laughter.

"Please tell me that's not real."

He reappeared before the camera, wiping beneath his eyes.

All of a sudden I felt myself nearly overtaken by an urge to be there, with him, sharing the silly moments that I enjoyed as much as I enjoyed the romantic ones.

"Saw it in the flesh," he managed, straight white teeth flashing in a grin that made him look like a hell-raising little boy despite the weekend-scruff look he had going.

"Well, speaking of flesh, that *would* be the tux to wear if you wanted to fend off the zombie hordes—" Better prepared now, I clicked on the link once more and took a closer look at the orange horror. Good God, it even had a ruffled shirt— that matched perfectly. So. Very. Wrong.

"Seriously, even the undead have standards."

"Judging by the tastes of some of the girls I go to school with, not really."

I winced. "Ouch. That's wicked harsh, Eddie."

"Truth hurts, baby."

Oh, he was making this entirely too easy. "Yeah, well, didn't some of those girls used to date *you?*"

He flinched, but the glint in his eye gave away his enjoyment with our game. "*Dayum,* girl. Low blow."

"Truth hurts, baby." I blew on my fingernails and buffed them against the front of my T-shirt. "Bow before the master."

Instead of bowing, he propped his chin in his palm and stared so intently, it was almost as if he was right *here* beside me. "That's why I love you, Peyton." His voice was soft, giving weight to the feeling of him being right beside me, yet making the distance between us feel even more enormous.

My hand froze against the front of my shirt. "Why? I mean…I'm not trying for props, I'm really not, but I just zinged you and you up and…and say *that* and…and…why?"

And there went the unfortunate tendency to babble when I got nervous.

That was the thing about Eddie, though. From the moment we'd met—him with his mouth stuffed so full of *pastelitos* he looked like a six-foot-tall chipmunk, and giving Claudia grief, because that's what boy cousins did in her family, according to her—he hadn't ever made me nervous. Much.

In fact, the only instance of honest-to-God actual nervousness between us that I could recall was two weeks ago—the first time he said he loved me. Except then I hadn't had enough time to *be* nervous—at least, not in his presence. All I could do was glance back over my shoulder as Claudia dragged me through security, to where he stood, watching me go and looking like he wanted to run right after me and keep me from going.

It wasn't until I was actually on the plane and leveled out at our cruising altitude of 35,000 feet that I'd finally freaked, because, *hello?* He said he loved me.

Me.

And I hadn't had a chance to say it back and how did I really feel and…and…*why?*

I mean, on paper, Eddie Abreu and I had absolutely nothing in common. He was a fun-loving, good-looking, Cuban-American jock, while I was an uptight, intellectual nerd from one of the snobbiest, elitist families in the country. Who had red hair.

He was smart, sure, because I couldn't ever see myself dating someone who didn't have some functioning gray matter, but he wasn't an academic wonk and as far as any athletic prowess on *my* part? Well, I was the person who held the singular distinction at Warrington of having broken my leg during the fitness rope climb…before I'd ever gotten off the floor.

See? Nothing in common.

But that was on paper. In real life we shared the same

twisted sense of humor and liked a lot of the same music and movies and—once I'd gotten over my snotty assumptions/shock that a baseball player liked reading—books. But even those were little things. I had those same things in common with half the guys here at school. Guys who, on paper, should have been perfect for me. Which was one of my very first lessons in learning that when it came to people, facts and figures and statistical probabilities didn't necessarily add up to the right answer. Eddie and I—we just…fit. All our outward differences, rather than being negatives, seemed to add up to giving us a never-ending source of conversation and avenues of exploration. Maybe he wasn't an intellectual wonk, but Eddie…he was curious about everything and wasn't shy about expressing his interest and enthusiasm.

Eddie just took such *joy* in everything. And that joy and enthusiasm were, I confess, addicting—especially for a cold, repressed WASP like me who'd spent her life taking comfort from numbers and their reassuring predictability.

That was the intangible we shared—the thing that made us so perfect together when on paper, we never should have worked beyond a holiday hookup between the Hot Popular Jock and the Nerd Who Was a Curiosity.

"Why do I love you?" he asked.

"Um…yeah." I toyed with the end of my braid, twisting strands around my fingers. "I mean, you only said it once so I wondered if it was maybe an impulse. That you, um…regretted."

His brows lowered. "And when have you ever known me to regret anything I say?"

"Never," I admitted. "But then, we've barely known each other four months."

"And I feel like I've known you my whole life," he snapped.

"It's like with Claudia and David, Peyton—I can tell you things I've never told anyone else. And you know what? I've never told anyone else I love them, either."

"You tell your mother."

"Peyton."

"Sorry, sorry…I'm nervous."

"And you think I'm not?"

"You don't seem like it."

"I am." He shoved a hand through his hair, leaving it sticking up in a wild disarray of ink-dark spikes. "Okay, in order to give you the precision you seem to crave—" He paused and pinned me with a dark stare. "You paying attention?"

"Yeah."

"Okay. I have never told anyone I'm dating or involved with or who's not a blood relative or David, who might as well be a blood relative, that I love them."

I was torn between laughing and melting, because, you know, cocky Cuban-boy jock or not, he looked so impossibly sweet and nervous, staring into his computer's camera.

Battling what felt like a Cirque-du-Soleil troupe doing aerials in my chest, I finally managed, "Neither have I."

After a pause, he quietly said, "You still haven't."

"I know." I'd wondered about that. If we'd had more time, would I have said it back at the airport? I wasn't completely sure, but I *think* I would have. I knew the way I felt about him was different from how I'd ever felt about any other boy. It was…more. And I was pretty certain it was love. I just didn't quite trust myself to be able to recognize it, was all. I didn't exactly have a huge amount of practical experience with it— at least, not in the no-holds-barred "love and fight and make up with equal intensity" sort of way that I'd observed in Claudia's family.

Not exactly how things were *done* in the Chaffee family.

There was, one thing, however, about which I was absolutely sure.

"When I say it, Eddie, I want it to be face-to-face."

My voice was so soft I could barely hear it over the blood rushing through my ears. I could feel my lips and tongue moving and could only hope I'd actually said the words I was thinking. Because that was another bad side effect of being a babbler—the unerring ability for my mouth to spew something completely different from what I was thinking.

Thankfully the roaring subsided enough for me to hear his tentative, "But you want to, right?"

Not completely trusting my stupid mouth, I merely nodded, but it was enough, judging by the relieved expression that crossed his face and the "Good" that was as much a sigh as a word.

When I finally felt as if I'd regained control over speech functions, I ventured a soft, "You still haven't told me why, though."

Before he could, though, Claudia burst through the door, more wet than dry and with her sweatshirt on inside out.

Drops scattered everywhere as she grabbed my laptop, turned it to face her and said, "Yo, cuz, save the tender goodbyes for another time—Peyton's gotta go." She slammed the lid shut, cutting him off in the middle of an outraged squawk.

"Claudia, what the hell? Have you lost your mind?"

"Head's up. Your parents are here."

I stared. "My what?"

"Your parents. You know, the people with whom you allegedly share genetic material? Although I maintain you were switched at birth or hatched in a lab or something, because you are *so* not like them." As she spoke, she bustled around the room, shoving the bags from our shopping expedition into the closet and straightening our ever-growing piles of books into something that wouldn't topple into an avalanche.

I watched, too stunned into immobility to move—or, you know, breathe. My "How do you know they're here?" came out more like an unintelligible wheeze than actual words, but luckily, Claudia and I had been roommates long enough she had no trouble translating.

"I ran into Jenny McIntyre in the bathroom. She was over at Main talking to Dean Winchester when they showed up. She said they looked überserious and hastily beat a retreat into the drawing room with the dean."

The fact they were here was bizarre enough. But here, on a random Tuesday night, and talking to the dean?

"But…*why?*"

At that moment, the room's intercom buzzed. "Peyton, you there?"

Casting a sympathetic look my way, Claudia crossed to the unit. "Yeah, she's here. What's up?"

"She has guests…" A pause. "Her parents. They're waiting in the drawing room in Main."

And with a hiss and crackle that brought to mind *Macbeth's* witches, the disembodied voice cut off, leaving behind a silent void that echoed ever more loudly with the question I'd asked Claudia.

Why?

four

claudia, loyal roommate that she was, offered to walk over with me. Nice of her, but not really necessary. Shock and curiosity at their unexpected appearance aside, my parents didn't make me nervous.

At least, not any more than talking to polite strangers made me nervous.

I knocked on the heavy carved wooden door and waited for the dean's melodious "Enter" before pushing it open.

Dean Winchester, very elegant and French, even after thirty years in the States and almost that many years of marriage to a Texas-born neuroscientist, smiled. "*Bonsoir,* Peyton."

"*Bonsoir,* madame." My smile faded as I turned to the couple seated by the fireplace. "Mom, Daddy... What a surprise. I thought you were in—" I paused, kind of wishing I'd thought to check my calendar before I hoofed it over here, then mentally shrugged and said, "Brisbane."

"Buenos Aires, actually."

Whoops. Still, though, at least I had the Southern Hemisphere part right.

"We arrived back in town this morning." With a smile, Mom tilted her head slightly, the summons clear. I stepped forward and placed a dutiful peck to her porcelain-cool cheek, still smooth and unblemished, thanks to some tasteful and very expensive work she thought no one knew about.

"You must be exhausted, then." As if from a distant corner of my mind, I could hear my voice taking on the clipped, patrician cadence with which I'd grown up. A cadence that had been fading more and more of late. "Which begs the question, why are you here?"

Daddy stood from his chair to give me his kiss, perfunctory and somewhat distracted. So that was as usual. Moving to stand before the fireplace, he studied me with a pale blue intensity that was incredibly familiar and yet not. I'd seen that gaze thousands of times—discussing a business deal, the America's Cup, a new vintage of Bordeaux, or how to perfect his golf swing. What *was* unfamiliar was seeing that gaze focused on *me*.

Honestly, I wasn't sure the man had ever looked at me so intently in my entire life. It left me with the distinct sensation he was actually *seeing* me for the first time. Maybe ever.

"In part, Peyton, because of the email I received from the bank regarding a substantial withdrawal from your trust, paid to Johnson & Wales University. An institution that frankly, I had no idea even existed, let alone that you had any intention of attending."

Oh, *crap*. I mean, I knew I'd have to tell them eventually. I'd just hoped maybe to put it off for a while. Like, until graduation.

Not from Warrington—Johnson & Wales.

Hey, a girl can dream, right?

"I had no idea you were still being informed of the activity on my trust account now that I'm eighteen."

His eyes narrowed. "While you have control, we still maintain a supervisory interest until you turn twenty-five."

"Ah." *Crap.* "It might have been nice to know that."

"Would that knowledge have changed anything?"

I tilted my head as if considering. "No…not really."

And, hey, listen to that. My voice was steady and cool, with just a hint of the distance I'd heard him employ on countless business calls throughout my life. As if there were no real questions to be posed and I was just the slightest bit bored.

Never mind that my heart was pounding and a knot the size of Plymouth Bay had appeared in my stomach. If they were still being informed of the movement on my trust, did that mean they could also reestablish any measures of control? Because if they could, I was, in a word, *screwed*.

I fought to keep my swallow unobtrusive. I could play this stupid, but not only would that not fly, it really wasn't my style.

"You have an objection to my postsecondary plans, then?"

Dad's gaze narrowed further, but instead of answering me directly, turned to Dean Winchester instead.

"Were you aware of any of this, Hélène?"

She leaned back against the front of her desk and crossed her arms. What did she see, I wondered? Certainly not a happy family unit—not in the traditional sense at any rate. Ironic, really. While my family and its name stood as a bastion of American tradition, it was likely the last word anyone would use to describe us.

"I was," she finally said. "Peyton came to me when she was weighing her decisions and asked for some advice and guidance."

"And she didn't listen?" Mom's voice reflected as much emotion as I'd ever heard from her. Guess she had listened all those times I expressed admiration for my school's headmistress.

Dean Winchester lifted one shoulder in a quintessentially Gallic shrug. "I advised her to carefully weigh the pros and cons of what she was considering."

"So she didn't listen," Dad muttered.

"And," Dean Winchester went on, with an added sharpness that suggested she didn't much appreciate being interrupted, "I told her that ultimately, it was her decision and she had to choose what she felt would make her happiest."

"Oh, for God's sake," Dad exploded. "Do you know what she wound up choosing?"

The dean nodded calmly.

"And you didn't think there was anything *wrong* that a girl with her academic credentials chose a goddamned cooking school?"

The only indication that Dean Winchester was at all shocked by Dad's outburst was a subtly raised eyebrow. While I, on the other hand, stood there gaping like a landed trout. Dude, I'd *never* heard my father's voice hit that sort of volume—not even when watching the Red Sox from his box at Fenway.

"I will admit, Richard, it did come as a surprise when Peyton expressed her interest in culinary school. Frankly, I had no idea she even knew how to cook."

"Neither did I," Mom murmured.

Not such a surprise. In my family the kitchen was where you went to microwave something. If you could get to the thing before a servant appeared to ask if you needed help pushing the buttons.

"But the more I thought about it, the more I thought it a splendid idea for her. The students here, they're so focused and directed and that's a true joy, do not get me wrong. However—" she paused, her gaze turning inward "—these years they should also have adventure. New worlds and people and exploration. Quite honestly, Peyton is the last student I would have ever thought would embark on such an adventure, and perhaps was one of the ones who needed it most."

She turned my way. "Rarely have I ever encountered such a determined, single-minded soul in my entire life, which is admirable—" she smiled "—but perhaps a bit limiting at so young an age?"

"All this soul-searching sounds lovely and might be fine if Peyton was an average or even above-average student," Mom said. "But Hélène, we both know Peyton's intellectual gifts are exceptional. It was bad enough she was determined to waste them on remaining in academia rather than joining any of the family's businesses. But at least a tenured professor position at a top university carries with it a certain cachet."

I watched as Dean Winchester's eyebrow rose a fraction higher. Whether it was at the sideways slam at academics or the overall snobbery, I wasn't sure. Probably the slam at academics, given that Warrington drew its student body from snobbery of all stripes.

"Moreover," Dad added, "I did not gift this school with an extremely generous endowment in order for you to send my only child off to become a…a…*servant*. Preparing food for the masses."

"Oh, for God's sake, you make it sound like I'm going to be wearing a hairnet and asking 'Do you want fries with that?'"

I couldn't be sure, but I *thought* I heard Dean Winchester make a noise that almost sounded like a laugh. Covered up an instant later by a cough and Dad's aggravated, "You stay out of this, Peyton."

Oh, he did *not* just say that. "Stay out of it?" I spluttered. "Stay *out* of it? It's my *life*. And since when do you give a shit about it anyway?"

"Peyton—" Dean Winchester's voice remained outwardly mild, but I could hear the warning.

"But Dean—"

She held up a hand. "In a moment." To Dad she said, "Richard, I understand how upsetting Peyton's change of heart must be—how…disappointing, even. However, the simple fact of the matter is that for a student of her magnitude, the Oxfords and Harvards will always be there and will always be fighting to have her attend. What is the harm in allowing her to explore this newfound interest?" A canny expression crossed her face. "With Johnson & Wales's position as a traditional university as well as a top-notch culinary institute, she could also earn a business degree. Quite valuable if she's to open her own restaurant, as she expressed interest in eventually doing."

Oh, she was good. Hit Dad right where he lived. Naked ambition wasn't necessarily a desired trait—so…*common,* darling—but a sound plan executed with solid business acumen?

How could he argue with that?

An equally canny expression crossed Dad's face—an expression echoed by Mom as they exchanged glances, and an uneasy shiver skittered along my spine. Because Dad, he was good, too. A master, really.

"You make sound points, Hélène," he began in a cultured, affable tone.

Crap.

I knew that tone.

"Especially about the schools still being there should she opt to attend at some date in the future."

"However—" Mom picked up the narrative with a small smile and my heart rate escalated to something approximating mambo speeds "—one could argue the reverse is also true. That, after completing a degree at, say…Oxford, for example, that culinary school would still be there, yes?"

Dean Winchester looked remarkably unperturbed. The random thought that I'd hate to face her across a poker table flitted in and out of the transom of my mind. Never mind that I had no clue how to play poker. Had never even had an interest in playing poker.

I wondered if this was what a breakdown felt like.

"One could argue that most effectively, yes," Dean Winchester said. "But ultimately, this is a decision that lies with Peyton, would you not agree?"

It felt like a chess match was being fought—and I was the key pawn in the middle.

Still, a pawn was never without some power.

"Out with it."

Three heads turned to face me.

"You've got something in mind." I looked from Dad to Mom. "So quit tiptoeing around and just spit it out already."

Dad's eyes narrowed again and oh, my, was that actual shock? "You're going to need to learn a bit more finesse Peyton, if you're to succeed in business."

"I've got time." I crossed my arms. "Well?"

Dad resumed his seat beside Mom. A power play. While some thought that looming over your opponent was a sign of strength, it was actually the other way around. Kind of like royalty on the throne. Handing down decrees.

Or death sentences.

"We have a proposition."

Or…worse.

FIVE

"YOU aren't seriously going to do this."

"What choice do I have?" I typed a name into the browser's search window while Claudia wore a hole in the rug between our two beds. I wanted to tell her to stop with the agitated pacing, but not like I had room to talk—not with the way my foot was twitching, hard enough I could barely keep my laptop from taking a header to the floor.

She froze, midpace, and hit me with a hard stare. "You *could* say no."

My hands froze on the keyboard. "I know," I said slowly, my cheeks burning. "But Claudia, they're expecting me to fail and I can't. Not at this."

This, being the proposition my parents had presented me with.

See, there was this charity dinner they'd soon be hosting to benefit… Hell, I couldn't remember if they'd even said. No doubt some fashionable cause that had captured their fancy, was politically advantageous and would provide a nice tax write-off. A high enough profile event for them to have secured the services of one Kai Belizaire—very French, very accomplished and currently one of *the* hottest young chefs on the planet.

Dude had cooked for heads of state, rock stars *and* Johnny

Depp, all before most people in this country were of legal age to drink.

Well, what with my interest in cooking and in the restaurant world, wouldn't this be just the *perfect* opportunity to see if I had any real aptitude for it?

That little tidbit delivered with a smile that clearly conveyed what *they* thought.

So they'd approached Chef Belizaire with a request: allow their aspiring-chef daughter a place on his cooking team for the charity event.

I might have expected a chef of Belizaire's stature to respond to that sort of high-handed request-that-really-wasn't with a hearty, "Oh, *hell* no." Or maybe more accurately, given what I'd heard about the man's temper, something like, *"Bite my shiny French ass,"* in some creatively profane combination of the multiple languages in which he was allegedly fluent.

No doubt massively insulted that a chef of his magnitude was being asked to babysit some overprivileged neophyte who hadn't yet had so much as a formal cooking class.

There was *no* way he'd ever agree.

Except…he'd agreed.

I couldn't help but wonder how much of an investment they'd promised for whatever his next new restaurant venture would be.

Cynical?

You bet your sweet bippy. I might not have had an interest in finance or business as a career choice, but it didn't mean I didn't understand how the game worked. I was a Chaffee, after all.

Which meant I also understood Mom and Dad's game even before they finished fully outlining it.

What it boiled down to was simple: succeed, by Belizaire's

famously exacting standards, and Mom and Dad would lay off and cease all interference with my plans to attend culinary school.

Fail, and I'd give up my place at Johnson & Wales, relinquish control in my trust until I turned twenty-five—so as not to make any further rash decisions—and enroll at Oxford, which was *their* first choice for me. Oh, and forget mathematics and an academic career. I'd be enrolling in the business school so I could employ my gifts to their fullest extent and to the benefit of the family, as was right and proper.

Their faith in me was touching, really, it was.

"I feel you—and you know I totally get where you're coming from." She lowered herself to sit at the edge of my bed. "But Peyton…what happens if you do fail?"

My hands clenched into fists. "I gave them my word."

She shook her head. "Girl, I keep telling you, there is some Irish in your woodpile, what with the red hair and the crazy-ass stubbornness."

"Or maybe it's just a genetic predisposition toward insanity." I sighed. "I mean, there are a few cousins and great-aunts who are only spoken of in polite whispers."

She grinned. "See, another difference between you starchy WASP types and Cubans—we don't hide our crazy relatives. We put them out on display and do a compare and contrast."

I drew my brows together and let loose with a haughty sniff. "Oh, my dear, that would be entirely too tasteless."

She waved an airy hand. "Tomato, tomahto—what's tasteless and outrageous to your family passes for any given Thursday night dinner in mine."

She skewered me with that dark brown gaze—long enough to leave me squirming just a little. With a nod, as if satisfied, she finally said, "Okay, what gives? What *haven't* you told me?"

With a sigh I closed the laptop and set it aside, exchanging it for one of the oversize throw pillows littering my bed. "The night of the dinner."

"What about it?"

"It's a week from Saturday."

I watched the comprehension dawn.

"Son of a *bitch*."

I clutched the pillow tighter. "More or less my reaction, as well. For which I was chastised, because 'such language, Peyton.'"

She rolled her eyes. "Do you think they knew about prom?"

"I don't think so—" I sighed "—but after I mentioned it, it turned out to be a convenient piece of leverage for them."

"Proof of how much you really want to do this."

Claudia's face reflected the equal amounts of anger and frustration I had felt as I'd watched my parents' expressions shift. They'd exchanged these glances that left me feeling like a piece of chum dropped straight into shark-infested waters.

"Yeah." I wasn't ashamed to admit I'd gotten just a little desperate. "I offered to take their challenge on any other day. Asked why it had to be *this* particular event—I was sure they'd have others or I could even apprentice in a kitchen of their choice during the summer, but they were adamant. Said they knew me well enough to know I'd want to challenge myself with the best—"

"And right now, the best is this guy."

"Yep." I shoved a hand through my hair, impatiently pulling my ponytail free of its elastic. "Hoisted by my own petard, as it were."

"Yeah, but this is beyond unreasonable. Even for them."

"I know…" I hesitated. What had also emerged during that segment of this evening's festivities was ugly and kind of made my skin crawl, and yet shouldn't have come as such a huge surprise. "Which made me think one reason they dug their heels in was because of Eddie."

Claudia's eyes widened so far she almost looked like a manga drawing.

"Come again?"

"Turns out they're not happy I've been seeing someone they don't know." How they even knew I'd been seeing *any-one* had been a mystery until they mentioned that a friend of a friend had seen me looking "rather cozy with someone we didn't recognize, darling. Appeared to be a local," on Lincoln Road Mall. The way Mom relayed it, you'd have thought I was caught on camera in a compromising position with a leper.

Her wide stare narrowed. "Someone they don't know or a Cuban boy not of their perceived station?"

Thank God for a friend who just *knew* things without my having to spell them out. And who didn't judge.

Hugging the pillow closer I quietly said, "It doesn't matter to them that your family is as successful and well-established in their community as mine is—they're…"

"Cuban," she said flatly.

"I was going to say *different*."

She shrugged. "Why beat around the bush?"

"Because it's *embarrassing*." My skin flushed with uncomfortable heat as I went on. "I mean, it's one thing for the Relatives of a Certain Generation—" I intoned it like the title I'd always imagined it to be, "to be prejudiced and intractable, but my parents aren't *that* old. Why should they care?"

"Because your parents grew up in a protected, elitist bubble." She shrugged. "My family might have been every bit as bad if they hadn't had their entire lives uprooted by Castro and had to start over, albeit under better circumstances than a lot of their contemporaries."

Because the Abreus had already long since expanded their jewelry business to Miami and Europe by the time Castro came to power, while they lost what they had in Cuba, they still had a solid foundation from which to start over.

"Their worldviews were shaken up just enough that it left them a little more open to possibility." A surprising grin crossed her face. "Still didn't stop the men in the family from thinking they knew what was best for me or bartering like camel dealers in Damascus in order to engineer a relationship between me and David."

I couldn't help but laugh. "Yeah, talk about 'be careful what you wish for.'" Since both she and David, who turned out to actually *like* each other, had not only started dating, but were taking off for Stanford in the fall, both to pursue academic careers light years from the roles their families had imagined for them. The likelihood they'd ever be returning to Miami on a permanent basis was stuck somewhere between "slim" and "not a chance in hell."

We fell quiet for a few seconds, then she said, "So what're you going to do about Eddie?"

"Well, I'm not breaking up with him if that's what you're asking— *Ow!*" I threw my arm up to protect myself from yet another unprovoked pillow attack. Maybe it wasn't such a good idea to have so many pillows on my bed.

"I know that, you ninny. Jesus!"

"Sorry." I tossed the pillow back at her and resumed clutching mine. "I guess I'm still stuck in What Mom and Dad Want Me to Do–Land."

"Well, let's zip on back to What Peyton Wants to Do– Land."

"What I want is to go to Miami with you and go to prom with Eddie."

"But you're not going to."

I shook my head.

She sighed and looked so sympathetic, I felt tears prick the backs of my eyes.

"I do get it," she said softly, making the tears threaten even more powerfully. "Do you want me to beat a retreat for a while so you can call Eddie?"

Still struggling to fight back the tears, I shook my head.

Her eyes widened. "You want me to stay?"

I shook my head again, leaving her looking mildly confused.

Taking a deep breath I said, "I think this is something better said face-to-face." I sighed. "I'll just switch my plane ticket to this weekend and fly down to see him."

"Do you need me to go with?" she immediately offered.

I shook my head. "It'll be okay. I hope."

"Eddie'll be cool with it. I mean, he'll be disappointed, but not because he'll be missing prom." The look she gave me then had another one of those hated blushes rising and her laughing—the bitch.

"I'll call *Mami* and tell her to make sure your room is ready."

"Claudia—"

She cut me off with one of those looks she'd inherited from her grandmother. Scary effective, it was. "Listen, you, even if you weren't dating Eddie, you'd be family. Haven't you figured that out already? God, for such a smart girl, sometimes you are such a dope. *Mami* and *Abuelita* would skin both of us alive if you went to Miami and *didn't* stay there. I don't know about you, but I'm *so* not willing to risk it."

Seriously, I was going to cry. And I *never* cried. I'd long ago learned there was no benefit to crying and that it was only considered a sign of weakness. Of course, these days, I knew better, but old habits were hard to break.

Luckily, Claudia—as if knowing just how close to an uncomfortable edge I was hovering—chose that moment to roll to her stomach and prop her chin on her fists.

"So tell me more about this chef dude and what makes his *crudités* so special?"

I laughed, a little watery around the edges, but it was enough to make the hated tears back off. Reaching for my laptop, I opened it and clicked on the first link my search had returned.

"Chef Kai Belizaire—Hawaii-born and French-raised—initially burst onto the cooking scene as a young teenager." I skimmed the bio, summing up the highlights. "Owned his own place by the time he was eighteen and became the youngest chef ever to earn two Michelin stars for his eponymous New York restaurant."

"That's good, I take it?" Claudia asked.

"*Really* good."

She grunted, clearly not entirely convinced, and waved a hand, indicating I should go on.

"He's only twenty-two and considered on a level somewhere between enfant terrible and rock star—one reviewer said his manner is 'brash and abrasive enough to make Gordon Ramsay seem like the world's kindest, gentlest kindergarten teacher by comparison.'"

"Gordon Ramsay?"

"*Hell's Kitchen* guy."

"Oh, the screamer."

"Yeah."

"And this guy's worse?"

"Apparently." I clicked on another link. "You know what makes him even worse?"

"What's that?"

"You look at Ramsay and you can just *tell* the dude's a walking time bomb. I mean, he has perpetual Aneurysm Face."

Claudia snorted. "So I'm guessing Mr. Cranky French Chef does *not* suffer from Aneurysm Face?"

"Not exactly." I turned the laptop so we could both see it.

"Oh."

"Yeah."

"Wow."

"I know."

"That is some powerful genetic soup."

"I *know*."

"Peyton, can I give you a piece of advice?"

"Could I stop you?"

"No."

"Well then—"

She sat up and clicked through the series of photographs in the gallery, shaking her head slowly as each one revealed in loving, full-color, high-def detail the fact that Kai Belizaire, offspring of a Hawaiian mother and French-Moroccan father, was, in a word, *hot*.

Maybe more appropriately, *scorching*. Hard-bodied, dread-locked, tattooed and with piercing green eyes that reached through the screen with a stare that seemed to say, "I'm fucking awesome and I know it, *mais oui*."

She clicked on an image that showed him wading through sparkling turquoise Hawaiian waters, looking like some bronzed warrior from a bygone era. A spear and crown of leaves on his head and the image would've been complete.

We stared in silent appreciation for a few moments before I said, "Claudia?"

"Hmm?"

"Advice?"

"Oh, yeah…" She shook her head as if emerging from a fog. I could relate. "Don't show these to Eddie."

I snorted. "Don't be ridiculous."

Her eyebrows rose. "What, you think Eddie's not above being jealous?"

"No, I'm saying why would he be? I mean, *look* at this guy." I gestured at the screen, my fingertips inadvertently brushing against the chest with the tribal tat swirling around one pec and oh, dear God, was that a *piercing?*

"I can tell without even knowing a thing about him that I am so not his type." Nor was he really mine. I mean…pretty, yes. Very, very pretty, come to think of it—but while I could admire him, he just didn't seem like a very *comfortable* person to be around.

"Girl, it doesn't matter." Claudia clicked on the picture, enlarging it further and oh, dear God, it *was* a piercing.

"Cuban boys, for all their bravado, are pretty fragile creatures, ego-wise. Mr. Cranky French Chef's not a whole lot older than we are and is crazy successful, which means there's also a fair amount of intelligence there, as well. Add in the mondo talent in a discipline in which you share an intense interest, plus the looks, plus the many, many hours you're likely to be spending in close proximity to him?" She shook her head. "I guarantee, it's gonna drive Eddie crazy and then he's gonna start driving everyone else crazy, by which I mean it's *me* he's going to be driving crazy, because it's *me* he's going to be calling 24/7 to whine at."

"Oh, come *on.*"

"I'm serious."

"You're nuts."

"Be that as it may—" she drew her legs up to her chest and rested her chin on her knees "—I also happen to be right."

"Are you saying he doesn't trust me?" Because seriously— I was the redheaded math wonk, Eddie was the smart, hot jock. It really should go the other way, except I *did* trust him.

She wrinkled her nose. "He trusts you with his life. He just wouldn't be able to understand how the rest of the world doesn't necessarily see you the way he sees you. He thinks you could have anyone you want—yet you want *him*. But he'd worry that could change and in Mr. French Chef—despite the circumstances and despite the excess of cranky—he might see the perfect storm of possibility."

"My wanting Eddie is *not* going to change." No matter how hot, tattooed and pierced Kai Belizaire was. He just couldn't compare to Eddie. No one could.

Claudia's expression was sympathetic. "I know. All I'm saying is just make sure Eddie knows it, too."

I was a worm.

No, worse. I was the slimy underside of a worm after it slithered through a rain puddle that had sat stagnant long enough to develop that disgusting oily green film. So gross, even seagulls, those notoriously indiscriminate scavengers, would pass me by as too low and disgusting even for them.

That's how much of a worm I was.

I stared out at the waves as I sifted sand through my fingers, wishing I could just dig myself a hole and disappear. Since, you know, even the birds wouldn't want me.

I'd take Eddie with me, of course—provided he didn't utterly and completely hate me.

"You hate me."

"I already told you—six times—I don't hate you."

Eddie's hand captured mine, trapping sand between our palms in a way that made me shiver. Not that sexy times on the beach had ever figured prominently in any of my fantasies because (a) unless you had your own beach, the possibility for getting busted for public indecency was kind of high and (b) the potential for sand to creep into some seriously uncomfortable places, no matter how many towels and blankets you had spread out? Also high. Still though…feeling the grit and rasp of the sand between our palms, hearing the music of the waves as they crashed against the shore and watching the last of the sun glint like diamonds on the water, I could understand why sex on the beach remained such a highly used trope in books and films.

"Your parents, on the other hand…"

I sighed. "Yeah, *them* I kind of hate right now, too." And actually articulating it out loud probably wasn't winning me any points with the universe. I looked at Eddie—free arm draped across his upraised knees, profile etched in strong lines against the oncoming twilight and dark gaze focused on the horizon, and you know what? At this point the universe could bite me. Far as I was concerned, it owed me. Big time.

This was so monumentally unfair. A thought I'd expressed approximately seventeen thousand four hundred thirty-two times in the five days since my parents had handed down their Proclamation of Doom. Dean Winchester even made a point of pulling me aside Friday before I left for the airport and saying she'd tried—*again*—to get my parents to see how unreasonable they were being, but they wouldn't budge. To their way of thinking, I was wasting not only countless opportunities, but my intellect. I was willfully throwing away my future and they would be remiss in their duties as parents if they didn't do their best to get me to see the error of my ways.

They picked a hell of a time to take an interest in my life and start acting like actual parents.

Never mind that a huge chunk of my interest *was* intellectual—not even so much the math and chemistry of cooking, as I might have imagined, but rather, the humanity of it. I mean, the more I thought about it, the more I realized that a large part of what had drawn me to Cuban cooking was not only the *ermahgerd* amazingness of it—and yes, "ermahgerd" was a technical term—but its societal significance. How it served as a common tie within the community and brought together multiple generations. It was a common thread I discovered as I learned more about regional cuisines beyond Cuban—a thread I found lacking within my own background. Of course I was aware New England had a long culinary tradition, what with Pilgrims and all, but it wasn't one that had served in any way to draw my family together, so the personal connection just wasn't there.

Needless to say, the academic in me was fascinated by these threads. It was a course of study I was actually considering investigating further—something I felt would be an exciting corollary to my culinary education.

Needless to say, my parents were *so* not impressed.

I believe the phrase "and the point of learning the history of cooking peasant food for the masses?" had been uttered, at which point I waved the white flag.

The sad part was, under different circumstances, I'd be jumping at the opportunity they were providing even if they didn't realize I'd see it as such. Because seriously? Getting a chance to learn from a master like Kai Belizaire at such an early stage in my education? It could only be a good thing.

If only it hadn't been provided with the express intent to have me fail.

"It's just one night, Peyton."

"But it was supposed to be a special night. *Our* night. I gave my parents every opportunity to administer their so-called test at any other time, but they were all 'My way or the highway.'" I stared out over the water until spots began dancing in front of my eyes. "It's so hypocritical, Eddie. They say they're doing this for my best interests when my best interests—what's important to me, whether it's with respect to my career or my relationship with you—are clearly at the bottom of whatever their agenda is."

"Their agenda's pretty simple, baby." Eddie released my hand and wrapped his arm around my waist, urging me close enough to drop my head to his shoulder. "They have these rigid, fixed ideas of what your life should be like, based on standards set by generations before them. Trust me, I have a lot of experience with those sorts of expectations."

The last was uttered so softly, they were nearly lost within the waves rushing ever closer as the tide came in.

I lifted my head. "What's up?"

It wasn't the first time this weekend he'd alluded to something going on—oblique as it was, this statement was the closest he'd come to actually admitting something was going on.

"And don't go all boylike and say 'nothing.' To quote your esteemed cousin, 'That shit don't fly.'"

His mouth snapped shut as a light blush stained his tanned cheeks. Once again, I found myself looking at him and wondering *how?*

Okay, yeah, I dissed my redheadedness and my braniac tendencies, both of which had earned me my fair share of teasing over the years, but at the same time, I'd had enough guys express interest in me—couple of girls, too—to know I wasn't without my own appeal. Maybe not universal, but there was at least *something* reasonably attractive there. However, the Eddies of the world so hadn't been the type to ever express interest before—nor, if I was being completely fair, were the Eddies of the world the type in which I would have expressed interest. Tall, dark and cocky had never really been my cup of tea— but I guess tall, with a goofy sense of humor, seal-dark hair that was equal parts brown and black, and a smile that started at dark, deep-set eyes and seem to suffuse his entire being?

That I was a complete sucker for, apparently.

"Peyton?"

"Yeah?"

He wrinkled the nose that would've been too perfect if not for the bump he confided David had put there with an errant swing of a baseball bat when they were seven.

"Don't quote Claudia."

"Why not?"

"Because it just sounds *wrong*. Sort of like me trying to say, 'Did you pahk the cah in Hahvahd Yahd?'"

I blinked. "Eddie, not even Boston natives say that."

He shrugged, clearly unconcerned. "Just trying to make a point."

"Which is?"

"I like the way *you* sound. The things *you* say. The way *you* say them."

"Oh."

"Yeah." A smile turned up just the edges of his full mouth—his cat's expression, I called it, since for some inexplicable reason, he reminded me of the pictures I'd seen of big, dark jungle cats. But before he could lean in completely and kiss me to distraction—something at which he excelled—I put my hand on his cheek.

"What's going on?"

His mouth opened and I could almost see the "nothing" forming, but at my look, he caught himself. "Okay, yeah, there is something and I did want to talk to you about it. Nothing bad," he added in a hurry as he clearly felt my hand tremble against his cheek. "Just wondering what my odds are on getting the deposit back on the orange tux."

He turned his head and kissed my palm, his perpetual weekend stubble scratching the sensitive skin in a way that nearly made me lose track of the conversation.

Almost.

"You're an ass."

"And you're adorable."

Seriously, if his hair weren't so short, I'd be yanking it out in big, painful clumps right *now*.

"Eddie—"

Another kiss to my palm—another shiver on my part.

"Peyton, it's nothing that can't wait until after you're done with your version of *Kitchen Nightmares*."

I sighed, my mind immediately returning to the impending test. Impending doom. "I'm hoping it won't be that bad."

"From what you've said about this guy?"

Please, to be noting—*said*. I'd shown Eddie no pictures and I was hoping he wouldn't get it in his head to Google Belizaire. While I still thought Claudia had maybe overexaggerated Eddie's possible reaction, I really wasn't hot to test the theory. I had too much else to deal with.

"Yeah, I know." I slid my hand around to his neck and leaned my forehead against his. "This sucks."

He tilted his head up just far enough to place a gentle kiss on my forehead. "I promise I'll make it up to you," he whispered.

A choked laugh escaped. "Shouldn't that be my line?"

"Does it matter?" A single finger traced a line along my jaw and down my throat, the calloused pad of his finger pleasantly rough against my skin. "We're in this together, Peyton. Right?"

I leaned back far enough to meet his gaze, seeing in it not only a rare seriousness, but an even more rare uncertainty, only strengthening my suspicion that something was up. But I knew him well enough by this point to know he wouldn't tell me until he was good and ready.

Until then, I'd have to trust him—just as much as I could see he trusted me.

Eddie trusted *me*.

So few people, as evinced by my parents' own behavior, ever had.

seven

"Again."

Not for the first time did I wonder how many years evisceration carried with it as punishment.

But I said nothing—at least not out loud—and merely grabbed another large onion, hacking viciously at the ends and slicing through the first layer of skin with a deft, sure stroke.

Check that—I had to say something.

"What was wrong this time?"

Chef Kai looked up from where he was in discussion with the produce wholesaler, his pale, critical gaze flickering over the small mountain of sliced Vidalias in front of me. "Not thin enough," he said, his voice colored with the lilting accent that was equal parts Hawaiian and French.

"Can practically read the damned newsprint through these," I muttered as I cut the onion in half and began rapidly slicing thin, uniform slices of the "acceptable substitutes" for the Mauis he was having flown in to use in the actual dishes come Saturday night. To think, Claudia had mocked my obsessive watching of Julia Child's *The French Chef* videos—along with more than a few viewings of *Julie & Julia*. Maybe I hadn't had a formal class...*yet*—but it didn't mean I was utterly lacking in instruction. No, French cuisine wasn't Cuban, but Julia had used classic techniques to cook for real people. *That* was the secret.

"You shouldn't have time to read the newspaper with all you need to accomplish before Saturday."

I jumped, narrowly missing slicing my thumb. Swear to God, the man had ears like a bat and could move with the stealth of a fox through a henhouse and could I come up with any *more* hoary clichés?

"Do you *mind?*" I grumbled irritably as I resumed slicing onions.

"It's my kitchen. Of course I mind."

"Technically, not your kitchen," I shot back because seriously, after less than forty-eight hours, I was already *so* over Mr. High-and-Mighty Cranky Bad-Ass French Chef Kai Belizaire.

A typically French noise, low in his throat, was his only response. I probably should have been worried, but honestly? I just didn't care.

Done, I used the blade of my knife to shove the mound of onions to the side of the giant butcher-block island where I worked and automatically reached for another. I ignored the ache in my palms and fingers and the telltale chafing that signaled a blister would be developing if I wasn't careful.

Yesterday had been proving I could julienne and brunoise and chiffonade. *Hours* of proving I could julienne and brunoise and chiffonade with a modicum of skill. Grudgingly— and only after more than a few sharp "agains," and grumbling insults in French I don't think he realized I could understand or, more likely, didn't care—he'd finally admitted I *could* manage those basics that any primary-schooler in France could. This morning, we'd moved on to slicing onions to his exacting standards.

Clearly, my role for this week would be on the line as a prep chef—fairly low on the totem pole and a role I was *more* than okay with. The rest of his team, including his *sous-chef* for the event, would be arriving from New York Wednesday night and spending Thursday getting acquainted with the expansive and thankfully well-equipped kitchen of the Boston Esplanade Yacht and Rowing Club—longtime hangout for generations of Chaffees and the setting for Saturday night's festivities.

Or as I called it, the Day of the Prom That Wouldn't Be.

The upside—sort of—was because I'd been excused from school for the week to participate in this asinine farce, I wasn't around to see Claudia in her pre-prom frenzy, packing and exchanging texts and hushed, giddy phone calls with David.

For as much as I never imagined I'd ever want to attend a prom, I was beyond disappointed to be missing it. I *wanted* a wrist corsage and to slow dance to some incredibly sappy song. I wanted to attend the after-party organized by the parents so we didn't get into *too* much trouble before moving on to the hotel suite the boys had reserved weeks ago. I wanted to spend the night with Eddie and watch the sun rise over the Atlantic and know that as much as prom was meant to signify a bittersweet ending, for us, it was all about beginnings.

I was aware, however, as excited as Claudia was, she was also feeling massively guilty about getting to experience all of that while I was stuck in a kitchen, undergoing a bunch of arbitrary tests designed to make me fail.

But how miserable are you, really?

Shut up. I am. This "test" is bullshit and you know it. And I miss Eddie.

He understands. And admit it, you're enjoying this "test" more than you thought you would.

Seriously, shut up.

Hard, bronze fingers curled around my wrist before I could lay waste to yet another defenseless onion.

"Wait." He kept my hand pinned to the cutting board as with his free hand he selected a slice of the most recent onion I'd decimated. Holding it up to the light, he examined it with a critical stare. So paper-thin and translucent, I could practically see his fingerprints on the other side, I nevertheless waited for yet another scathing critique.

My favorite so far? "You call this julienne? Lightning striking a tree produces more uniform cuts. *Again!*" Followed by more than a few colorful epithets in English and French for good measure. And that had been one of the *nicer* responses.

Turning the slice of onion to and fro, he nodded slowly, met my gaze, smiled and said, "Again."

And again, I wondered how many years evisceration would net me in the pen. Hey, I could always get a job in the prison kitchens. But then again, as Claudia reminded me last night when I was bitching to her on the phone, "Prison orange would *so* not be a good color for you, Peyton."

I swallowed a sigh—that particular response had garnered me another tongue lashing and a screaming invitation to leave if I found it all too tedious—and tried to pry my wrist free so I could reach for another onion. Before I could, however, his fingers tightened around my wrist.

"Oh, and make no mistake—so long as I am in charge, it *is* my kitchen. No matter what your name is or who your parents are."

Furious, I lifted my head and met his challenging gaze, clearly reading in the pale green depths his absolute awareness that he held my fate in his hands. In that moment, I didn't care how highly lauded a chef he was—far as I was concerned, he was nothing more than a toadying son-of-a-bitch bastard, selling out to the highest bidder.

It was entirely likely my fate was already sealed—in fact,

entirely certain—but again, I was *damned* if I was going down without a fight. In this case, however, graceful retreat was the most effective form of battle.

"Of course, Chef." Very gently, I pulled my hand free and reached for another onion.

For another hour I sliced onions, falling into an almost hypnotic rhythm, able to ignore the burning in my shoulders and the aches in my palms and fingers. As I worked, I vaguely noted the smell of olive oil heating up, followed closely by the unmistakable pop and sizzle of food meeting hot oil.

Done with the final onion in my pile, I lifted my head and wiped away the bead of sweat that had escaped the kerchief tied around my head. As my little personal bubble gradually expanded and burst, I noted the additional smells filling the kitchen—carrots, celery, the onions I'd been so diligently slicing marrying with the distinctive aroma of roast pork. However, rather than scented with sour orange and cumin, in typically Cuban preparation, there was instead a sweet, almost molasses-like aroma wafting through the kitchen along with a different sweetness—cinnamon and something... licorice-like. Anise. Yeah, that was it.

The one commonality I could perceive between a Cuban-style preparation and whatever he was making was garlic.

Lots and lots of garlic.

"How are you with sectioning chicken?"

One of the most basic lessons of cooking and one of the first I'd practiced. Ironically with help from a video tutorial taught by none other than Gordon Ramsay.

"Pretty good," I said with what I hoped sounded like confidence.

A heavy, dark brown eyebrow, bisected by a thin scar, rose. Like he could hear every ounce of terrified bullshit in my voice. "Fine. Try not to make them look like a pack of wolves attacked."

Through gritted teeth I muttered, "Yes, Chef," as I eyed the pile of chicken carcasses—at least two dozen. With a silent apology to my poor, abused palms, I pulled the sharpening steel from my case, gave my already-sharp chef's knife a quick honing and set to work.

After the first one, the lessons came flooding back and like with the onions, I fell into a rhythm. Pull out the drum, cut a slit in the skin at the thigh, cut through the joint, separate the drum from the thigh. Repeat on the opposite side, move to the wings, cut them away, then separate the breasts from the remainder of the carcass. Save all the remnants for stock because nothing needed to be laid to waste.

Lather, rinse, repeat.

From the edges of my peripheral vision I could see Chef Kai deftly measuring two different types of flour, combining them, then adding water in increments, testing the consistency of the dough after each addition. By the time I finished the final chicken, he was in a rhythm of his own, kneading the dough with powerful strokes that flexed the muscles and tendons in his forearms. His biceps strained the sleeves of his faded Green Day T-shirt, making his tattoos ripple like tribal warriors performing an intricate war dance.

Fascinated, I watched him roll the dough out with a long wooden pin, then use it to fold the dough over several times into a rectangle. Taking a wicked-looking steel blade, he trimmed the edges, then with a carved wooden board as his guide, used the same blade to cut uniform strips of dough. Every twenty strokes or so, he'd pause, separate the noodles and dust them with a bit more flour.

"Soba noodles," he said without looking up.

I didn't say anything because honestly, there didn't seem anything I could say that wouldn't leave me sounding like a monumental idiot. I continued silently watching even as I cleaned my knives and work station and washed my hands, wincing as the hot water hit the tender skin of my palms.

"Learned from a Gordon Ramsay video, did you?"

I glanced up from sliding my chef's knife into its slot in the soft leather case to find him studying my efforts. Again, I wasn't sure how to answer—for all I knew, he hated Ramsay. Thought he was a hack, which left me feeling oddly defensive. Terrifying as the man was in his reality-show persona, in the demonstration videos I'd discovered on YouTube, he was remarkably affable and a clear, concise instructor with an obvious love for his craft.

You know, screw it.

"Yes, Chef." After a pause, I asked, "How did you know?"

He lifted one of the carcasses. "You cut through the wishbone. One of his favorite techniques."

I shrugged. "Made sense the way he explained it."

"It does." He studied the rest of the chicken parts, arranged by meat color. "Well, at least the homeless won't mind," he muttered, lifting a drumstick, neatly trimmed, the knuckle cut away to ensure even cooking.

I breathed deep—in through the nose, out through the mouth, for once grateful for the yoga classes Claudia had dragged me to. "Homeless?" I finally asked and was proud when my voice didn't shake.

"You didn't think we were going to let this food go to waste, did you?"

No, I had no idea what the hell he had expected to do with the food he'd made me chop, slice, julienne, brunoise and chiffonade. For all I knew, he intended it as rabbit food for the little beasts he'd then turn into a nice, tender *lapin à la cocotte.*

He turned to one of the two enormous professional-grade gas ranges that dominated a wall of the spacious kitchen. "We'll use the stock I made last night. Bag the carcasses you sectioned and put them in the walk-in—we'll use them tomorrow to make more for the weekend."

With a nod, I followed his instructions and returned in time to see him pulling a pork loin from the oven, deep reddish-burgundy in color. Its mouthwatering aroma wafted through the kitchen and reminded me I hadn't had so much as a spinach leaf since my coffee and croissant this morning. But I instinctively knew better than to go poking around *his* kitchen for something with which to satisfy the munchies. Not without permission at any rate. And I wasn't about to interrupt him to ask. Food would simply have to wait until I got back to Beacon Hill tonight.

I sighed and gazed longingly at the pork he'd set aside to rest, before returning my attention to where he stood at the range searing chicken and humming under his breath in a surprisingly melodic voice. Honestly, I might as well have been one of the recently dissected chicken carcasses for all the attention he paid me.

Check that—he paid the chicken carcasses more attention. Soothing as the kitchen sounds—and lack of his bitching at me were—my natural curiosity couldn't help but rear its head. At the very possible risk of incurring his wrath I finally asked, "What are you making?"

The humming stopped. "Wondered when you'd get around to asking."

"I wasn't aware questions were permitted."

"Don't be an ass. Questions are always permitted. I'd rather have a question than have you fuck up." That same scarred eyebrow rose, nearly disappearing beneath the bandanna he had tied around his forehead. "Of course, it would be vastly preferable if you were well-trained enough to not have too many questions."

And he was calling *me* an ass?

Ass.

"Look, this wasn't my idea, you know."

"I know."

But nothing more. Just a resumption of that humming as he lifted a huge container of clear golden stock and poured it into the pot. With a jerk of his head, he said, "Cut the pork. Quarter-inch-thick rounds, then cubed."

As if on cue, my palms ached, but I told them to shut up as I did as requested.

"Try it."

I paused, my blade hovering over a tender slice of the pork.

He huffed out an impatient breath. "How can you know if it's prepared the way you want if you don't try?"

His warning about questions still ringing in my ears, I ventured, "How is it supposed to be prepared?"

"Should have a sweet, smoky flavor, good balance with the spices between savory and sweet. Make sure you taste the glaze."

I cut a long strip off the edge of the slice in front of me and cut it again in half, putting the second piece in his outstretched hand.

Oh, dear *God*.

I chewed slowly, in hopes of not diving in and gnawing on the entire loin like a rabid dog.

"What do you taste?"

I tried to weigh all the tastes lingering on my palate. "Light smoke, fruity sweetness, warm spices…cinnamon and anise, yeah?"

He inclined his head. "That's the Chinese five-spice—and the smoke actually came from a smoked sea salt that I used in the rub. Works in a pinch if you lack the time or equipment with which to actually smoke." He turned back to the pot. "The dish is called *char siu*—barbecued Chinese pork. A staple in the saimin."

I resumed cutting the pork and resisted the temptation to shove another piece in my mouth. "Saimin?"

"Hawaiian soup." He looked up briefly from the sausage he was slicing into neat disks. "Technically, this should be SPAM."

"SPAM?"

"It's considered a Hawaiian delicacy, man."

"No way."

"Way."

For the first time since we'd been introduced, a grin—an honest-to-God, teeth-and-all grin—crossed his face, softening the stern lines and also for the first time, revealing his true age.

"The classical French cooking, that came from my dad—the home cooking, though, that came from my mom. She'd take me to Hawaii every summer and I'd cook with her and all my aunties until I was fourteen when I started working in my dad's restaurant."

Which more fully explained the French/Hawaiian/Polynesian fusion cuisine on which he'd built his reputation.

"You have a car here, yeah?"

"Yeah."

"The produce guy, he told me where there's a shelter."

Not a question—not even a statement—just…an expectation. One I was clearly meant to accept. I should be annoyed with the high-handed attitude, and yet, understanding his intention, how could I? Not without feeling like a total Grinch.

Once again, I cleaned my equipment, watching as he added the sausage and pork to the chicken and stock, then after seasoning it, set about cleaning his own equipment.

"What about the noodles?" I asked.

"Not until the end—they're likely to sit longer in the broth than would be optimal, so no point in overcooking them excessively." He was sharpening his knife, the blade a silver blur, the steel humming with a high-pitched melody. "Ideally, I'd scramble an egg into the soup before serving or maybe add hard-boiled egg, but again, not optimal under these conditions."

"It's a nice thing you're doing," I blurted.

Not that he asked.

Not that he cared.

The blade paused for a split second. "Chef's just a title," he said quietly over the hum of the steel. "Hard-earned, yeah, but just a title for someone who cooks. A cook feeds people. We have a responsibility to our community—to keep them nourished." He glanced up, that piercing green gaze finding mine. "I may make a living off feeding the wealthy, but it's the community that feeds me."

I had the distinct feeling he was saying more than what the actual words were expressing. A feeling that increased as we drove to the shelter and I watched him pull on a pair of clear gloves and serve up bowls of soup, talking easily to those who passed through the line. Even though he hadn't asked, I nevertheless pulled on a pair of gloves and stood beside him, slicing up the loaves of day-old French bread we'd stopped on our way to the shelter to pick up—and when had he had time to make that connection, as well? I placed the bread on the trays alongside the plastic bowls of soup, content to not say much beyond "you're welcome." Oh, and the odd "thank you," to the older ladies who seemed to find my hair fascinating.

Back at the boathouse, I helped him finish up with the last of the cleaning, even though again, he hadn't asked.

Outside on the sidewalk, he pulled the tie restraining his dreads loose and rolled his head, allowing the golden-brown coils to settle around his shoulders in a comfortable disarray.

Rubbing his neck he said, "Four-thirty."

Already used to his abrupt speech patterns and the topics that sprang up, seemingly out of nowhere, I gaped. "A.M.?"

"Want to check out the fishmongers. The boats start coming back in by six."

I groaned. "But four-thirty?"

"You want the best, you got to be first. And these cats, they don't know me, so it's not like they'll know to hold the best aside."

"Four-thirty," I sighed, then yelped as he grasped my wrist, his hold every bit as firm as it had been during the onions. Turning my hand over, he studied the palm in the pool of light thrown by the weathered brass sconces illuminating the boathouse's doorway.

"Soak, but don't cover. Let air get to it." One long, graceful finger traced the blister that had finally made an appearance, sometime during the cubing of the pork. "Put a moleskin doughnut on it tomorrow."

I nodded, even though I had no earthly clue what a moleskin doughnut was. Maybe one of the household staff would know. Luckily, I wouldn't have to suffer through any comments from Mom and Dad about how if I was so delicate, perhaps I wasn't quite cut out for the professional cooking world. In fact, I wouldn't have to deal with them until Thursday when they were due to return from Napa, where they were making final arrangements for the wines and sommelier for the gala. Hell, for all I knew, they were buying a damned vineyard.

Whatever. With any luck I'd be so busy I'd be able to legitimately avoid them until after all was said and done.

"You hearin' me, girl?"

I was yanked out of my head to find him staring intently, his eyes paled to an eerie silver green in the lamplight.

"Yeah," I managed, realizing he was still holding my hand, but it had shifted from the peremptory grip to something not…gentle, per se, but rather, supportive. And clearly, I was exceedingly tired. Or cracked. Or both.

I stared up at him, focusing my gaze on that thin scar bisecting his eyebrow. Wondering how he got it. Not wondering why he was still holding my hand.

I'm sure it would be explained.

Maybe.

"Listen—"

Once again, I found my wandering thoughts reined in by that lilting voice. With some effort, I focused enough to meet his gaze.

"I don't need to have you with torn-up hands, so do as I say."

I nodded.

"And don't go staying up until all hours. You get yourself home, take a bath and go to bed. If you're tired, you're prone to stupid mistakes. You're enough of a rookie you'll be makin' plenty of them without being exhausted."

I nodded again, clearly incapable of speech.

"Four-thirty—here. Don't be late."

With that, he dropped my hand and loped off in the direction of his hotel while I stood there a moment longer shaking my head before I took off for home and hopefully, the discovery of what in the ever-loving *hell* a moleskin doughnut was.

Eight

"You're alive."

I cringed. "I'm so sorry."

"No, I know you've been busy, it's just—"

"It's just you've called and texted and I kept promising to call when I had a minute, but by the time I have a minute it's just so late and then I'm generally up by around five and—"

"Peyton—"

"And it's been insane and Kai's crew arrived yesterday and Mom and Dad returned today and just 'popped by' the boathouse, 'just to check on the progress and we do hope Peyton's not been too much of an imposition' like this is just some fucking lark they're indulging—"

"Peyton—"

"And I honestly have no idea what the hell Kai's thinking or what he might have said to Mom and Dad, especially after I killed that batch of duck confit and we had to start over from scratch. Luckily, we had the time to do so, but oh, my God, I thought he was going to tear me a new one. I mean, who knew the boathouse had acoustics like that—"

"Peyton."

I yanked the phone away, my ear ringing. "Sorry."

"S'okay."

"Is it?"

"Not really."

I sighed. "At least you're honest."

"Sorry, that was shitty of me." His sigh was long and full of all the frustration I was feeling. Actually, check that. All the frustration I *would* be feeling if it wasn't for the fact that I was way too freakin' tired to feel anything other than way too freakin' tired.

And...?

Not now.

Yes...now.

Okay, fine. And absolutely exhilarated.

Which prodded another emotion to the surface—guilt.

I *knew* I should be feeling guilty over missing prom but I... kind of wasn't. And I felt guilty because I...wasn't.

I did miss Eddie, though. A lot.

I wished I could be sharing more of this with him.

I wished he was *here.*

Do you, now?

Yes. Now, shut it.

I did wish he was there—I *did.* If only because everything had been so amazing and I wished I could share it with him and with Claudia and even David, because they would get it. At least, Claudia and David would. They'd understand, because they were of the same mind-set, how amazing it was to be immersed in something you loved beyond all imagining.

And Eddie... Well, even though he hadn't yet developed that sort of all-encompassing passion for anything, he'd understand because he understood me. Understood what this meant to me.

"Are you okay, really?"

"Yeah," I managed around yet another huge yawn. "Just wrecked." I rolled over in bed and reached for my Diet Coke. I probably shouldn't be drinking it at midnight, but then again, so…freakin'…tired. And I was going to have to be up by five-thirty, so I could be back at the boathouse by six.

"Aren't there labor laws in Massachusetts?"

"Sure. But I'd actually have to be employed. Technically, this is 'volunteer' work. Do you know my parents actually had the nerve to say that to me today? That it's the sort of thing that would look good on my university records." The can made a loud, metallic crunch as I closed my hand into a fist.

"Not even bothering to pretend, are they?"

"Nope." I yawned again, my jaw aching with the strain.

"Then why even bother showing up tomorrow? What's the point? You could always blow it off and come back down. That way you at least don't have to miss prom."

"The point is, so long as I show up and do my job, then I have a chance—infinitesimal as it might be—to win. Or at least make a point as to the seriousness of my intent."

"Do you honestly think they even care? And what makes you think they'll stick to the promise they made, even if you do win? If Mr. Cranky French Chef says you've got the goods to make it as a pro?"

Couldn't blame Eddie for asking. There was no guarantee they'd stick to their promise. Except, *I* knew if I did pass this test, I was going to cooking school—no matter what they decided. If I had to take out loans and work in kitchens washing dishes to do it, I was going. I'd figure it out. Cooking—it was in my blood now.

Whether my parents ever realized it or not, all they'd done is solidify my path.

"Doesn't matter," I slurred, the room fading in and out.

"Damn girl, you are twelve kinds of brave."

"Or twelve kinds of idiotic."

"I've heard it both ways."

I laughed even as I fought to stay awake. Kind of felt it might be a losing battle.

"Peyton?"

"Yeah?"

"Think I might be able to borrow some of that brave?"

I perked up momentarily. "For what?"

He hesitated—long enough for sleep to start pulling me under again. And much as I wanted to know—*knew* this was what he'd been dancing around for a couple of weeks now, and wanted to be there for him, wanted to be just as supportive and *there* as he'd been for me, I just couldn't. I was so drained and I just couldn't give him the attention he deserved.

"Peyton—"

I snapped awake.

"God, Eddie, I'm sorry, I'm just so tired."

His voice softened. "I know, baby. It's cool."

My eyelids already drooping again, I managed, "Tell me tomorrow?" before completely succumbing.

I woke up the next morning with a vague memory of hearing a soft "Promise," but beyond that, didn't have much time to think of anything that wasn't chop, slice, julienne, brunoise and chiffonade—not to mention stir, fetch, wash, baste, tie and plate, since I'd been assigned as the swing chef's assistant, basically doing whatever was needed. Which included staying the hell out of Kai's way, since he was in full enfant-terrible mode. He was a black-T-shirted missile as he moved from station to station, voice rising as he barked orders and got ever more scathing if they weren't carried out double-time and executed with the same amount of skill and finesse he demanded of himself.

Needless to say, the entire day was a blur. Well, except for the one, glorious moment when my parents swept in with their usual sense of entitlement, no doubt to see how "things were going," and had their asses absolutely handed to them. Kai's *sous-chef* had tried to usher them out with some grace and diplomacy, which had been met with predictable disdain. However, before the condescending expressions could even fully form, Kai had swooped in, chef's knife glinting dangerously, and told them to get the hell out of his kitchen.

Mom—not all that quick on the uptake—had started to protest. Dad, with a cautious eye on that knife, had merely said they'd return at the end of the evening.

I'd smiled for the next half hour, until Kai's screaming fit because we were falling behind schedule and where in the fucking fuck were the Vietnamese cinnamon sticks? No time to dwell on the Chaffee takedown or do much more than breathe as I slipped into a sort of twilight-zone state, my entire world narrowed down to whatever task I was charged with completing.

The kitchen chatter, the clink of crystal and china, the pop and sizzle of food, the smells, everything—it all faded into a hum that surrounded me in a protective bubble as I worked in my own little vacuum.

"Peyton—"

I would've jumped except I was restrained by a heavy hand on my shoulder.

"Dammit, would you quit it with the stealth act?"

Kai's brow rose and before he could say it, I sighed. "Yeah, yeah…I know. *Your* kitchen."

To my surprise, he grinned—that big, full-out grin with the teeth.

"Time to take a break."

"But—"

"Crew's got this in hand."

Before I even fully registered what had happened, I found myself outside, breathing deeply of the cool night air and realizing, for the first time, just how hot I was after hours spent in the confines of the kitchen. The room that had been comfortable with only two cooks in there had turned into something approximating Dante's Inferno what with the cooktops, rotisseries, ovens and salamanders going full tilt for hours. Not to mention all the bodies from the cooking team down to the waitstaff, bussers and cleanup crew making the cavernous room feel as if it had shrunk to the size of a bathroom stall.

Ever aware, Kai pressed a bottle of water in my hand as he urged me onto the wood-and-wrought-iron bench across the street from the kitchen's entrance. With a sigh of relief, I sank down, the wood slats providing welcome support. Only now did I realize just how rubbery and achy my legs were.

"You should go to CIA."

I blinked, not quite processing. "The Central Intelligence Agency?"

With an impatient sigh, he poured water into his hand and flicked it in my face.

"Hey!"

"Wake up—Culinary Institute of America."

Still not quite processing. But just as he was preparing to flick more water in my face, the pieces finally fell into place.

"You're saying I'm good enough to do this." Because it would just be a waste of time to be coy and ask him to spell out what he was saying. A week of exposure to Kai had rendered me familiar with his speech patterns—and his lack of patience.

Coy wouldn't cut it with him.

"I'm saying you have potential. And it should be nurtured."

He leaned back against the bench and stretched his arms out along the back.

"But my parents—"

The eyebrow rose. "Thought it was a done deal, eh? That they had me in their pockets?"

"Pretty much."

"No one owns me."

"That's going to come as news to them." I sighed. "Not that it'll matter." I knew in my gut Eddie was right—regardless of outcome, they weren't going to stick to their promise.

In the lamplight, his narrow gaze took on that eerie silvery-green cast, rendering them even more startling than usual against his skin. "Do you want to do this or not?"

I nodded. "I won't lie—it would be a lot easier if I had their support, but since that's *never* going to happen, lack of inter-ference would work."

He made that noise low in his throat that translated to some-thing between scorn and agreement.

"So now what?"

I shrugged. "I guess I contact Johnson & Wales and start seeing about student loans and scholarships."

"I've got contacts at CIA. Could get you scholarships. And you could work for me."

Again, I struggled to process. "But…Johnson & Wales—" And Cuban cooking and Miami and the Abreus, who were more family to me than my own, and Eddie.

Oh, God, Eddie.

"It's a good school, but CIA is *the* school. And New York is the epicenter of the culinary scene. Anything you want to learn about cooking—you learn it there. It's an education in and of itself."

"I…"

He made an abrupt shift, turning to face me. "Girl, listen to me—you've got potential, but more important, you've got the heart and the *soul* for food. You've got the passion for it." His hands closed around my hands in that oddly supporting grip I recalled from the other night.

"Word 'round the kitchen is you missed your prom to do this."

No point denying or even asking how he knew. He just did. All he wanted was absolute confirmation.

"Yeah."

"Yeah." He nodded slowly. "So you've got the nerve for this, too." His eyes narrowed. "This is a hard bitch of a business, girl. It's husband and lover combined, consuming you from the bones out, understand?"

Swallowing hard, I nodded.

"There's no guarantee you'll make it—but what I *can* guarantee is with my help, you've got a better shot."

No doubt. But, you know, I was my parents' child when it came down to it and I was nothing if not a cynic.

"Why are you helping me?"

He snorted. "You think I got something to gain?"

I lifted a shoulder—if he wouldn't spell things out, neither would I.

"Maybe I do." The thumb of one hand ran over the moleskin—as it turned out, a soft felt doughnut—protecting the blister on my palm. "You remind me of me. You know my dad, he didn't want me to leave Paris to start my own place?"

"I didn't know."

His deep breath stretched his T-shirt tight across the expanse of his chest. "He's okay with it now, but it was rough for a while."

"Two Michelin stars only makes it okay?"

"Three would've been better."

"You need to get on that, then." And was I seriously sitting here, with my hands resting in Kai Belizaire's, and joking?

"A chef's only as good as his team."

Once again, a lot was left unsaid, but nevertheless clearly spelled out. If you knew what to listen for.

"You really think I have that sort of potential?"

"Yeah." Releasing one of my hands, he lifted his face to mine, brushing back a tendril of my hair that had escaped the tight French braid. "I'd really like to be part of your journey, Peyton. Show you all the possibilities."

So much left unsaid. Yet nevertheless clearly spelled out.

My head was reeling with all that was said and unsaid and all the emotions rushing in and pulling with the strength of a powerful undertow, threatening to sweep me under. Feelings I'd kept tightly restrained all week and refused to allow myself to acknowledge they even existed because I was too busy trying to prove myself. Feelings I couldn't allow to interfere with my end goals.

But…while the end goal hadn't changed—and wouldn't be changing—could *how* I got there be shifting? I didn't know.

I just didn't know.

What I did know was that Kai was leaning in a little closer and I was leaning in a little closer, my free hand coming to rest on his chest right over the piercing that had so intrigued me, while his breath ghosted along my cheek, drawing me ever closer. But in the instant before my eyes drifted completely shut, I caught a flash of movement from the edges of my vision.

"Eddie," I breathed as I jerked back from Kai. He stood across the street, illuminated by a diminishing wash of light as the kitchen door slowly swung closed behind him. Frozen into immobility, I stared as he stood there a moment longer, then turned and disappeared into the shadows.

Nine

"I'm a worm."

Claudia looked over her shoulder. "I've been telling you all week, I'm not going to disagree with you." She returned her attention to the closet, riffling through the items haphazardly shoved in there. The beginning of any school year we started out with the best of intentions, but by May, it generally resembled a black hole of despair.

"Why are you even still speaking to me, then?"

"Because if you're a worm, then Eddie's a jackass."

Would my stomach ever stop that horrible swooping sensation it experienced every time I heard his name? Saying it did horrible wrenching things to my heart, so I tried to utilize it as little as possible.

She looked over her shoulder again. "Is he still not returning your calls or texts?"

"I quit trying after Wednesday."

"*Nothing* from him?"

"Not so much as a homing pigeon dropping off a note."

She blew a strand of hair from her face with an impatient breath. "Jackass."

I rolled over onto my side, clutching a pillow to my chest. "What he saw, though?" I tried not to think about how my speech patterns had taken on shades of Kai. Whom I'd heard from once since Saturday—a typically brusque text telling me to let him know what my decision was.

What *was* my decision?

While I wasn't exactly sure, I had to admit I was leaning a particular direction.

"Admittedly not one of your better moves," she said, the words clear, if a bit muffled by the depths of the closet.

"I can't even say with any certainty nothing would have happened."

Claudia sighed. "I *so* had a feeling about that guy."

I hugged the pillow tighter and tried not to think about how Kai's chest had felt beneath my hand. "Yeah, well, that only makes one of us." Even after what had sort-of-kind-of-but-not-really happened, *I* still had trouble believing it. There were times the past week I'd almost convinced myself it was nothing more than a mirage brought on by utter exhaustion and prolonged exposure to sliced onion fumes.

Then I'd remember the feel of Kai's chest beneath my hand—and the expression on Eddie's face.

Rolling to a sitting position, I shoved a hand through my hair.

"Seriously, though, why aren't you more mad at me about this? Eddie's your cousin."

"And you're like a sister to me." Hooking a pair of hangers over the closet door, she dropped onto the bed beside me. "Okay, first, not like Eddie's been a saint in the past with girls—so it's not such a bad thing for him to get dosed with a little of his own medicine—and second, it's not like you actually *did* anything." Her narrow amber gaze, *so* like Eddie's, studied me. "You *haven't* done anything, have you?"

"Claudia—" When I could unclench my teeth enough, I

said, "When would I have had time to do anything? I was back here practically first thing Sunday morning."

And spilling my guts to her Sunday night before she'd barely crossed the threshold, all alight with after-prom glow the likes of which should've made me crazy/stabbity jealous.

Instead, I was actually happy for her and David. *Definitely* guilty about Eddie. But I had to admit, overriding both was the incredible high from everything Kai had said about my professional future.

A door that had previously been merely cracked had been flung open wide for me this past week. I couldn't help but feel a tingle of…anticipation.

"Come on, girl—you and I both know a lot more could've happened *before* Sunday morning."

For the first time, I felt truly hurt and an honest burst of anger. "Jesus Christ, Claudia—how much of a cold bitch do you take me for? You really think I would've slept with Kai, not that I think that was actually an option, right after having Eddie see us nearly kiss?"

To my surprise, she didn't get offended or defensive—just merely nodded. "Just wanted to make sure is all."

"Why?" And I glanced at the closet. "And why in the hell do you have our prom dresses out?" Hers still covered in plastic from the dry cleaner's. Mine still bearing the tags from the store.

"Because." She heaved herself off the bed, and in the same smooth motion, pulled me up after her. "We are going out."

"We're what?" And when did she start talking like Kai?

"We're going out." She pulled my dress off the hanger and tossed it to me. "We're not letting a perfectly good dress go to waste—and if you're going to be spending the next however many years in a white jacket, whether it's in Miami or New York, who knows when you'll get to wear this."

"I—"

"Don't argue."

"But—"

"Seriously, shut it, Peyton."

"Claudia—"

"Didn't I say to shut it?"

And she accused *me* of stubbornness.

I couldn't even begin to imagine where we could go that we wouldn't look wildly overdressed, even if it was a Saturday night—but, you know, there was no point in even bringing that up as an argument with Claudia. She was bound and determined that we were going out, and short of barricading myself in a bathroom stall, we were *going out*. So I slipped on the dress we'd deemed perfect—seemed like a lifetime ago already—and the impossibly sky-high heels that were probably going to be the last truly expensive splurge I made for a long while and made up my face and left my hair falling long and loose around my shoulders.

There was a car waiting for us downstairs, Claudia clearly having been certain I'd acquiesce and also just as clearly wanting to make this a special night out.

Maybe not prom, but definitely *special,* and, you know, she was right—she was truly the sister I'd never had and I was going to miss her like crazy when she went off to Stanford in the fall. Guess the bittersweet endings that prom and graduation signified weren't just about romantic relationships after all.

Sitting in the back of the town car as it sped toward Boston, we laughed and toasted each other with sparkling cider and I knew—no matter where our journeys took us, we were indelibly linked. We'd always be a part of each other's lives.

I knew a lot of people made similar declarations on the eve of high-school or college graduations and they maybe even meant it, but this was different. It was a deep-seated sense of how things would *be*. I could see us, years down the line, still laughing and toasting each other. Who would be by our sides, if anyone, I couldn't tell you—but Claudia and I, we'd be there.

The car pulled to a stop—an instant later, a valet had the door open, revealing the distinctive red-brick facade of the Revere.

"Ritzy," I muttered as I took the valet's hand and stepped from the car.

"No, that's around the other side of the Commons," Claudia shot back.

"Smart-ass."

"And you are *so* gonna miss it when I'm not around."

Despite my absolute certainty we'd remain in each other's lives, I felt that pang of loss again. "Yeah...I am."

"Me, too, *hermana*."

Claudia looped her arm through mine, but rather than head, as I expected, toward Rustic, the hotel's acclaimed restaurant, she instead made a beeline for the elevators.

"Claudia?"

"Patience, grasshopper."

Not that I had much choice, with the grip she had on my arm and her determined strides that left me taking two for every one of hers. Damned long legs.

Somehow, I wasn't surprised to see her hit the button that would take us up to Rooftop. I'd been there in the past for events and it was one of my favorite places in all of Boston, allowing for views of the Commons and the lights of Back Bay. I maybe wasn't expecting to ever return to Boston to live, but that didn't mean I didn't appreciate my hometown. Who knew? Maybe one day I'd return to open my own restaurant.

One day.

When the elevator doors slid open, Claudia surprised me yet again—instead of heading toward the already crowded restaurant/lounge area, she instead veered off to the area reserved for private parties, where one final surprise waited.

"Eddie."

And David, too, both of them decked out in tuxes and waiting with flowers while behind them, the candles in hurricane-glass lamps flickered on a pair of exquisitely set tables placed around an area clearly meant to evoke a dance floor.

"We wanted you to have a prom," Claudia whispered, even as she met David's gaze and blushed. And so did he. Oh, for heaven's sake. You'd think they'd be so over that already, but there they were, staring at each other like they were happily stranded on their own little island.

Which left…

"Eddie."

I pulled away from Claudia and approached where he stood, tall and handsome in a sharp dark gray tux with a black shirt and no tie. Not traditional, but somehow completely perfect for him. Stopping a few feet away from him, I waited for him to make the next move because honestly, after a week of no contact, I wasn't sure what he was doing here at all.

Taking the hint, along with a sharp elbow from David, he crossed to me, hands clutched around a clear plastic florist's box. Inside, I saw the most perfect single calla lily—not white, as I was accustomed to seeing, but rather a deep purplish black. Like his tux, not traditional, but an unerringly perfect com-

plement to my pale aquamarine beaded cocktail dress—the
dress both Claudia and I had known was absolutely perfect.

"You look beautiful," he finally said.

Lips pressed together, I nodded.

"Uh...this is for you." He fumbled with the box, finally
wrestling it open, and removed the flower. "Do you want me
to or do you—" He turned it over, revealing the elastic band.

Still unable to speak, I merely extended my hand, palm
down, indicating he could slip the corsage onto my wrist.
With a clear sigh of relief, he set the box aside and took my
hand in his.

Tough to say whose hands were clammier with sweat.

Even after he'd adjusted the corsage, he kept hold of my
hand—not too tight, as if giving me the option to retreat. Or
pull it free in order to slug him a good one.

I kept my hand in his. Not that slugging him wasn't tempt-
ing.

"I'm sorry," he finally said.

"I think maybe that should be my line. It *would* have been
my line if you'd given me a chance to explain." I looked down
at our hands.

"Why are you here, Eddie?"

"We wanted to give you a prom."

"Bullshit." Now I pulled free and wandered over to the
roof's edge. "That can't be the only thing."

"It's not." He joined me at the roof's edge, resting his arms
on the smooth metal railing. "Claudia says there's nothing
going on with you and the chef dude."

"I would have told you the same if you'd actually answered
any of my calls. Or texts. Or emails."

He winced and leaned back far enough to grab the railing
with his hands, knuckles turning white.

"Why did you show up there last week anyway?"

He turned his head and met my gaze. "I wanted to give you some support. I knew you had to be upset with your parents."

I sighed. "More resigned than anything."

"Claudia said they definitely reneged on their promise."

I nodded, fist of fear over what my future might hold twisting low and painful in my gut.

"She said, too, you might have…other options."

I nodded, but chose not to elaborate, because I sensed this was more of a conversational gambit for himself.

"I think…" He swallowed, hard enough I could see his Adam's apple moving nervously up and down the tanned column of this throat. "I think maybe you need to seriously consider those options—especially if they'll open more doors for you professionally."

I studied him for a long moment. "I'm guessing this has something to do with what you wanted to tell me last week, doesn't it?"

Color rising in his face, he nodded.

For the first time since the elevator doors had slid open and I'd seen him standing there, I felt the urge to reach out and touch him. My fingertips skimmed along the wash of red streaking along his cheekbones before dropping down to take his hand in mine.

"What's up, Eddie?" The same words I'd said to him weeks earlier when he'd first hinted at something going on.

Even so, it took him a few seconds of staring out over the Commons before he finally said, "It looks like I'm getting drafted in June."

"Drafted?" I repeated. "As in…baseball?"

"Yeah."

"But…I had no idea you even wanted to play profession-ally."

Wide shoulders rose beneath the fine wool of his tux. "I had no idea I had a chance in hell."

"Why not? You're a fantastic player."

"I'm a *good* player. David's always been the fantastic player."

But David, who'd long been lauded as one of the top play-ers in the country, was forgoing a sure top pick in the draft for an academic scholarship to Stanford and a career in astrophys-ics. Which was neither here nor there with respect to Eddie.

"You've been on all the same teams as David. Made a lot of the same all-star lists."

"As second team, while he's been first."

"Only because his cumulative stats are better, but your fielding percentage is a good fifteen points higher than his and your slugging percentage a few points higher. Plus, you can play every position in the infield and emergency catch, as well."

Eddie's grin was wide and very white in the flickering candlelight. "Six months ago you could care less about base-ball and now listen to you."

"Eh, the math of it was always easy—I just needed a good reason to be interested." His hand tightened on mine at my teasing. Breathing a little easier, I asked, "Why didn't you ever say you wanted to play professionally?"

"With David around, who was going to take me seriously?" he said without any anger toward David, just stated as fact. A fact that I guessed was probably pretty well-founded.

"I long ago quit thinking it was a possibility, so I decided to just have fun as long as it lasted. Figured I'd get my last hur-rahs playing at UM before I settled into being an adult and working for the family business."

His thumb traced a pattern over my knuckles. "Then a couple of the scouts who were checking David out made a point of coming up to me. Asked what my future plans were—finally I asked one of them if he thought I really had a shot and he said yes. I'll probably start in a developmental league and have to work my ass off, and even then there's no guarantee, but…it's more of a shot than I ever imagined having."

His gaze looked out over the city, oddly enough, in the direction of Fenway Park—as if he just instinctively knew.

"I wanted to talk to you about it. I mean, I knew you'd made your decision about going to school in Miami at least in part because of us—but then I realized, I couldn't let that dictate my decision." Dark and apologetic, his gaze found mine.

"I really want to do this, Peyton. I know it's a hell of a risk and not fair to you, but if I don't do this, I'll live my whole life wondering."

"I get it." My free hand rose to his face and cupped his cheek, feeling again all the reasons we'd been such a perfect fit. "You *need* to do this."

The worried expression that had clouded his eyes faded, leaving them the clear, dark amber of a caramel sauce.

"You, too, huh?"

I nodded. "New York. Culinary Institute of America."

"And Mr. Chef Dude," he guessed.

"He's the best at what he does. And he's offered to mentor me."

I might have expected Eddie to make some snarky comment about the nature of the mentoring, especially given what he'd seen, but once again, he surprised me.

"Wouldn't be fair to stay together, would it?"

I felt tears prick the backs of my eyes. Unlike every other

time they'd threatened, I allowed a few to fall as I silently shook my head.

Taking both my hands in his, he stared down at me. "I am going to miss you so damned much, Peyton."

"Me, too." I gripped his hands tight, the velvet softness of the calla lily brushing against my skin. "You never know what might happen, though."

A small smile—the cat's smile—turned up the edges of his mouth. "No. You never know. After all, I sure as hell never expected to fall in love with you."

"Me neither." For the first time, I was able to say it. "I do love you, you know."

The grin broadened. "Dude—of course you do. How could you not?"

And there he was—the cocky goofball jock on full display, even though his eyes reflected a new, grown-up sadness. The same sadness I could feel in my heart. But this was the right decision. For both of us.

A slow, sweet song began drifting from the direction of the rooftop lounge.

The goofy grin faded into a gentle smile that made my heart ache, just a bit more.

"Dance?" he asked.

I blinked away the tears and returned his smile, feeling as I did that our story—mine and Eddie's—wasn't over yet. Somehow—some way—our paths *would* cross again.

Until then, though, we'd have this one last dance.

★ ★ ★ ★ ★

A very special thank you to Tracy Sherrod, for her faith in my work, and for asking me to be a part of this project.

Glenda Howard, it was refreshing to work with an editor with such infinite patience, and a true understanding that the creative process takes time.

Thanks to Katy Butler with www.thebullyproject.com for providing valuable tools and resources with which parents, students, and educators can use to recognize, prevent, and stop bullying.

Last but not least, thanks to my husband, Richard, for the infinite support and encouragement, and for being on #TeamDeidre for all these years. You really "get" what being the spouse of a writer is all about, and for that I am eternally grateful. XOXO

PROM AND CIRCUMSTANCE

Deidre Berry

one

DEANNA PARKER

I was in Mr. Baisden's fourth-period social studies class the day Principal Ellerbee made the announcement that entirely changed the remainder of my high-school career.

It was senior year, with only one month left to go before graduation, and like most seventeen-year-olds, I couldn't wait to put high school in my rearview mirror so that I could get on with the fabulous life I had planned for myself, plans that included attending a prestigious college, followed by law school. After an illustrious career practicing criminal law, the next step in my life plan was to become a criminal-court judge. I'd retire at the ripe old age of fifty-five and then live out my golden years as *Supreme Court Justice Deanna Parker.*

Yep, sounded like a good plan to me.

But life is funny that way. Just when you think you have things all planned out, fate steps in with a monkey wrench and jacks up all of your plans. Just to keep you on your toes, I guess. Or, just to remind you that fate always has the upper hand whether you like it or not.

Unaware of the meteor that was about to collide with my life in a few short minutes, I sat at my desk anxiously tapping my pen against my notebook as Mr. Baisden gave us the guidelines for his latest assignment, which was worth a whopping 30 percent of our final grade.

Compare the accomplishments of a historical figure to someone who is currently making a similar impact on today's society.

"And," Mr. Baisden continued, "for this final assignment of the year, you'll be working in teams of three."

My heart sank and I groaned out loud along with the rest of the class.

I despise group papers. In fact, I hate them so much that I invite whoever invented the concept to take a flying leap off of the highest cliff that they can possibly find.

Don't get me wrong, I work well with others. I really do. It's just that I was striving to keep my grade point average above 4.0 so that I could become valedictorian of the graduating class, and at this stage in the game I would've preferred for my fate to be solely in my own hands, instead of partially in the hands of two other people who may have already mentally checked out for the year.

My heart sank even further when I found out that Mr. Baisden paired me up with Chad Campbell and Shelly Bennett.

Shelly was one of those moody, goth-punk girls who had the reputation of not being smarter than a fifth grader. She rarely talked and wore all black everything, including lipstick and nail polish. Chad was a fairly smart kid, but he was also top jock of Brookfield High, and I noticed that he didn't quite seem to know what to do with himself now that the school year was winding down and all of the sports seasons were over. I objected so strongly that I immediately walked up to Mr. Baisden's desk and quietly pleaded with him for other partners.

"In the real world you don't get to choose who you work with, Deanna," he said in a hushed but stern tone of voice. "Besides, I like for the more advanced students like yourself to work with the ones who are struggling. Look at it as your chance to be a leader and teach."

But isn't that your job? I started to ask, but didn't, because I realized it was a losing battle.

As I made my way back to my desk, Mr. Baisden addressed the class: "All right everyone…for the remainder of this hour, I'm going to let you guys break off into your respective groups to brainstorm topics for the assignment."

Instantly, a lot of shuffling and desk-scooting went on throughout the room, as kids arranged themselves with their assigned group members.

"Well, does anyone have any ideas?" I asked Shelly and Chad, poised to take notes on my laptop. I waited for a response that never came. Instead, Shelly just sat there doodling on a sheet of notebook paper, while Chad played some kind of video game on his cell phone. It must be a good one, because he hadn't bothered to look away from the screen once.

Mr. Baisden must have felt a teensy bit guilty about the predicament he'd put me in, because he tapped Chad on the shoulder and said, "This assignment is critical, so put the phone away and get focused, son."

Chad sighed, placed his phone on his desk and just sat there with the blankest of expressions.

Okaayyy…

Chad and Shelly's lack of interest confirmed that I was in for a bumpy ride with these two geniuses. As I looked at them, trying to get them to engage in the process, I could almost see the dust clouds blowing through their heads. And one thing became crystal clear: if we were going to get an A on this paper that was worth 30 percent of our final grade, then I had to accept that most of the work was going to be on my shoulders.

So there I was, deep in thought, trying to come up with an A-worthy idea, when Principal Ellerbee's voice came blasting through the PA system, breaking my concentration.

"Good afternoon, Brookfield student body… It is my pleasure to announce the nominees for this year's senior-prom court…"

"Oh, goody!" I muttered sarcastically. As I said that, I looked around the room and noticed that some of the other girls in class were giddy with anticipation, and a couple of them even had their fingers crossed.

But not *this* girl. At the time, I couldn't have cared less about the actual prom itself, let alone who could possibly be crowned prom queen. The way I saw it, prom was just another idiotic high-school ritual designed to bestow even more love and adoration onto the popular kids who already think they're better than everyone else. My mind was preoccupied with other, more important things, like the fact that it was early May and I still hadn't received an acceptance letter from any of the five colleges that I had applied to.

"The prom king nominees are…Chad Campbell…Justin Reynolds…Manny Gomez…and Jamal Davis…"

No surprises there, I thought. All of those guys were extremely popular and were constantly being nominated for stuff like homecoming court, student body president and things of that nature.

I looked over at Chad to give him a thumbs-up, but he looked so nonchalant, I wasn't sure if he'd even heard that he had just been nominated for prom king.

Principal Ellerbee's announcement was temporarily interrupted by the piercing sound of audio feedback, caused by being too close to the microphone.

"Ah, come on!" Tanya Walker said impatiently, as if she fully expected to hear her name called.

"Sorry about that, everyone," Principal Ellerbee continued. *"And the nominees for prom queen are…Aubrey Garrett…Judy Reeves…Tiffany Boyd…and Deanna Parker. Congratulations to all the prom nominees!"*

"DEANNA PARKER?" My classmates shouted in unison, most of them looking just as surprised and confused as I felt. Me? Nominated for prom queen? No. Freakin'. Way.

AUBREY GARRETT

Right after Principal Ellerbee said "Aubrey Garrett…" my home-economics class exploded with loud cheers and applause. Even my home-economics teacher, Mrs. Cowell, was thrilled for me. "Way to go, Aubrey!" she said cheerfully, and gave me a pat on the back. That really meant a lot coming from her, because I've never seen Mrs. Cowell get hyped about anything other than a nice roll of cloth that she'd gotten for a good price down at the Jo-Ann Fabric store.

My entire high-school career had been storybook-perfect, and now I had the chance to wrap it all up on the highest note of all: prom queen of Brookfield High. In my opinion, being named prom queen is the highest honor a girl can receive. But more important than the crown itself is winning what comes along with it, which is respect, prestige and confirmation that you are the number-one queen bee of the entire school, and all the other girls need to bow down and pay homage.

Yay for me! And "yay" for my boyfriend, Chad, for being nominated for prom king. If we both managed to win, it would be the coolest thing ever.

For the rest of the school day, Brookfield High was all abuzz with the news that I had a 99.9 percent chance of becoming the school's next prom queen. Out in the halls, everyone I passed congratulated me as if I had already won, and at my locker between fourth and fifth periods, my best friends Mia, Jessica and Kimberly greeted me with a swarm of hugs.

"Those other chicks are so beat up from the feet up, they don't stand a chance!" Jessica said, giving me a high five.

"That's right, Aubrey," Mia added. "You might as well be running unopposed, because clearly, you already have this thing in the bag!"

Not bragging or anything, but Mia was right. Out of all the other nominees, I was the one with prom royalty flowing through my veins. Being prom queen is a Garrett family tradition that goes back several generations. My older sister, Angela, my Mom, my aunts and my grandmother were all prom queens when they were in high school, so naturally it was expected that I would bring home another family crown to add to the collection.

I was happy about the nomination, but I can't say that I was all that surprised. I'd been named homecoming queen back in the fall, and the way it goes at our school, whoever wins homecoming is practically an automatic shoo-in when it comes to prom.

What did surprise me about the prom queen nominations is who the other nominees turned out to be. Tiffany Boyd, Judy Reeves and Deanna Parker. *Really?*

Obviously, someone had just pulled off one of the greatest pranks in Brookfield history, because I just couldn't take any of those three girls seriously.

I don't have anything personal against any of them, it's just that we're all really different. First of all, Tiffany Boyd was a female jock who dressed like a boy and had the nickname "Baby Shaq" because of her height and imposing physique. Not only was Tiffany the tallest girl in school, she was the tallest student, *period*. Tiffany was cool in my book. We had a lot of mutual friends and often ended up at the same parties, but to be honest, she isn't exactly what you'd call promqueen material.

Secondly, Judy Reeves, also known around school as "Judy Cootie," has a face full of acne and braces caked with whatever she had to eat that day. Ever since elementary school, Judy's had this unquenchable thirst to be popular and will do just about anything for attention and recognition. Her attempts to dress and act cool are laughable, almost always fail and only result in making her the butt of even more jokes, and that's exactly what her nomination appeared to be—a joke.

And then there's Deanna Parker. I really don't know that much about the girl besides the fact that she wears these huge, Steve Urkel-style glasses, and constantly goes out of her way to show everybody how smart she is. Kids like Deanna annoy me with the way they sit at the front of every class, and are always first to raise their hands to ask or answer a question. People only know of Deanna around school because she participates in all the nerd activities like debate and science club, where she's always winning some competition or award, but when it comes to a social life, she doesn't have one, as far as I can tell.

Deanna and I were actually kinda cool for about ten minutes during sophomore year. I tried to befriend her and bring her into my circle, but it just didn't work out. I liked her initially, but we just didn't have enough in common to maintain a friendship.

For instance, I think everyone should always leave the house looking like they're ready to hit the red carpet, with hair, makeup and outfit—done! Deanna obviously doesn't share my point of view because she keeps her hair pulled back in a ponytail, and jeans and flip-flops are her standard, everyday uniform. Shallow? Maybe…but it's totally not my fault that I was dropped as a baby into a pool of awesomeness and glitter. My mom won Miss Texas back in 1993 and happens to be a former Dallas Cowboys cheerleader, so I got my fabulousness from her, and learned early in life that image is everything.

But anyway, back to Deanna. To her credit, she has a decent personality and would look a lot like Kelly Rowland if she put in the time and effort. When we first met, I saw potential in her and tried to help up her swag game, but you can only help those who want to be helped. Deanna was obviously content with going around looking like a lost cause, so I just had to let go and let God.

So, that was my competition, in a nutshell. If it's true that snagging the prom-queen title is nothing but a popularity contest, then out of the four girls in the running I was slated to win this thing by a landslide. I've heard that you should never count your doughnuts before the yeast rises, but I think it's safe to say that the election is just a mere formality. I mean, unless there's some sort of glitch in the matrix, there's just no way that I can lose.

DEANNA PARKER

I kept thinking: *Nah…it can't be. There must be some mistake!* And then I remembered that every year, four girls are nominated for prom queen, and at least one of the nominations is considered a joke to the rest of the student body. So after getting over the initial shock of being nominated, I laughed long and hard, because I figured I was the one who had been selected for the gag. Then when I found out that my friends April, Kristen and Trish went behind my back and collected the fifty signatures that were necessary to land me on the ballot for prom queen, I laughed even harder.

"Ha-ha. *Funny!*" I told them during Spanish class, where

they confessed what they'd done. "The joke is on me. Now can we please get on with life?"

"No, the joke isn't on you," Trish said sincerely. "We didn't put you on the ballot because we thought it was funny, we did it because you actually do deserve to be prom queen."

"And since you've been all work and no play, we were hoping that the nomination would be the spark you need to finally start enjoying senior year," Kristen added.

"Look, I appreciate what you guys tried to do, so I'll attend prom if my dad lets me, but I'm not entertaining the shenanigans of running for prom queen," I said. "That's just not gonna happen."

"And why not?" April asked, more than a little annoyed with me. "No girl in her right mind would turn her nose up at the prospect of being prom queen."

"Then obviously you don't know me very well, because if you did, you'd know that I find the whole thing so petty and so...*high school*," I said.

"*Hello!*" Trish sang out. "In case you haven't noticed, you're in high school, and while you're here, you should start doing things that only high school kids get to do, like go to prom, and be silly, and have fun."

"And run for prom queen," April added.

"That's right, Deanna," Kristen said. "It's time to let your hair down and be carefree, because this time next year we'll be off in the real world with real responsibilities, and I just don't want any of us to look back on these days and regret not taking full advantage of the opportunity to go out with a bang."

"Face it, Deanna, it's time to come out of that comfort zone of yours and live a little," Trish told me. "You only have one life to live so you might as well do it big!"

Mr. Martinez walked past our desks and casually said, "I

think you should go for it, Deanna," which surprised us all because we had no idea he'd overheard our conversation.

"Yeah, Deanna, go for it!" Kristen said excitedly. Then they all started chanting, "Go for it! Go for it! Go for it!" over and over again, as if that was supposed to make me change my mind. It didn't.

"Sorry, guys, but it's just not that important to me," I told them. "I'm more concerned with the next phase of my life."

"Well, the prom court assembly is in three days, so you have until then to decide if you're going to accept or decline the nomination," April informed me. "So just promise us that you will at least take some time and really think it over."

I promised them I would, but at the time I had every intention of declining the nomination. I'm not a follower. I've never been one to tag behind the crowd, and hopefully I never will be. My friends, of all people, know that I try to stay away from things that are negative and unproductive. But none of us knew that the prom-queen scenario would get so negative, so fast.

The trash-talking began immediately.

I was on my way to sixth-period biology class when Ethan Cohen, the school videographer, stopped me in the hallway with his video camera rolling. "Hey, Deanna, you were nominated for prom queen earlier today. What do you think of the betting pool that has Aubrey winning this thing by a landslide?"

I was humiliated, but tried not to let it show on my face. "It's no big deal," I said right into the camera. "People are entitled to waste money on whatever they choose, so to each their own."

Ethan's brow wrinkled. He looked disappointed that I hadn't given him something more controversial to stir the pot and add to the rumors that were already spreading like wildfire.

I'd overheard lots of things throughout the day, but to sum it all up: Tiffany Boyd, who had a reputation for being a big-time prankster, had somehow cheated her way onto the ballot to incite prom anarchy and make a mockery of the whole thing. Judy Reeves was only nominated for comic relief, and the only title I had the chance of winning was "queen of the geek squad."

Ouch! That stung a bit, and was super rude, but the more I thought about it the funnier it became. *Queen of the geek squad...* Yeah, I'll take that. One thing to know about me is that I don't view the words *nerd* or *geek* as insults. So-called geeks are the ones who build social networks, cure diseases and otherwise change the world for the better. So go ahead and call me a geeky nerd all you want. I don't mind.

But what did bother me about the trash-talking was the common belief that Aubrey Garrett, and only Aubrey, was fit to be queen.

Oh, really? I had a problem with that. A HUGE problem. Just because I don't cake makeup on my face every day or walk around like I own the world, doesn't make me any less worthy than Aubrey, who actually should've been running for the title "queen of mean."

Seriously, nothing about her impresses me. Not that she could pass for Meagan Good's younger sister, or even the fact that her parents gave her a brand-new Jeep for her sixteenth birthday.

My dad's being a recruiter for the United States Marine Corps is the reason that I've been to six different schools in the last ten years. Before moving to Dallas two years ago, my family (Mom, Dad and big sister Erica) lived in Germany,

Hawaii, San Diego, Omaha and North Carolina. Throughout all that traveling and moving around from place to place, I have never met anyone quite like Aubrey Garrett. That girl is truly a piece of work…and I don't mean that in a good way.

There are lots of words I could use to describe Aubrey, but if I could choose only one word to sum her up best it would be *superficial*. You just shouldn't look down on people who don't have what you have, or dress exactly the way that you dress. At least that's what my parents taught me, but hey, that's Aubrey Garrett for you.

Believe it or not, the two of us were actually friends for a short time during sophomore year, back when I first transferred to Brookfield High. At that time, I tutored Aubrey in math, and we became fast friends until Aubrey suddenly stopped talking to me and started passing me in the halls as if I'd somehow developed the superpower of invisibility. Aubrey never had the guts to tell me why she defriended me, but I can only guess that she buckled under the pressure from her mean-girl group of friends who labeled me as "not cool enough" to hang out with. Not that it bothered me. I couldn't have cared less, actually, because by that time I'd realized that Aubrey doesn't really want genuine friends. She wants groupies—people who suck up to her and constantly tell her how great she is. And if those groupies act, talk and dress exactly like Aubrey, then that's even better.

I wasn't interested in playing that game, because I for one was nobody's groupie. Least of all Aubrey Garrett's.

TWO

AUBREY GARRETT

Chad knew how hectic my day had been and that I needed to unwind, so he took me to Taco Hut after school to celebrate our nominations for prom king and queen. I absolutely love Taco Hut. It's one of our favorite restaurants because they serve the best Tex-Mex in the whole city of Dallas, and it's also where Chad officially asked me to be his girlfriend back during sophomore year. We have been dating for two years, but have known each other since we were little kids. Not only did we attend the same church, but our mothers were members of the same professional women's organization, so we always wound up running into each other at some of the same high-society events like art auctions and fashion-show luncheons. So with seeing each other so much both in and outside of school, it was inevitable that Chad and I would eventually become a couple.

Right before we were about to dig into our chicken enchilada platters, Chad raised his glass of strawberry soda in the air and said, "Congrats, babe, not only are you the queen of my heart, but now you're going to be the queen of Brookfield High… All hail the queen!"

I smiled and giggled, thankful to have a boyfriend who was

so thoughtful and romantic. I tapped my glass against Chad's and said, "To the queen *and* king!"

"Hear, hear!" he said drily, taking his nomination in stride as he does with most things that have nothing to do with sports. In addition to being good-looking, Chad is also a jock. But not just any old jock, he's *the ultimate jock* who dominates in every sport he plays. Not only does Chad run track, but he's also captain of the football team and is Brookfield High's leading scorer on the basketball court. If there were a Wikipedia page defining superstar high-school athletes, Chad Campbell would be used as the prime example.

"So how's your dress coming along?" Chad asked, shoveling a forkful of Spanish rice into his mouth.

"It should be ready any day now," I said, referring to the gown that was being custom-made just for me by Jules Jamison, an awesome designer who made a huge name for himself after designing a dress for the first lady of the United States.

Every girl wants her prom to be over-the-top amazing, and everything starts with the dress. There was no way I would even consider wearing a dress straight off the rack, so six months ago, my Mom and I traveled all the way to New York to meet with Jules.

I didn't know about the other girls, but my dress was going to be fifty shades of fabulous. It was a yellow satin sweetheart gown with a full skirt, and a bodice embellished with hand-beaded multicolored jewels. Not only was it gorgeous, it was *everything!*

Having a glamorous mother and a father who is a successful engineer has its privileges, so I was looking forward to having the most perfect prom experience ever, and the price tag wasn't cheap.

To go along with the dress, Chad and I had these awesome plans to rent a Hummer limo with three of my closest friends and their dates, so it would be a total of eight. We were going to start the night off at Mia's house for a pre-party where we'd take tons of pictures before heading off to dinner at a fancy restaurant. After dinner, we'd hit up the prom for a few hours and then go to my house for an all-night after-party.

It was going to be *the* ideal prom, and a very expensive night.

"So are you going back to New York to try it on or have it altered, or anything?"

"No," I replied. "They have all of my measurements and everything, so they're just going to ship it here by FedEx when it's done."

Chad shook his head and snickered. "You're so high-maintenance."

"Yeah, but you love it, though," I teased.

"Yeah, I do," he said, dipping a tortilla chip in salsa. "But if we get married one day, I don't know if I'll be able to afford you."

I thought he was just kidding until I looked up and saw that he had a concerned look on his face. Like the thought that he couldn't afford me really worried him. "Aww, that's so sweet." It touched my heart so much that I leaned over the table and kissed him on the lips. "Don't worry, when the time comes for us to get married, you'll be a professional athlete raking in tons of moolah, so affording me will not be an issue."

"I sure hope so...." he said, still looking a little unsure. My poor little Tink Tink. The week before, Chad had gotten word that his basketball scholarship to Georgetown University had fallen through because his grades weren't up to par, and he'd been down in the dumps ever since, worried that no other schools would want him.

I'm not the best at consoling people, so I thought it was best to steer the conversation in a lighter direction.

"So what about your tux and all that other good stuff?" I asked, helping myself to a heaping spoonful of his corn cake.

"Everything is all set," he assured me. "All you have to be concerned about is looking fly and having fun on prom night."

"Done and done!" I smiled, relieved that he had things under control on his end.

We left Taco Hut and walked hand in hand back to my black Jeep Cherokee.

"When are you finally gonna let me drive this thing?" Chad asked, playfully trying to wrestle the keys from my hand.

"Umm, it'll be three days after never," I joked. "I promise!"

Chad had been dying to drive my truck since my parents surprised me with it last year for my 16th birthday, but the vehicle came with the stipulation that I could never let anyone else drive it. Not even Chad, whose own parents flat-out refused to buy him a car until he graduated from high school.

As soon as we got in the Jeep, Chad pulled me close and attacked me with kisses all over my face. "I'm so lucky," he said as he breathed in the scent of my hair.

Chad was always telling me all the time how lucky he was to have me, but I thought I was the lucky one. He really was every girl's dream, but the downside to having such a keeper is that tons of other girls want him, too. Even though everyone knows that I'm Chad's girlfriend, other girls are constantly throwing themselves at him and trying to sabotage our relationship. We've broken up and gotten back together more times than I could count or remember, but somehow, we always ended up finding our way back to each other.

★ ★ ★

I made it home and found my mother in the living room surrounded by posters that read AUBREY GARRETT FOR PROM QUEEN and VOTE FOR AUBREY!

I had texted her earlier in the day when the nominations came out, and apparently she'd taken the news and ran with it all the way to Hobby Lobby. There were posters of every size and color, all of them with my smiling face on the middle of them, and with a sparkly tiara on top of my head. My mom works as a buyer for Nordstrom, but drawing and graphic design are among her many talents.

"Thank you, Mommy," I said, examining her handiwork. "These are so fabulous… I love them!"

"You're welcome," she said, looking up at me from where she sat on the floor. "And I'm glad you like them. I'm going to take them down to the printer tonight and have them laminated. That way you and your friends can put them up before school starts tomorrow morning."

I frowned. "That means I have to get to school at least an hour early in order to get all these up before first period."

"Hey," she shrugged. "A girl's gotta do what a girl's gotta do, if she wants to win prom queen."

My mother has always taken an interest in my activities and supported me in everything I do, but when the divorce became final a few months ago, she morphed into supermom and started to overcompensate for the fact that my father had drifted further and further away from me since he'd left, despite giving me his word that we would remain close.

I really hadn't planned on doing any over-the-top campaigning, because that's how sure I was of victory, but my mother convinced me that politicking was necessary because it would generate goodwill among my classmates and prove that I deserved to win.

"You can't take anything for granted, Aubrey, especially your competition," she warned me. "Confidence is great, but overconfidence can lead to a downfall."

She was officially in prom-mom mode. I'd watched her do the same thing last year after my sister, Angela, was nominated for prom queen. Mom had orchestrated the campaign from *A* to *Z*. She single-handedly created the posters, baked five hundred cupcakes and produced a personalized video with Angela listing all the reasons she deserved to win the title.

It was a thrilling moment when Angela returned home from prom wearing the crown. All of my mother's hard work had paid off then, just as it would with me. I almost felt sorry for those other girls, because they had no idea what they were in for.

DEANNA PARKER

I got to school the next day and saw that Aubrey's face was everywhere. Literally. She had littered the entire school inside and out, with what seemed like hundreds of tacky color posters of herself, wearing that smug look of entitlement that irks me to no end. What a narcissist! You would've thought she was campaigning for some important political office instead of prom queen, a title that holds little to no importance in the real world.

While I still didn't take my nomination seriously, Judy Reeves took hers seriously enough for the both of us. After lunch, she ran up to me in the hallway and hugged me so hard we both almost fell over. I was surprised by her display of affection, because Judy and I weren't tight like that. I mean, we had a couple of Advanced Placement classes together, but that's about it.

"Congratulations, Deanna! Isn't it great? Aren't you excited about the nomination?" Judy grinned, with something orange stuck in her braces, which I guessed might have been the buttered carrots that had just been served for lunch in the cafeteria.

"No, I'm not really all that excited." I sighed. "I'm so over all the hoopla already, but it sure looks like you're enjoying it."

"Gosh, are you kidding?" she gushed. "This is the most amazing thing that's ever happened to me in my life!"

Judy looked the happiest that I've ever seen her look, and I was happy for her, even though I'd heard through the grapevine that her nomination was just another extremely cruel prank that some of the kids at Brookfield enjoyed playing on her.

Poor Judy. You come to school one time smelling like cat pee, and they never let you live it down. It certainly didn't help that her father was a mortician down at Overland Funeral Home, so most kids considered Judy creepy by association. It's mean, and totally unfair to ostracize someone based partly on what their parents do for a living, but hey, it's high school. What are you gonna do?

As Judy and I were talking, Eric Taylor, one of the cutest guys in school, walked up to us and asked, "Hey Judy, will you go to prom with me? Pretty please?"

Judy blushed and smiled as if one of her secret dreams had just come true. As soon as she said, "Yes!" Eric yelled, "Psyche!" and then ran off down the hallway with his friends, all of them laughing hysterically.

"I'm sorry about that," I said to Judy, feeling as bad for her as if it had happened to me.

She shrugged it off and said, "No, it's okay…."

But I could tell that Eric's cruelty had crushed her. I'd seen the tears that welled up in her blue eyes, but then were gone in an instant. She had literally sucked it up and moved on from the incident within 8.5 seconds, which was amazing to me. Had it been me, or anyone else, we probably would've had to go home for the rest of the day to recuperate, but Judy Reeves was resilient if nothing else. Had to give her bonus points for that.

"So anyway," Judy continued, as if the awkward incident with Eric had never happened. "Aubrey's probably going to win, but it really does feel great just to be nominated, doesn't it?"

Before I could answer "No!" I saw Aubrey coming down the hall with her squad of minions: Jessica Hendricks, Kimberly Harris and Mia Carson. They were walking the way they always did. Side by side, and shoulder to shoulder, which forced people to get out of their way or risk getting run over. The four of them stopped right in the middle of the hallway, lined up in formation, and started doing the type of step-routine that sorority girls do.

"KA-BOOM! Team Aubrey just stepped in the room, filling all the haters with doom and gloom… Oh! We forgot to mention, when it comes to our girl there's no competition! A–U–B–R–E–Y, there's no one who's quite as fly as Aubrey… yeah, yeah…as Aubrey! She's super tight and extra lean, so vote for Au-brey for prom queen… Yes, Aubrey… Vote, vote, for Aubrey!"

Kids who had stopped and gathered around cheered and applauded Aubrey and her crew, and Judy cheered loudest of all.

I, on the other hand, refused to clap for that mess. Instead, I snickered and shook my head, because it was typical Aubrey Garrett. Tooting her own horn was a skill she had mastered to perfection. Since I've been in this town, and at this school, I've learned that everything really is bigger in Texas, including Aubrey Garrett's ego and overinflated sense of self-importance. Not only was she a legend in her own mind, but she also reminded me of a piano with only one flat, and very off-key, note.

Aubrey locked eyes with me, and clearly noticed the unimpressed look on my face. "Uh-oh, hater alert!" she said, pointing me out to her friends.

"Oh, don't mind her," Mia said. "She's just mad because you're gone-with-the-wind fabulous, and she's just plain ole gone with the wind."

"Or could it be that prom isn't even here yet, and she's already lost?" Aubrey asked innocently.

"Boo-hoo!" Jessica rubbed her eyes like she was crying. "Too bad, so sad!"

"Well, you don't necessarily have to be a beauty queen to win prom queen, so maybe she does have a shot," Kimberly chimed in. "Wait...did I just say that out loud? Oops!"

Because my father taught me never to take crap from anyone, for any reason, I have never been one to let people walk all over me. And I wasn't about to start then. When I started marching over to Aubrey and her goon squad, I noticed that Judy Reeves had disappeared like a thief in the night. It was okay though, because I didn't need Judy or anyone else to help me fight my battles.

"I see you're all wearing your mean-girl panties today," I said to Team Aubrey. "But I can promise you, I'm not an easy target."

"Ooooh!" They all shivered like they were cold, and laughed.

"It seems like *you're* the one with *your* panties in a knot," Mia said with a smirk.

"They tend to get that way when people talk trash, and don't know the first thing about me," I said.

"Calm down, girl. It's really not that serious," Aubrey said to me. "As a matter of fact I was just about to come congratulate you on the nomination and wish you the best of luck."

"Thanks," I replied. "But I'm not accepting the nomination."

"Well it's probably for the best," Kimberly said, flipping her long black hair. "Since you really don't have much of a chance of winning, anyway."

"And what makes you think I don't have a chance of winning?" I asked.

"Come on, Deanna, you know you're not that girl..." Aubrey said with pity. "You're a smart cookie, so I'm sure you know the odds of you actually winning are stacked higher than Mount Everest."

"Excuse me? Oh, I'm sorry...I didn't realize you all were experts on my life and how I should live it," I said, folding my arms. "Please continue while I take notes."

"Actually, I think she should accept the nomination and campaign," Mia said to Aubrey, as if I weren't standing there. "I mean, thirty years from now, it's probably going to be the highlight of her life."

"No, that's where you're wrong," I corrected her. "The highlight of my life will be practicing law and making a positive difference in this world. You see, running for prom queen doesn't matter one bit to me because I have lots of other things going for me. Unlike some people..."

Aubrey's crew all gasped in unison, as if I had just committed a mortal sin. It was common knowledge that Aubrey wasn't the brightest bulb on the Christmas tree, and she hated for anyone to dare point out that particular flaw of hers.

"I mean really, Aubrey," I continued. "You shine socially, but I excel scholastically. And in the long run, which one is more important?"

"Oooh…no she didn't!" Mia said under her breath.

I knew I'd gotten to Aubrey, because her almond-colored complexion turned a funny shade of red. Ha! As much as she dishes it, you would think that she'd be able to take it. Then again, Aubrey is one of those girls who is not used to being challenged. This was new, uncharted territory for her, and I was thrilled to be the one to introduce her to it.

"Yeah, you're about that geek life," Aubrey said when she finally recovered. "But nobody is impressed by that…at least not anybody that I know."

Aubrey spit out the word *geek* as if it were the dirtiest of all four-letter words. She was trying her best to get under my skin, but I wasn't fazed. Not one bit.

Initially, I had no intentions of entertaining the shenanigans that come along with running for prom queen, but at that very moment I decided to enter the race and really give Aubrey a run for her money. If she came out victorious over me, then so be it. But at least she'll have actually earned something for once in her life.

"You know what?" I said. "I've changed my mind,"

"Oh, so you're running for prom queen, after all?" Aubrey asked.

"That's right, I'm entering the race, and I don't plan to lose," I told them.

"Wow, it looks like somebody just grew a pair," Jessica said. "And right before our very eyes!"

"Yeah, how about that?" Kimberly added with fake amazement.

"Okay, turn it up, then!" Aubrey said, sharing another laugh with her friends at my expense.

"Oh, I plan to turn it all the way up," I replied matter-of-factly.

"Well best of luck, and may the best woman win…" Aubrey offered a handshake, but I left her hanging. She was talking a good game, but I could tell by her body language that she wasn't too pleased by this new turn of events.

The warning bell sounded, signaling that we only had five minutes left to get to class.

"Ladies, I enjoyed this little talk," I said, not even close to being sincere. "Let's do it again sometime, shall we?" I gave the goon squad a wink before turning and walking away.

I had no idea what it took to run for prom queen, or even where to start. All I knew at that point was that Aubrey Garrett should have looked both ways before she crossed me.

three

AUBREY GARRETT

DING-ding!

The battle for prom queen just got real. If it was a fight Deanna wanted, then it was a fight that she was going to get.

Not only was she in over her head, but that girl obviously had no clue what she was up against.

Deanna might have the nerd vote locked down, but unfortunately for her, the nerd vote doesn't carry much weight at Brookfield High. Everybody knows it's the popular vote that truly counts, and that was my world and realm of expertise.

Frankly speaking, though, Deanna Parker was a nonfactor in the grand scheme of things.

A more pressing situation had been brewing for way too long, and I needed to get it straightened out once and for all.

The deal was that while Chad may have had some of our prom arrangements handled on his end, there was still one major loose end that I needed to tie up before the big night.

Besides the fact that my dress wasn't finished yet, the party planner responsible for putting together my all-night after-prom party was demanding $2,500 dollars within the next few days, or we would lose our $500 deposit and there would be no party. The problem was that my father, who had agreed to bankroll the party, was suddenly missing in action.

I'd called and texted my dad so many times without reaching him that I could no longer deny the fact that he was purposely avoiding my phone calls. So after school that day, I drove downtown to Dad's engineering firm, Garrett & Associates, hoping to finally catch him face-to-face. My father's company was in the Comerica Bank Tower, one of the tallest skyscrapers in Dallas. When I got off the elevator on the fifty-first floor, Carol the receptionist was busy handling a bunch of calls, so I acknowledged her with a nod, then walked directly to the huge corner office that said "Steven Garrett, President and CEO."

Dad was seated in his executive swivel chair, behind a massive mahogany wood desk. He was working on the computer when I walked in, so he didn't notice me right away.

"Hey there, remember me?" I said, to get his attention.

Dad looked up and smiled, and said, "Of course I remember you," but I didn't get the feeling that he was overjoyed to see me.

Things had been strained between us for months, because for some reason he assumed that I'd taken my mother's side after they separated. And maybe I had, without even realizing it. Admittedly, I was still a little pissed about the way he broke the news to me that he was leaving Mom. Dad had taken me to the Bahamas last July for my seventeenth birthday. I should have known something was brewing because he always lets me take at least one friend with us whenever we travel, but for that trip Dad said he preferred that it just be the two of us.

"But what about Mom?" I asked, thinking that it wouldn't be a true birthday celebration unless all of us were there.

"Jeannette won't be coming along with us. We already talked it over and mutually agreed that you and I are long overdue for some father-daughter time."

It was just the four of us: Mom, Dad, Angela and me. We were a small family, but we were tightly knit, and our bond was unbreakable. Or so I had thought. On the third evening of that Bahamas trip, Dad and I were out on the beach enjoying a sunset dinner of fruit salad, conch fritters and lobster caught fresh from the ocean just hours before, when he suddenly launched into a "people are in your life for a season, a reason or a lifetime…" monologue. I was confused at first, but when it finally sank in that he and Mom were getting divorced, I got so nauseous that the entire contents of my stomach ended up right there in the sand. My father tried to calm me down as best as he could by hugging me, wiping my tears and shushing me while I cried.

"Don't worry, my sweetheart, it's not the end of the world," he whispered in a comforting voice. "It's going to hurt at first, but eventually you'll be fine…"

As far as I know, that is the first lie my father ever told me. We weren't going to be a family anymore, so it *was* the end of the world, as I knew it. And things haven't really been "fine" ever since.

Mom puts on a brave face and acts like she's "fine," but I know her better than she thinks I do. The divorce was finalized nine months ago, but she still wears her wedding ring more often than not, and I've noticed the sadness in her eyes and around the corners of her mouth that wasn't there before. She also didn't laugh as easily as she used to, which was a clue that Jeannette Laverne Gilbert-Garrett was more devastated by the divorce than she let on. She missed my dad like crazy. I knew, because sometimes I'd hear her crying in the middle of the night. On those occasions, I'd go into her bedroom and lie in the spot where my father should have been, and stay there for the rest of the night. Sometimes my mom would immediately stop crying when I came into her room, and then there were times when she just let the tears flow until she was all cried out.

Sitting there in my father's office, I was prepared to make awkward small talk about school and stuff like that, but Dad cut right to the chase by asking, "How much money do you need now, Aubrey?"

"Whoa, wait a minute," I said. "The way you just said that was like all I see you as is a walking ATM, and that's it."

"Well, you have definitely inherited your mother's taste for the finer things in life, and when you call me, nine times out of ten it involves money, so let's 'keep it real,' as you kids like to say."

I didn't like where this conversation was going. It felt as if I was on trial for something I didn't do, and my father was the coldhearted judge who was about to throw the book at me.

"Well, keeping it real, I actually came by to see how you are, and to talk to you about the rest of the money I need for prom…"

"See, there you go! Just like your mother!"

I couldn't help but take offense. During the year leading up to the divorce, my parents were constantly fighting about money. He thought she spent too freely, and she thought he was a "tight-ass" who needed to learn how to loosen up the purse strings and live a little.

And there I was, caught in the middle.

"She'll probably never admit this to you," Dad told me. "But Jeannette almost spent us into the poor house while we were married, and I'm still trying to recover from all the money she wasted trying to keep up appearances."

"But what does that have to do with me, Dad?"

"You are your mother's daughter, and apparently the two of you think money grows on trees."

"All I'm asking for is what you promised me for prom—nothing more," I said.

"And certainly nothing less! You've been pampered your entire life, but what you need to understand, Aubrey, is that we're in a recession now and times are tough. The firm hasn't been doing as well as it has been in the past and things are a little tight for me financially, because in addition to a mountain of debt, I'm also paying for Angela's college tuition and monthly living expenses."

I blinked and frowned. *Tight* was a word that I'd never heard my father use in reference to his finances. And then it occurred to me that he'd had to make a choice between my prom and Angela's education, and Angela's education had won. I may have been the baby girl, but my sister was clearly my father's favorite. It was Angela who was following in Dad's footsteps. She was the one with the beautiful mind who was away at MIT studying engineering, and I thought it was pretty ironic that money never seemed to be an issue when it came to whatever Angela needed for school, and otherwise.

I loved my sister and certainly didn't resent her in any way, but it was kind of hard not to resent the way that my father kept glaring at me as if I were a stranger. That's what hurt me the most.

"You divorced Mom," I said tearfully. "But why is it that I'm starting to feel like you divorced me, too?"

My father softened up when he saw my tears. He came from around his desk to give me a hug and kiss me on the top of my head the way he used to do when I was little. "Sweetheart, I'll never divorce you. It's just time for some tough love."

Dad went on to lay out my options for me, which were

to scale back my prom plans or get the money that I needed from my mother. "Sorry, baby girl," he said somberly. "But I'm all tapped out."

I ran out of the offices of Garrett & Associates in tears. I wasn't crying because my father suddenly couldn't afford to give me money toward prom; I was upset because our relationship had disintegrated to the point where he no longer saw me as Aubrey, his daughter. Instead, he viewed me as an extension of my mother, and he really hadn't been feeling her too tough lately.

He had divorced me whether he wanted to admit it or not. My hero had abandoned me when he'd promised me he wouldn't, and at a time when I needed him the most.

Mom went into a blind rage after I told her what happened with Dad. She picked up the phone and thoroughly cursed him out without letting him get a word in edgewise. The conversation wasn't on speakerphone, but I got the gist of it just by what I overheard Mom say:

"You should have manned up and told her weeks ago, instead of making her track you down like a damn fugitive!"

"And what's that supposed to mean? You knew that senior year was going to be expensive, and more than that, you've promised since she was a little girl that she could have whatever she needed and wanted to make her prom night special...."

My mother has the heart of a lioness. She will go to war for me in a heartbeat, and often put me and my feelings before her own. My prom plans were in shambles, and that was all she cared about in that moment.

Not the fact that she was arguing with a man she was still in love with. After twenty years of marriage, Daddy had moved out and moved on with his life. He was now living in a new town house, driving a shiny new convertible and dating Heather, a woman much younger than my mother, and who looked as though she had just gotten off the pole down at the local strip club.

"I'm aware that money doesn't grow on trees!" Mom yelled at Dad over the phone. "But prom comes around only once in a girl's life and Aubrey shouldn't have to suffer because you're crying broke…"

I'd heard enough. I went into my bedroom, flopped down on the bed and sent out a mass text message informing everyone I'd invited that the after-prom party at my house was canceled. Afterward, I put my headphones on and zoned out to some new tunes on my iPod.

The music soothed my mind and body to the point where I was able to think clearly for the first time since I'd left my father's office. I realized that despite everything that was going on, the prom court assembly was scheduled for the next day and I had to get ready for it.

I opened a new document on my computer and the words just started flowing.

I've heard that you should never do anything in the heat of anger, but since I couldn't take what I felt out on my Dad, I put all those emotions into my campaign speech.

When I finished writing, I realized that adding a video to my presentation would really capture the audience and help make the big splash that I was hoping for.

Ethan Cohen, the school videographer, was the only man for the job, because he had unlimited access to the kind of footage I needed. He was also a genius when it came to looping, editing and all that other technical stuff. So much so that an hour after inviting me over to his house, Ethan and I had our finished product.

"Are you absolutely sure you want to go through with this?" he asked with both eyebrows raised.

"Yeah, I'm sure," I replied, but I honestly hadn't thought through the consequences of what I was doing, or how other people would feel about it.

I didn't know how the video would come across, but one thing would be for sure after tomorrow. Everyone at Brook-field would know that I was in it to win it, and that I wasn't taking any prisoners.

Four

DEANNA PARKER

The run-in I'd had with Aubrey brought out my competitive nature, and I was ready to win at all costs. But before I could officially start my campaign, I had to break the news to my parents that I'd even been nominated for prom queen in the first place.

Two days had passed since Principal Ellerbee announced the candidates for prom royalty. It took me that long to work up the nerve, because prom had been a touchy subject in our household since my sister got pregnant on prom night three years ago. We were living in San Diego then, and Erica was a senior at Washington High, a school that made an even bigger deal about prom than Brookfield. The prom tradition at Washington High was the more extravagant, the better. You had to go big or stay your butt at home, so it wasn't unheard of for kids to arrive to prom in helicopters, vintage Rolls-Royces and even horse-drawn carriages.

At the time, Erica had just gotten a full-ride scholarship to Xavier University, so our parents agreed to let her go as big as she wanted. No expense was spared.

My parents bought Erica a fancy dress and paid to have her hair and makeup professionally done. They rented a limo and a deluxe suite at a swanky hotel for her and her friends. Erica said she'd had the time of her life. Seven months later, she came home from her first semester at Xavier and had clearly gained more than her fair share of the average "freshman fifteen." In her case, it was more like the freshman forty. My parents took Erica into their bedroom and closed the door behind them. After a nearly all-night badgering session, Erica confessed that she was knocked up with her prom date's baby, a guy who she hadn't seen or heard much from since prom night.

Erica's scholarship ended up going to waste because she had to drop out and take a crash course in motherhood and responsibility.

My father was so heartbroken that he didn't speak to my sister for almost two whole months. He couldn't even look at her. It wasn't until my niece Jayla was born that my dad was able to get over Erica's pregnancy and move on.

Dad forgave, but he didn't forget. Since then, the rules about prom in our house became the same as *Fight Club*.

First rule: you do not talk about PROM.

Second rule: you DO NOT talk about PROM.

Third rule: you DO NOT talk about PROM—EVER!

The unspoken message was that since Erica betrayed my parent's trust, there would be no prom for me, so don't even bother asking. I didn't like it, but I accepted it. Just as I accepted not being allowed to date until I turned seventeen, which happened recently. I was now able to date, but it came with the requirement that I could only go out in groups of at least four people, and even then, my father had been known to pop in and check up on me, which was mortally embarrassing.

He was so scared that I'd follow in my sister's footsteps that he lived in a constant state of terror that history would repeat itself. For instance, I gained a few pounds during the holidays last year thanks to Mom's irresistible caramel cake, and Dad gave me the same crooked side-eye he'd given Erica when he suspected that she was expecting.

"I think you need to schedule an appointment with Dr. Sayers to have Deanna checked out," I overheard him tell Mom. She refused. My mother is the voice of reason between the two of them, and she holds me down when Dad's fears and suspicions get too out of control. He gets so paranoid sometimes that I actually feel sorry for him. It's like, it's so hard for him to just sit back and chill, instead of worrying about me so much.

So there we were at the table, my parents and I, eating a dinner of roasted chicken, mashed potatoes and green beans. I waited for my Mom to finish filling us in on how her day had gone at the public health clinic where she worked as a nurse, then jumped right in with, "So, a funny thing happened at school the other day…." When I finished telling the story, all that could be heard was the sound of utensils scraping against plates, and *Wheel of Fortune* on the television in the living room.

After what seemed like an eternity, Mom finally said, "That's nice, Deanna… I'm so proud of you…."

"Thanks…" I said, surprised that it came out barely above a whisper. I was so scared of what my father would say that I'd lost my voice.

We both looked over at Dad, whose whole attitude and demeanor had changed from happy-go-lucky to ticking time bomb. His eyes narrowed, his jaw clenched and that vein in his forehead started throbbing as it always did when he's heated about something.

"Say something, Anthony," Mom urged, but Dad stayed quiet, showing more interest in his dinner than the conversation at hand.

Mom reached over and gently tilted his chin up, forcing him to look directly at her. They exchanged glances, and I could see her silently pleading with him not to go flying off the handle about this. He's a military guy, so he can be intense without even trying to be, and is capable of going from zero to a hundred in ten seconds flat.

Dad pushed away from the table and stood up. He glared down at me as though I had just become the enemy and said, "Congratulations… Just don't come home pregnant!" He spat out the word "pregnant" as if it left a bad taste in his mouth, and then stormed out of the room without another word.

"He'll come around," Mom assured me apologetically. "You just go on and do what you have to do, and let me know how I can help. Okay?"

I nodded and breathed a sigh of relief. I think it went well considering the fact that I was still breathing, but I had a feeling that the subject wouldn't be officially closed until Dad had his say. It was coming. It was just a matter of time.

AUBREY GARRETT

After lunch on what had to be the hottest day of the year, four hundred kids crammed the gymnasium for the prom court assembly. The purpose of the assembly was for the candidates to officially accept the nomination, and to introduce themselves to the student body in hopes of winning their vote.

Eight folding chairs were lined up in the middle of the gym floor. Filling those chairs were Chad, the other three prom-king candidates and those of us in the running for prom queen. I'd been a cheerleader since seventh grade, so being in front of a large crowd wasn't unnerving to me, unlike some of the other nominees who looked like they were scared out of their minds.

When everyone was all settled, Principal Ellerbee talked briefly about why we were all there and then turned the floor over to the prom-court candidates.

In the tradition of ladies first, Tiffany Boyd, Judy Reeves, Deanna Parker and I all took to the lectern to speak. Tiffany approached the lectern with the enthusiasm of a stand-up comic about to launch into a comedy routine. Her speech, if you could really call it that, was short and to the point. "Hey everybody, vote for ya girl Tiffany!" she hollered into the microphone, and then did a little two-step like she was at a party. Always the class clown, Tiffany raised the roof while her supporters chanted "Tiff! Tiff! Tiff! Tiff!" over and over.

The racket quieted down a little when Judy Reeves replaced Tiffany at the lectern. Judy was a trembling, sweaty mess before she even uttered one word, and I don't think it helped that a few kids started yelling out "Judy Cootie!"

The crowd was rough, worse than the one at the Apollo Theater on amateur night. The heckling increased, along with a mixture of boos and laughter. They were trying to break her, but Judy just stood there and took it, which only made things worse. It got so loud and rowdy that Principal Ellerbee had to yell "Knock it off!" into the microphone and threaten the offenders with suspension before Judy could start her speech. She wiped away the sweat on her forehead and then started reading from the sheet of notebook paper that fluttered in her shaky hand.

Don't ask me what Judy's speech was about, because I have no idea. I don't think anyone did, because her voice was so low you could barely hear her, even with the microphone. It was torture having to sit there and endure all that incoherent mumbling, but there was light applause when she sat back down, because we were all relieved that it was over.

When it was my turn, I approached the lectern with confidence and a huge smile. "Okay, people, can we get serious now?" I asked, causing the student body to roar with laughter.

I sensed that this was my crowd, and they were on my side, so I jumped right into my speech. "Just about every girl in America wants to be prom queen, but what qualities make a girl truly deserving of that title?"

I signaled for Ethan Cohen to dim the lights, and then went over my PowerPoint presentation titled "What Is Prom Queen Material?"

The main points were:

1. Likability;
2. Leadership skills;
3. Outgoing personality;
4. A great sense of style.

"I have been captain of the varsity cheer team for two years in a row, so even those of you who know the least about me know that I possess all of these qualities and more," I continued, noting that kids were actually listening and no one was goofing off. "But ask yourself if my fellow candidates for prom queen possess them, as well."

I signaled for Ethan to replace the PowerPoint presentation with the video I'd sweet-talked him into helping me put together.

It was a collection of all the other nominees' most embarrassing moments that he'd caught on tape since he'd been school videographer. It started with Tiffany's not-so-secret-after-all infatuation with Coach Kelly. Coach K was gregarious and handsome, and all the students liked him, but apparently no one liked him quite as much as Tiffany. And according to the rumors that had been swirling around school for months, the feeling may have been mutual. The clip Ethan used was of

Tiffany smacking Coach Kelly on the butt after a win against Booker T. Washington High and saying, "Way to go, sexy!" with a suggestive wink. Coach K duplicated Tiffany's actions, which Ethan put on a twenty-second loop for dramatic effect.

Next was footage of Judy, just being Judy: awkward, uncouth, and desperately seeking attention anywhere she could find it.

And I was especially happy that Deanna Parker had been caught in all of her nerd glory. At the science fair last January something went wrong with her experiment, causing it to blow up in her face and singe her bangs to a crisp. Hilarious! And most recently, footage of Ethan asking her: "Hey Deanna, you were nominated for prom queen earlier today. What do you think about that?" to which she shrugged and replied, "It's no big deal!"

The very last frame was of me flashing a winning smile. "I'm Aubrey Garrett," I said right into the camera. "And I approved this message!"

FIVE

DEANNA PARKER

Embarrassed, humiliated, and downright pissed off were just a few of the emotions I felt at that moment. Imagine being slapped in the face, followed by a hard, *Mortal Kombat*-style uppercut. That's exactly how I felt after watching that piece of trashy propaganda that Aubrey had cut-and-pasted together.

If it was Aubrey's intention to shake things up and get tongues wagging, then she had definitely succeeded. By the time the video finished and the lights came back up, the buzz in the gymnasium was so loud you could barely hear yourself think.

First of all, Tiffany and Coach Kelly deserved to be put on blast because that incident was highly inappropriate, but what Aubrey had done to Judy and me was just downright evil.

And Ethan Cohen wasn't any better. He'd edited my section of the video to make it seem like I had given the middle finger to the entire student body, when that wasn't the case. The part when I'd said it was "no big deal" was in response to his question of how I felt that people were taking bets that I would lose to Aubrey, not in regard to the nomination itself. True, I didn't care much about the nomination in the beginning, but Ethan didn't know that, and besides, a girl has the right to change her mind.

Aubrey had tossed down the gauntlet, and it was my turn to pick it up and run with it.

All eyes were on me, but I wasn't nearly as nervous as I thought I would be after being humiliated in front of the entire school. Besides, years of being on the debate team had prepared me for public speaking, and I was ready to give the speech of my life.

Kristen was my self-appointed campaign manager. She took that duty on the second I announced that I would be running for prom queen, and I felt totally secure with that appointment, because she had dreams of being a crisis-communications expert like Olivia Pope, from the television show *Scandal*. No matter what kind of chaos was going on around her, Kristen always stayed in complete control, and her organizational skills were amazing. Kristen was the one who suggested the campaign slogan "the prom queen who cares," so the speech I'd written in my bedroom two nights before began with all the substantial contributions I've made to my school and community via social activism and volunteer work.

"So, who is Deanna Parker, you ask? Well for starters, I have earned over one hundred hours of community service by volunteering with the Special Olympics and helping to construct playgrounds for underprivileged children..."

A couple of kids in the audience said "Awww!" But it wasn't clear if they were actually making fun of me or not. Either way, I forged ahead, reciting my speech from memory. "I also volunteer with a local food bank, as well as the senior citizens' annual Meals on Wheels banquet. I am president of the math club, and a proud member of the NAACP Youth Council, as well as the National Honor Society. But enough about me.

Let's talk about you, and how you fit into the social pecking order here at Brookfield," I said. "If you're like me, chances are you don't easily fit into the popular, cool kids' category, so to separate us from them, they put labels on us like nerd, dork, band geek, slacker, freak, loner, loser, outcast, burnout and theater geek. If you've been tagged with one of those labels, then *I* represent *you*. A vote for me is essentially a vote for yourselves, so vote Team Deanna, and let's become prom queen of Brookfield High, *together!*"

When I finished, a large portion of the crowd jumped to their feet and applauded. Some of them were grinning and high-fiving. The "Team Deanna" chant started as a murmur, and then got louder and more enthusiastic.

It was then that I knew I had a real shot at winning the crown. And judging by the pained expression on Aubrey's face, she knew it, too.

In order to maintain momentum, Kristen spread the word via social media to all of our mutual friends that #Team-Deanna would be meeting in the multipurpose room after school. One and all were welcome to come join us to discuss campaign strategies.

Shelly Bennett, the goth-punk girl from social-studies class, showed up, along with about two dozen other kids, which totally blew me away. So-called nerds, dorks, band geeks, slackers, freaks, loners, losers, outcasts, burnouts and theater geeks all came to show support and help in any way they could. I stood at the front of the room and thanked everyone for coming, and then we got down to business brainstorming ideas for posters, fliers and T-shirts.

It turned out to be a very productive meeting. Several kids volunteered to set up tables in the school lobby and distribute baked goods on behalf of #TeamDeanna every Wednesday afternoon, which I thought was a sweet gesture and awesome idea.

Michael Turner, a kid some would consider a technology geek, pulled out his laptop, and it took him less than ten minutes to set up a Facebook page titled "Vote Deanna Parker for Brookfield Prom Queen." I looked over his shoulder as he did it, and was amazed that the page got more than 300 "likes" in less than an hour.

It wasn't long before Aubrey's name came up.

"How cool would it be if we created a video with some of *her* most embarrassing moments?" asked a guy in a wheelchair.

A girl with pink hair and multiple face piercings cosigned. "Now that's a great idea!"

"No, guys, we can't stoop down to her level," I said. "Let Aubrey play dirty if she wants to, but we're keeping our campaign as classy and positive as possible, because when it's all over, we want to look back and feel good about what we did individually and collectively."

Several kids mumbled "Okay," but it was clear that the majority of people in the room would have loved nothing more than to see Aubrey get what she deserved.

At the end of the meeting, some students told their own personal stories of being negatively labeled, and expressed pride in the movement that we were creating.

"Well you, guys," I said. "I think this calls for a team cheer."

We gathered in a big circle, and everyone put their arms in the middle.

"Team Deanna on the count of three," Michael said. "One…two…three…TEAM DEANNA!"

#TeamDeanna was now a tangible force to be reckoned with, and there would be no stopping us.

AUBREY GARRETT

I had to give Deanna Parker her props. Playing on the sympathy of the disenfranchised was a brilliant move on her part. My favorite part of her speech was when she said something to the effect of, "Yes, nerd tribe, the prom can be for you, too!"

LOL…

That really cracked me up. I'm all for people going after their dreams, but come on now. Let's be realistic.

Deanna's rant reminded me of one of those old teen movies where the nerds try to rise up and dethrone the popular kids. The only thing is, it rarely works out for the nerds in the movies, just as it won't work for Deanna in real life.

Like it or not, the status quo at Brookfield will never change. The cheerleaders, jocks and other popular kids will always be at the top, with everyone else lagging behind.

To those who have a problem with that, I say, don't blame me. I don't make the rules, I just live by them.

Deanna's speech was hilarious, but what wasn't so funny was the aftermath of my video presentation.

It was business, nothing personal. I knew when Ethan and I were putting it together that the video would be controversial, but I didn't know it would reach the level of scandal that it actually did. Ethan and I were immediately called into the principal's office where he grilled us relentlessly about the footage of Tiffany and Coach Kelly. He wanted the five W's (who, what, when, where and why).

I must have said "I don't know" about a thousand times. After about an hour, Principal Ellerbee finally let me go when he realized that Ethan was the only one who could give him the information he wanted.

My parents weren't happy with me, and neither was Chad.

"Not only did you humiliate Deanna and Judy, but you just

totally ruined two other people's lives," Chad said to me the next day, as if he were a father disciplining a child. "Coach Kelly is being put on administrative leave as we speak, and Tiffany's parents have pulled her out of school, so she won't be back at all this year."

"Well, is she gonna be allowed at prom?"

"Are you serious?" Chad asked me with a mild trace of disgust in his voice. "Look, I don't know if Tiffany will be allowed at prom or not, but she's no longer in the running for prom queen, which is all you really care about, anyway!"

I said, "That's not true..." but I didn't sound convincing, not even to myself. Chad knows me better than anyone else, so he saw right through me.

"Yes, it is!" he said. "That's what the video was all about, right? Why Aubrey Garrett deserves to win prom queen, and why those other girls don't?"

"Well, at least you were paying attention," I said jokingly, trying to lighten the mood.

But Chad didn't laugh. Instead, he stood there looking at me as though he was seeing me for the first time and didn't really like what he saw.

"You know, you haven't been the same since your parents got divorced," he told me.

"Don't you even dare go there..." I warned him.

Throughout my parents' separation and eventual divorce, I was extra grumpy and just generally not a nice person to be around. I did not play well with others, and I wasn't the best girlfriend to Chad back then, with all the almost constant snapping and complaining I was always doing.

Throughout it all, I thought that Chad understood what I was going through, but obviously he still hadn't totally forgiven me.

"No, seriously, Aubrey," Chad said huffily. "You've turned into such a mean girl it's like I don't even know who you are anymore."

"I'm the same girl you've known almost all your life. I haven't changed."

"That's not true and you know it. If you're not gonna keep it real with me, at least keep it real with yourself. If you think it's okay to ruin people's lives, careers, their futures and reputations just to become prom queen, then you're not the person I fell in love with, and definitely not someone I want to continue to be in a relationship with."

"Okay, so I made a mistake with the video, but I really don't like the way you're talking to me right now," I told him. "So you really need to check yourself!"

"I'll do you one better than that, and check out of this relationship. How about that?"

"What's that supposed to mean?" I asked, folding my arms.

"You're not a complete idiot, Aubrey, I'm sure you can figure it out."

"No, I need you to spell it out!"

"Okay, I will…. We're finished, Aubrey, it's a wrap," he sneered. "You and I are over for good this time…O-V-E-R!"

SIX

DEANNA PARKER

Aubrey's blind ambition to become prom queen had blown up in her face like the science project that accidentally caught my hair on fire.

Coach Kelly was more than likely going to lose his job, and Tiffany mysteriously vanished from school. It was unfortunate, but prom was quickly approaching, and as they say, the show had to go on.

Aubrey still had plenty of supporters, but she was no longer considered the front-runner. The race was now neck and neck thanks to #TeamDeanna, who showed up in full support and produced three times as many posters as #TeamAubrey.

Made by some very creative and artistic people, my promotional posters were flashy and eye-catching. A couple of days after the prom-court rally, Kristen and I organized a crew and early one Saturday morning, we decorated the school with fliers and posters that had catchy sayings like: VOTE FOR DEANNA: QUEEN OF OUR HEARTS and DEANNA FOR PROM QUEEN! No surface was safe. We covered every locker, hallway, and bulletin board, as well as the same places that Aubrey had put hers. Only ours were bigger, better and much more interesting.

It took us about four hours to get it all done. "Thanks

team, job well done!" I said, giving a high five to each and every one of them. We left Brookfield and all headed over to Shakey's Pizza for lunch, which was my treat for all the hard work everybody had put in on my behalf.

The whole time we were eating, all everybody talked about was prom. What their plans were, what they were wearing and stuff like that.

"What are you wearing?" Trish asked me, and all I could do was shrug.

It was ironic that I was actively campaigning for prom queen, but I hadn't given any thought to what I would actually wear on prom night. I had to get on that ASAP but in the meantime, something Michael Turner said caught my attention. "Hey everybody, why don't we all pitch in and rent one of those party buses and go to prom together?" he suggested.

"You know, I never would have thought of that, but it's actually the best idea ever!" I said.

And we unanimously agreed. We were all in this together anyway, so we might as well take it all the way to prom night. *Together.* That was the theme, and we were sticking to it.

Later that Saturday afternoon, my sister and I were sitting at the kitchen table leafing through a dress catalog that was filled with one hideous monstrosity after another. "Oh, no, look at this one!" Erica pointed out a flowery pink-and-white dress that looked as if it came from another era.

Like, before the Civil War.

"I mean…really, dude? Seriously?" I closed the catalog in disgust. "There's no way I'm going dressed as Little Bo Creep who lost her sheep on the way to prom."

"Well, if push comes to shove, you're more than welcome to wear my dress," Erica said. My sister's old prom dress was a dark blue chiffon number with a short skirt, and white sequins weaved across the entire top half of the dress. She'd looked liked a Barbie doll in it, but seeing the dress on me just might send my father into cardiac arrest.

"Thanks, but no thanks," I told Erica. "There's so much bad luck associated with that dress, I'm surprised Daddy hasn't burned it by now."

"I know, right?" Erica laughed, but her laughter had a bittersweet undertone to it.

My sister had been through a lot in the last three years. She'd had a kid, and ended up losing the full-ride college scholarship she had worked so hard for. Thankfully, she was back on the right track. She now had her own apartment and a full-time job, and was set to graduate from community college with an associate's degree in journalism in a few months. Things were looking up for Erica, but I could clearly see where she could be much further in life if she had just protected herself from getting pregnant, or better yet, kept her legs closed altogether. Some of these reality shows make being a teen mom look more glamorous and less complicated than it really is. First off, babies are so expensive. I love my niece, but I'm not about that life. Not until I'm at least thirty-five.

Since the catalog had been a colossal fail, there was no choice but to hit the mall and see what we could find. My Dad wasn't home to object, and fortunately, he hadn't said a word about prom since the night I broke the news. He may not have been 100 percent on board, but at least he wasn't dead-set against it.

My mother rode with us to the Galleria, and couldn't resist taking a walk down memory lane. "You know, Grandma Ann was a seamstress, and she spent weeks sewing my prom dress for me," Mom said wistfully. "I sure wish I could find that dress, but we've moved around so much over the years that it got lost somewhere along the way. It's too bad though, because your grandma put her heart and soul into that dress. It was so beautiful."

I'd seen the pictures numerous times. My parents were high school sweethearts and went to prom together in 1988. In their official prom picture, my mother looked pretty in pink, in a strapless satin dress covered with white lace. She had on these sheer white stockings, pink-satin heels and white lace gloves with the fingers cut off, which I'm sure was inspired by Madonna when she first hit the scene way back then. Mom's pink eye shadow matched her dress perfectly, and her hair was feathered and teased high to the heavens. Dad stood next to Mom looking stiff and uncomfortable. He was decked out in a canary-yellow tuxedo with a white ruffled shirt. His hair was a Jheri-curl mullet that was an eye-catching creation I hoped would never come back in style. The prom theme engraved at the bottom of the picture read "A Night to Remember…"

Hmm…I'll bet!

Anyway, shopping with my mother was something close to torture. We searched high and low in every dress store in the mall, but we just couldn't seem to see eye to eye on anything. She hated every dress I picked out, and vice versa. Our running dialogue of the day went like this:

Mom: "No, that dress is too risqué for someone your age. Plus, it's so tight I can see your heartbeat!"

Me: "Well, what about this one?"

Mom: "That's cute, but the fabric is a little too flimsy—what do you think about this one?"

Me: "Too cheesy…"

Mom: "This one?"

Me: "Too old lady…"

Mom: "Okay, well how about this?"

Me: "Cheesy old lady!"

Mom held up a pink dress that closely resembled the one she'd worn to her prom. "I think we may have a winner!" she said, smiling from ear to ear. And she was dead serious.

"No, Mom," I sighed for the hundredth time that day. "*Please* put that thing back on the rack…"

We were five hours in and I had tried on dozens of dresses, but none of them were right. Finding the perfect prom dress was starting to look hopeless, and I was on the verge of giving up all hope when Erica screamed, "Deanna, come quick!"

My mother and I raced to the back of the store and found Erica holding the pinnacle of prom dresses. It was a pale peach silk charmeuse gown with crystals covering the front and back of the halter-style bodice. The bottom was pleated and flowed like running water whenever the fabric moved.

I gasped when I saw it, because it was chic, sophisticated, fun and flirty; everything that I wanted in a dress. It was also so timeless that I probably wouldn't cringe in the years to come when I looked back at my prom pictures and saw what I wore that day.

Mom, Erica and I were all ecstatic until we checked the price tag. Talk about sticker shock! Fifteen hundred dollars to wear one dress, one time, was a bit much.

"It's way too expensive," I said, highly disappointed.

"Says who?" Mom asked with a bit of an attitude. "If that's the dress you want, then that's the dress you're going to get— now go try it on."

I gave Mom a big hug and then dashed into the dressing room. The dress was made just for me. It fit like a glove, and didn't need any alterations at all. I smiled at my reflection in the mirror. I wasn't even all done up with hair and makeup, but I felt like a queen already.

seven

AUBREY GARRETT

I really hate fighting with Chad. Especially about random, petty stuff that has nothing to do with us as a couple. I mean, I could understand that Tiffany was his friend, but I was his girlfriend, and that should trump everything—even friendships.

People make mistakes. You forgive them and move on, not shout "It's over!" for everyone within listening distance to hear. How embarrassing.

It was pretty ironic that Chad brought up my father during the argument, because he sure reminded me of him, now that I thought about it. They both had the bad habit of making promises and then not making good on those promises. Promises like, "Nothing will ever come between us," "Don't worry, things will be fine" and "I'll love you forever." Lies, lies and more lies!

Chad's breaking up with me out of the blue sent me spiraling into such an emotional tailspin that I went straight home and cried on my mother's shoulder. My mom is my best friend. We're so close, I can tell her anything, and she never judges me.

Mom consoled me while I cried, and then called things as she saw them. "Honey, this is just my opinion, but you and

Chad have been close since you were little kids, but now that you're older and on the brink of adulthood, it's easy to see that you two are outgrowing each other."

My mouth fell open. I was shocked that she had come to such a terrible conclusion about my relationship. "We had an argument, Mom. It shouldn't be the end of the world."

"The fact that you two are even arguing at all is the problem. I've noticed the way that you and Chad have been snapping back and forth at each other lately, and I've also noticed that you're not as patient with each other as you used to be."

"Well, no relationship is perfect," I said in our defense. "Chad and I have our bad days just like any other couple."

"And what about the cheating—have you forgotten about that?"

Okay, so Chad wasn't exactly a saint. As I've said before, the hardest thing about being with a popular guy is that plenty of other girls are waiting in the wings trying to get his attention.

The last time Chad cheated on me, which was two months ago, I caught him red-handed sending flirty text messages to another girl. The things they were saying back and forth to each other were very intimate, so I didn't buy that "She's just a friend" crap that he wanted me to believe.

I broke up with Chad, but Mom was going through her own issues with Dad, so she wasn't all that sympathetic toward my plight. "Teenage boys are fickle," she said. "They run hot one minute and cold the next minute. One day they profess their undying love to you, and five minutes later they're texting other girls. That's just how they are."

"But Mommy, he promised to be faithful to me. Doesn't that count for anything?"

"If some married men can't manage to be faithful to their wives, you really can't expect much more from a teenage boy,"

Mom replied, wiping my tears. "And I don't care what he says, or how sincerely he says it. It's just not going to happen."

That time, it took about two weeks for Chad and me to eventually get back together, but now we were on the outs again, all because of that stupid video.

"So what should I do?" I asked Mom. "Just let the relationship go?"

"If it's really over as far as he's concerned, you have to have enough dignity and self-respect to let it go. You're young, so heartbreak is inevitable. But the good thing is, you have your whole life ahead of you, and believe it or not, Chad is just a tiny blip on the radar screen of your entire life."

It wasn't necessarily what I wanted to hear, but my mother has way more life experience than I do, so perhaps she was right. Maybe young love doesn't always conquer all.

I didn't know how things would work out with Chad, but Grandma Garrett's favorite line came to mind, which was, "When one guy walks away, sometimes the best thing to do is open the door for another one."

After talking to my mother, I invited my friends over to discuss the latest development with Chad. It was a typical muggy day in Dallas, so Jessica, Mia, Kimberly and I were all outside eating frozen yogurt and dangling our feet in the swimming pool.

"You and Chad will patch things up and get back together soon, just like you always do," Mia assured me.

"No, I don't think so," I replied. "I've seen Chad mad, but never like that. Plus, I've been calling and texting him like crazy, but he just keeps blowing me off."

"So are you two still going to prom together?" Kimberly asked me.

"I don't know. I haven't even had the chance to talk to him about it," I said. "But one monkey doesn't stop a show, so I'm going to prom with or without Chad."

"Do you have anybody else in mind?" Mia asked.

"Not really," I said. "I'm gonna try to work things out with Chad, or at least convince him that prom is too close to back out now, so we should just go ahead and still go together as planned."

"Yeah, but that's not going to be any fun for the rest of us if you two end up bickering and arguing all night," Jessica said.

"I agree," Kimberly said. "I think the best thing to do at this point is find an alternate date."

I palmed my face and sighed. This was not supposed to be happening right now. I'd been planning my senior prom night for months, almost as if it were my wedding, and now that the day had almost arrived, it looked as though I might have to switch "grooms" at the last minute.

For a split second, I thought about calling the whole thing off. Chances were very high that prom was going to suck without Chad by my side. The two of us had been to tons of dances together, and we always ended up having a blast, even if the event itself was super boring.

For example, Chad escorted me to my debutante ball last December where fourteen other girls and I were introduced to society. I won "Miss Deb" that night, along with $5,000 toward college, but the most fun I had that evening was dancing with Chad for the debutante-escort waltz.

The event was held in the ballroom of the Four Seasons hotel. All of us debutantes were dressed exactly alike, in the same white ball gowns with white arm-length gloves, satin silver shoes and rhinestone accessories. All of the fathers and escorts were also dressed identically in black tuxedos with tails, white shirts and bow ties and white gloves. It was all very grand and extremely formal, but Chad kept me laughing the entire time, cracking inside jokes, and talking very proper like a high-society aristocrat.

"My, Miss Garrett, you look quite smashing this evening, I must say!" Chad whispered as we twirled across the dance floor.

It was so hard not to burst out laughing, but that's how it was most of the time when we were together—just fun times and lots of laughs. But Chad had gotten so serious and moody lately, it was almost as if he had two different personalities. If he thought I'd changed in the last few months, then so had he. It didn't take much to set him off these days. Chad could go from zero to a hundred in the blink of an eye, just as he had during our argument earlier in the day.

While sitting there on the edge of the pool, splashing water around with my feet, I had one of those *Aha!* moments that Oprah's always talking about.

If things were truly over with Chad, then I just had to accept it and move on to plan B, which was to score a new date for prom. But any old prom date would not do. I needed a high-status hottie who was worthy of being on my arm for what would be the biggest night of my life so far.

And I knew just who to call.

Eight

DEANNA PARKER

It turns out that I wasn't wrong in assuming that working with Chad Campbell and Shelly Bennett would be an uphill battle.

A whole week after Mr. Baisden had given us the assignment, my group was still trying to compromise on a topic. Unbelievable! For starters, Shelly hadn't been to class in four days even though I'd seen her around school, and Chad was there, but he wasn't really *there*, if you catch my drift. He'd just sit in class, not really saying much, and looking as if he only had six brain cells left in his head. The poor guy was obviously going through a rough patch, and I couldn't help but wonder if it had something to do with Aubrey. I wouldn't have been surprised if she was the source of his troubles, because she tends to bring out the worst in people. Just saying.

The point of group papers is to exchange ideas and see how well you can work with others. It's kinda hard to do all that when everybody who's supposed to be there doesn't show up.

Luckily, Shelly had decided not to skip social-studies class for the fifth day in a row, so it was a chance for the three of us to finally get down to business.

The second we scooted our desks together, Chad asked, "So what are we gonna do, you guys?" which surprised me because he was apparently finally ready to do more than just take up space and oxygen.

"Madame C.J. Walker and Oprah Winfrey," I announced with great pride. I thought it was an excellent choice, and practically a no-brainer, but Shelly shot me down right away. Since becoming a part of Team Deanna she had finally found her voice, and was more vocal and opinionated than I had ever known her to be.

"Madame C.J. Walker is so three hundred years ago," Shelly told me. "How about Janet Jackson and Rihanna?"

"At least one of them has to be a *historical* figure," I said as patiently as possible. "And last time I checked, Janet and RiRi are both very much alive."

"Shelly's right," Chad piped up. "Oscar Micheaux was the very first black filmmaker, so I think doing the paper on him and Tyler Perry would be a better choice, because with all due respect, Madame C.J. Walker didn't invent the hot comb, she just introduced it to black women."

"Which is something I'm sure your girlfriend really appreciates, especially with all of that weave in her head," I quipped. Yeah, it was kind of mean, because I'm not 100 percent sure if Aubrey wears a weave or not, but I just couldn't resist taking a shot at her.

"Aubrey's hair is all natural, and she's not my girlfriend anymore," Chad replied casually.

Oh, so she was the problem!

"Sorry to hear that," Shelly said super-sarcastically, but Chad didn't seem to care.

"Anyway," I said, determined to keep us all on track. "Whether Madame C.J. Walker actually invented the hot comb or not is a moot point. It doesn't take away from the fact that she was a self-made woman who inspired countless other women, just like Oprah, not to mention she was this country's first black millionaire."

Chad gave me a slow, sarcastic hand clap. "Bravo for doing your homework, but I don't think you can argue that Tyler and Oscar are just more interesting."

"I most certainly can, but since I'm a huge movie buff, and enjoy the challenge of learning something new, I say let's go with your idea," I conceded.

"And I second that motion!" Shelly said.

With that finally out of the way, Chad, Shelly and I had just begun discussing the pros and cons of our topic when Aubrey walked into the classroom. She whispered something to Mr. Baisden, who then signaled Chad to the front of the room. When Chad followed Aubrey out into the hallway, I looked at Shelly and said, "Just what we need right now…more distractions, and more drama."

"You got that right," Shelly said, shaking her head. "Aubrey Garrett is nothing *but* drama!"

AUBREY GARRETT

The day after my argument with Chad, I arrived at school low on energy. I'd tossed and turned in bed all night, and couldn't get to sleep because I was so upset. It was senior year, and I was supposed to be having the time of my life, but my dream year was slowly but surely turning into a nightmare. My dad was being a jerk and my boyfriend wouldn't talk to me, despite the fact that I'd blown his cell phone up with dozens of calls and texts.

My fourth-period class was right across the hall from Chad's, and since I hadn't seen him all day I decided to take a chance and ask Mr. Baisden if I could talk to Chad for a minute. When I walked into the room, I noticed that Chad didn't look happy to see me; in fact, he looked annoyed. And I was annoyed by the fact that he was sitting so close to Deanna Parker. The two of them were smiling, laughing and looking so chummy, it almost made me lose my lunch.

"Hey, what's up?" Chad asked, once we were out in the hallway.

"You tell me, because that's exactly what I've been trying to figure out for the last twenty-four hours," I said. "And if you're still mad because of that campaign video, you're taking it way too far."

Chad sighed and rubbed the top of his head. "Do we really have to do this right now?"

"Yes, right now. Because I need to know exactly where we stand as far as prom is concerned, and most importantly, where does our relationship stand?"

"Okay, where we stand is that it's not just about that video, it's about *you*. I'm highly stressed right now, and instead of comfort and support, all you can manage to bring to the table is your never-ending, high-maintenance diva antics. It's exhausting, man, and I just need a break…for real!"

"We were just talking marriage a few days ago, and now you want a break? Get it together, Chad, because I'm sick of being on this roller-coaster ride where one day you know what you want, and the next day you don't."

"You know, Aubrey, it must be nice living in that bubble where everything revolves around you," he said nastily. "You talk a lot about yourself, but you rarely ask questions about others. If you did, you would know that I got rejected from my top three colleges because my entrance exam scores were too low, and the way things are looking, I'll be lucky to get accepted into a junior college way off somewhere in Timbuktu."

I knew he was bummed about not getting a basketball

scholarship to Georgetown University, but I had no idea that Michigan State and Kansas University had rejected him, too.

"I'm sorry if that went over my head, but I have a lot of things going on, too," I said.

"Yeah, I know, like running for prom queen," Chad said, again with that same nasty tone.

That was it for me. If he couldn't be civil to me when I had come in peace, then I was no longer interested in trying to save a relationship that was apparently already dead, as far as he was concerned.

"You know what, I get it," I told Chad. "It was nice knowing you…peace out!"

"Yeah, you, too," he said, chucking me the deuces before heading back into his classroom.

I needed confirmation on where we stood, and I'd gotten it. While standing in that empty hallway trying not to cry, I had an overwhelming feeling that someone was watching me.

I looked up and there was a big five-by-five-foot poster of Deanna looking down on me. I knew it was just a poster, but it felt like Deanna herself was actually laughing at me, relishing the fact that I'd just gotten dumped by my first love only one week before prom.

I took a black marker out of my book bag and drew a squiggly mustache on her upper lip, then blacked out every other tooth so that she resembled a jack-o'-lantern. I only drew on that one poster out of anger and frustration, but by the end of the day almost all of Deanna's posters had mustaches and blacked-out teeth. It wasn't my intention, but it was kinda funny. Oh, well, chalk it up to the strength of #TeamAubrey.

NINE

DEANNA PARKER

I walked out of social studies class and saw a small cluster of kids laughing and pointing at something on the wall. When I saw that it was a poster of me with a mustache and missing teeth, it wasn't hard to figure out that the culprit was none other than Aubrey Garrett. She had stood outside the classroom arguing with Chad in the very spot where the poster hung, and it was right up her alley to do something so silly and childish.

My picture had been defaced, but it was #TeamDeanna's collective hard work gone to waste that bothered me the most. Kids had spent their own money and put a lot of time and creativity into making those posters, only to have them ruined by Aubrey and her team of mindless followers.

Kristen was livid. "We can't let them get away with this," she said when we met up in biology lab. "Payback is a must!"

"What do you have in mind?" I asked.

"I'm not sure yet, but please believe that retribution will be swift, and it will be strong!" Kristen's green eyes were bulging out of her head and shining with the mere idea of sweet revenge. I looked at her, highly concerned that she and a few others on our team were a little too invested in this race for prom queen. This wasn't politics out in the real world, but some kids were treating it as if it were life or death.

I put on my white lab coat and safety goggles and went to my station, where one of Kermit the Frog's poor little relatives awaited the autopsy I was about to perform.

I picked up my scalpel and was poised for the first incision when Michael Turner walked into the classroom all dressed up in a suit and tie. He had an acoustic guitar strapped around his body and was also carrying a single red rose. All dead giveaways that some lucky girl was about to get a prom proposal.

I liked Michael. He was a pretty cool guy who had been down with #TeamDeanna since day one. He and Kristen had been working together closely on the campaign, so I just naturally assumed that he was there for her.

"Excuse me everybody, can I have your attention, please?" Michael asked the class.

When all eyes were on him, Michael began strumming the music to Jay-Z's song "Excuse Me Miss."

And then Michael started half singing, half rapping, "Excuse me miss, what's your name? Can you come hang with me? Can I take you out to prom? 'Cause I see a lady tonight that should be hanging with Mich-ael Turn-er!"

Everyone laughed and started clapping along to the rhythmic beat, even though no one knew exactly who Michael was singing to. As he continued, Michael eventually locked eyes with me, and slowly made his way over to my station. I looked behind me to see if he could've possibly been looking at someone else, but there was nothing behind me but a large window overlooking the school parking lot.

Michael stood right in front of me strumming and singing his tall, lanky heart out, and then handed me the rose.

"Miss Deanna Parker, will you do me the honor of going to prom with me?"

A chorus of "Awws" went up around the room. I put my hands over my mouth, in complete and utter disbelief. I was in a daze for a few seconds, and didn't snap out of it until Kristen yelled out, "Say yes!"

I was speechless, so I nodded "yes," and everyone clapped while Michael hugged me.

Being invited to prom by a decent guy is the equivalent of being asked for your hand in marriage, if only for one night. I had said yes to Michael's prom proposal, but it wouldn't be 100 percent official until after Michael met my parents and received their approval. Michael arrived at my house at five that evening, and the first thing he said was, "Man, I don't think I've ever been this nervous before!"

And I was nervous for him. Michael had a reputation for being a gentleman and a scholar, but Dad was a tough nut to crack. He's not always right, but he does always speak his mind, and that alone was cause enough for worry.

Besides, my father had barely gotten used to the idea that I was going to prom with a group of friends, so there was no telling how my being coupled up with a guy within that group would sit with him.

The four of us were in the kitchen: me, Mom, Dad and Michael. Dad was the only one who wasn't already sweating bullets. He sized Michael up and then pulled a chair out for him. "Have a seat, son," he said, in a manner that was more of a command than a request.

It was an hour-long Q&A session that consisted of Dad hurling a barrage of questions at Michael like, "What do your parents do for a living?" "Are you in a gang?" "Have you ever been in trouble with the law?" "Do you have any kids?" "No kids, but are you a virgin?"

Michael squirmed ever so slightly at the virgin question. "Well…"

"Don't answer that!" Mom said, taking Michael off the hook.

Michael looked relieved, but I was beyond embarrassed. But Dad didn't stop there. *Oh, no!* He just couldn't resist going into military recruiter mode.

"Have you ever considered a career in the military?" Dad asked.

"No, sir."

"How would you like to travel the world and get thirty days paid vacation for the first year, and a free college education?"

"That sounds good, Mr. Parker, but I've already earned a scholarship to Ohio University," Michael said politely.

"That's one of the biggest party schools there is, son!" Dad shouted like a drill sergeant. "I just hope you get a diploma at the end of all that partying!"

"I'm not going for the parties, sir. I chose that university because I want to be a doctor, and they have one of the best medical programs in the country."

Good answer! I gave Michael an encouraging nod and a re-assuring smile to let him know he was doing well under the circumstances.

"I'll be honest with you, Michael," Dad said gravely. "Game recognizes game, and I don't trust you or any other boy with my daughter."

I put my head down on the table, wishing a hole would open up in the floor and swallow me whole.

"No, I completely understand, Mr. Parker," Michael said. "My father is just as protective with my sisters."

"Anything can happen in the heat of the moment, especially on prom night," Dad continued. "It's a time when everyone's hormones are raging, and girls feel more pressure to give up the keys to the kingdom."

"Well, not me," I insisted. "I'm not giving up the keys to this kingdom until my wedding night."

"That's what your sister said," Dad snapped.

I threw my head back, and sighed. Here we go...*AGAIN!*

"Can we not have this conversation in front of company?" I pleaded.

"Yes, we can," Mom said. "Michael, it was nice to meet you, and you have our permission to take Deanna to prom."

"Just don't make me come looking for you," Dad warned Michael, and then went into the living room to watch the evening news.

When the interrogation was finally over, I fully expected for Michael to rescind the invitation, but he just chuckled and said, "Wow, that was *interesting....*"

"Yeah, I know my father can be pretty intense, so thanks for being such a good sport about it."

I walked Michael outside to the souped-up muscle car he was driving, which he said belonged to his older brother.

"So I'll pick you up next Saturday at seven p.m. sharp?" he asked.

"Seven it is." I smiled, trying not to blush.

Michael was such a cutie. I could tell that he wanted to lean in for a hug, but instead, he offered me a handshake. It was a smart move on his behalf, because Dad was standing in the living-room bay window, watching our every move.

ten

sometimes there are some real gems in the friend zone. All you have to do is stop, look and pay attention.

Julian Pearson was whom I had in mind to call if things didn't work out with Chad. Julian had been crushing on me since eighth grade, so when I asked him to escort me to prom, he jumped at the chance. "Of course, I'd love to! What color suit should I wear, what kind of corsage do you want and what time should I be there to pick you up?" he asked all in one breath.

Julian was the son of one of my mother's oldest and dearest friends. Just like with Chad, our families hung out together socially, and even though we didn't go to the same schools growing up, we had attended Jack and Jill together since we were four years old.

Because we'd known each other so long, Julian and I went through an adolescent period when we both thought the other was yucky. I hated to see him coming because I thought he was a dork who made Napoleon Dynamite look cool, and he got a kick out of saying mean things like, "Aubrey Garrett looks like a mangy ferret!"

However, Julian's teasing stopped around fourteen, when I

transformed from an ugly ducking into a beautiful swan with hips and curves in all the right places. A year later, I almost didn't recognize Julian when he showed up to our poolside Fourth of July barbecue wearing only swim trunks and a smile. I'd never noticed before, but his arms, back and chest were chiseled to perfection, causing me to wonder when, and how, he had gotten so buff. The last time I remembered seeing him with his shirt off, he was about fourteen playing ball down at the country club. Julian had a skinny little bird chest back then, but things had definitely changed.

There was a mile-long list of boys I could have called to replace Chad as my prom date, but none of them had the ability to get under Chad's skin like Julian did. Julian was someone Chad couldn't stand the sight of, which is exactly why I chose him. Those two were so much alike, you'd think they would be best buddies, but they couldn't be in the same room together for more than ten minutes without getting into an altercation.

Julian was his school's version of Chad. Brookfield High played against Glendale Academy several times a year in various sports, and those were the games everyone was excited to see because Julian and Chad were each other's most formidable opponents. They were insanely competitive against each other, both admitting that they hated losing to each other more than they loved to win.

Showing up to prom with Julian on my arm was sure to make Chad insanely jealous, and would hopefully cause him to see the error of his ways. I couldn't wait!

After talking to Julian, I gave some thought to what Chad had said about me earlier in the day outside Mr. Baisden's classroom. Was I really as self-absorbed as he claimed I was? Had my parents' divorce really turned me into such a bad person that my boyfriend/best friend couldn't stand to be around me anymore? Or had I always been that way, but Chad had been too blinded by love to see it?

I've had that "mean girl" accusation hurled at me plenty of times, but it was always done by random people who didn't really know the real me. Chad was the first person I knew and loved who had ever said that directly to my face. True, I have a mean streak that you don't want to mess with, but then again, most people do. If that was what Chad really thought of me, then it must be true to some degree because that boy speaks his mind, if nothing else.

I lay there on my queen-size four-poster bed staring up at the ceiling for the longest time. The thought of being a terrible person sank me so low, I felt that I needed to do something to redeem myself. I pulled an invitation out of my purse and read the details.

You Are Cordially Invited

Please join me as I celebrate my nomination for prom queen
on Friday, May 18th
The Home of
Judy Reeves
1783 Werner Road
Dallas, TX
7:00 p.m.–11:00 p.m.
Be there, or be square! :)

DEANNA PARKER

That week at school had been so wild and crazy, I don't think I'd ever been happier to see the weekend roll around.

Prom was one week away, and a party was exactly what I needed to unwind. For the last two days, Judy Reeves had gone around school passing out fancy invitations along with Number 2 pencils that were engraved with "Vote for Judy Reeves for Prom Queen!"

The party was the talk of the school, but I can't say that people were talking about it in a good way. Not that it mattered. Regardless of who else would or would not be there, I had promised Judy I would show up, so that was that. Done deal.

Not long after Michael left, I took a quick shower and changed into my favorite maxi dress and a pair of thong sandals. I took the time to curl my hair, which I rarely do, and even threw on a little makeup.

Judy lived in a modest house on a dead-end street not far from Brookfield High. Trish, April and I got to the Reeves' around 8:00 p.m., and were immediately a little creeped out.

For starters, a black funeral hearse was the only vehicle parked in the driveway, and there was no indication at all that there was a party going on. There were no decorations, no loud music thumping from inside and no people milling around out front. It was literally like a ghost town.

"Are you sure this is the right house?" I asked Trish as she parked her mother's Kia truck and turned off the ignition.

Trish pulled out her invitation and double-checked the address. "1783 Werner Road… Yep, this is it."

"I hope this doesn't turn out to be a waste of makeup and a nice outfit," April said, sounding a little miffed.

My heart sank for Judy. The fact that no one else was there an hour after the party started was not good. But since we were there, I decided to make the best of it. "Well, it's still early," I said cheerfully. "Come on, you guys, let's go turn it up!"

AUBREY GARRETT

I make it a point to arrive to parties fashionably late, because usually, things don't get crunk until it's close to closing
time, anyway.

It was a little after 9:00 p.m. when I arrived at Judy's house.
There were a couple of cars in the driveway, so I parked my
Jeep on the street and teetered up to the house in my four-
inch pumps. I was concentrating on trying not to fall, because
the driveway was on such a steep slope that it was almost like
climbing a mountain.

I rang the doorbell and waited a couple of minutes. When
no one came to the door, which I thought was odd for someone having a party, I eased the door open and let myself in.

"Hello?" I called out, but I didn't see anyone except an
old lady who had apparently fallen asleep on the couch while
watching an old episode of *Seinfeld*.

I heard music and voices coming from the basement, so I
followed my ears and walked downstairs into a nightmare.

Deanna Parker and a handful of other kids were looking
on in horror as Judy had a full-blown meltdown.

"Two hundred invitations and less than ten people showed
up!" Judy screamed tearfully. "Face it, Mom, I'm a loser!"

"Oh, honey, don't say that!" Mrs. Reeves said, trying to
calm her down.

"It's true! And I'm so tired of trying to fit in and be accepted by kids who are only ever going to see me as the girl
who came to school smelling like cat pee! And did you know
that the truly popular girls at school only invite me to functions on occasion so that they can have someone to laugh at?
Huh? Did you?"

Judy was in such a state of hysterics I thought she might
need medical attention.

Mr. Reeves grabbed his daughter by the shoulders and shook her. "Get a hold of yourself right now, and stop it!" he said sternly.

"Yes, please stop carrying on like this. It's not eleven o'clock yet, and people are still coming...." Mrs. Reeves said, pointing me out to Judy. "See?"

Judy whirled around and chuckled when she saw me standing there.

"Were your ears burning?" she asked me. "Because I was just talking about you!"

She burst into even more tears, and then ran past me out of the room.

It was a truly sad affair. Me and the other guests stayed for about twenty minutes hoping Judy would come back downstairs, but eventually, her parents apologized and said that the party was officially over. I left there feeling so bad for Judy, and for everything I'd ever said or done to add to her misery.

One particular incident that stood out in my mind happened freshman year. I had invited Judy over to a sleepover, and just like she'd said, it was solely for the purpose of live entertainment. I didn't ostracize her or treat her badly like some of the other girls, but I didn't defend Judy or make them stop, either. Looking back on it I could clearly see that those are the games that mean girls play, so maybe I was one after all.

I didn't feel good about that revelation.

Driving home from Judy's house, I made a vow to change my attitude and my ways, effective immediately. As my science teacher Mr. Faulker always said, "Don't make excuses, make adjustments."

Fifteen minutes later I was back at home, but the house was almost unrecognizable. It had been splattered with dozens of eggs, and the bushes, trees and even the flower beds were all covered with tons of toilet paper and Silly String. It was a mess of huge proportions.

I pulled into the driveway and my headlights revealed several disguised bandits. They all flipped me the middle finger and then ran to a blue Toyota parked across the street.

One of them yelled, "Team Deanna, beyotch!" Then the driver revved the car engine and peeled off down the street.

I couldn't tell who those kids were because they were wearing yellow bandannas around their faces, and I was shocked to see they had spray-painted "#TeamDeanna" across the garage door.

Eleven

DEANNA PARKER

There are no words to explain what went down at that party. Judy was fine when my friends and I first got there. In fact, she was the poster girl for perky, but when hardly anyone else showed up after us, her spirits dampened and her mood soured. The music, snacks and refreshments were all on point, so the few of us who were there were having fun until Judy just snapped.

"Why do people hate me so much?" she screamed, and started throwing meatballs and chicken wings against the wall. Her parents came running downstairs, but even they couldn't stop her ranting and raving. It went on for about ten minutes, and was really hard to watch.

From what I gathered, Judy had fully expected for it to be considered *the* party of the year. But when only eight people bothered to come, it was obviously too much for her to take.

Resilience was one of Judy's strong points, and I left her house hoping she would bounce back from this latest episode as quickly as she normally did.

Later that night my cell phone started ringing off the hook with back-to-back calls and texts about a certain video that had gone viral within just a couple of hours after being posted.

I clicked on a link and watched eleven minutes of footage that showed a carload of kids egging and TP-ing Aubrey's house.

Aubrey lived in a five-bedroom mini-mansion in the sub-urbs. The neighborhood was exclusive to the families of law-yers, doctors and other professionals who made big money. So more than likely, things like that don't happen very often out in that neck of the woods.

Seconds after the pranksters finish the job, Aubrey's Jeep pulls up to the house and whoever's filming catches her shocked expression before they drive off.

My heart dropped down to my toes. I knew then that the crap had officially hit the fan.

It was a typical prank, but I didn't think it was funny, espe-cially since they'd tagged the house with #TeamDeanna. But even if they hadn't, I still would've known who was behind the prank because I recognized the getaway car.

"She had it coming," Kristen said, when I called her for an explanation. "And trust me, as riled up as some of those kids were, Aubrey's lucky that was all that happened last night!"

Kristen had wanted revenge against #TeamAubrey for de-stroying our campaign materials, and she had jumped in that blue Toyota of hers and gotten it. And she was unapologetic about it, too. Kristen and I talked for almost an hour, but there was no getting through to her that the mayhem she had orchestrated was wrong. After talking to her, I hung up the phone unable to believe that the nastiness had gotten to this level.

There was a certain segment of #TeamDeanna that was out of control, and Kristen was a part of it. I didn't approve, but in their eyes, this movement belonged to them just as much as it belonged to me. Maybe even more. It was much bigger than me now, and as much as I tried, I could not control the monster that I had created.

AUBREY GARRETT

I was mad, but my mother was livid. When she saw the mess that had been made out in the yard, she demanded to know who #TeamDeanna was, and what reason they had to vandalize her house.

"It's Deanna Parker and her crew," I said. "She's one of the girls I'm running against for prom queen."

"Well, this *Deanna* needs to learn that decent folks don't go around damaging other people's personal property," she said, picking up the phone and punching in a number.

"Who are you calling?"

"The police, that's who!"

Minutes later, two officers from the Dallas Police Department were knocking on our front door. The policemen watched the video on my mother's iPad. When it was over, one of them shrugged and said, "I'm sorry, ma'am, but other than filling out a report, there's not much else we can do. We can't go out and arrest anybody because we don't know their identities, and we can't make out the license plate on the car."

"In other words," the other officer added, "there's no solid proof that this 'Deanna' was even involved in this occurrence. It could have been anybody…"

I had to admit that he was right. I left Judy's house before Deanna did, so there was no way she could have beaten me home and had enough time to do that much damage before I got there. Whoever had done the deed had to have been out there for at least forty-five minutes.

"Deanna Parker was halfway across town at a party when

this all happened, so there's no way that she could have been in two places at the same time," I said.

Mom looked at me as if I had betrayed her. "Now you tell me?"

The officers filled out a police report, took a few pictures and left.

Afterward, my mother called Hector, our handyman, to come clean up the mess, and then called Principal Ellerbee at home. They talked for a few minutes, and when she hung up, she seemed satisfied that the incident would at least be taken care of on his end.

That video was the talk of the school on Monday morning. Everyone had seen it, and it seemed that they were all laughing at me, which was a feeling I wasn't used to. I had never been made the butt of a joke like that before, and it made me sympathize with Judy Reeves and kids like her even more.

First period, 8:07 a.m.

Ms. Davidson was in the process of passing out geometry quizzes when Principal Ellerbee's voice came through over the loudspeaker. "Deanna Parker and Aubrey Garrett, please report to the main office…. I repeat, Deanna Parker and Aubrey Garrett, please report to the main office!"

The entire class said "Ooohhhh!" really loud, as they always do when they assume someone is in serious trouble.

"Turn your quiz over and leave it on your desk, Aubrey," Ms. Davidson said. "You can finish when you get back."

I got up to leave the room, and on the way out, I overheard a few snickers as I closed the door behind me.

To my knowledge, I hadn't done anything wrong, but making that trip to the main office still felt like a walk of shame to me. And my classmates' assumptions that I'd done something wrong didn't make me feel any better.

Deanna was already there. She sat in one of those blue plastic chairs, nervously biting her fingernails, but she stopped when she looked up and saw me. The awkwardness between us was so thick, you probably couldn't even cut it with a chain saw. We didn't speak to each other or make eye contact, just sat and waited for a couple of minutes until Principal Ellerbee emerged from his office and waved us in.

"Miss Parker…Miss Garrett…come in and have a seat," he said, then sat on the edge of his desk and got straight to the point.

"I've been brought up to speed about the fact that there has been quite a bit of unethical behavior throughout this race for prom queen. Threats, intimidation, and defacing posters and private property are all against the very nature of what being prom queen is all about. So if these activities don't stop altogether, you both will be disqualified, and your names will be withdrawn from consideration."

"But I didn't do any of those things!" Deanna protested, looking as if she was on the verge of tears.

"I don't know who's responsible for doing what, even though I have heard rumors," he said, sternly. "Either way, you are both still guilty by association, because if it wasn't you directly, then it was certainly members of your quote-unquote 'teams' who did the dirty work. Now, this whole thing has gotten completely out of hand, so I suggest the two of you get the word out to cut the crap…or else!"

"How are we supposed to do that?" I asked. "Lots of people are claiming Team Aubrey, but I don't know exactly who they all are."

Principal Ellerbee peered at me over his glasses for a few seconds, and then said, "Okay, I'll make it easy for you." He walked over to the PA system and made yet another announcement. "Attention members of Team Aubrey and Team Deanna! Some of you have directly violated rule number 412 in the prom handbook, which clearly states that it is against campaign rules to deface, destroy or remove another candidates' campaign materials. Pranks on, or off, school property are also considered violations, and if there are any continuing infractions the offenders will be suspended for three days and barred from attending prom…"

I don't know if my ears were playing tricks on me, or if I actually heard a collective groan echo throughout the entire school.

Suspension? No prom? What a wake-up call! Stakes were higher now than they had been since this thing started. It wasn't just my butt and Deanna's on the line anymore, but a whole lot of other butts, too.

DEANNA PARKER

One thing that never fails to get me mad enough to cry is being accused of something that I personally did not do. I understood that I was considered guilty by association, but that didn't make the pill any easier to swallow. Principal Ellerbee was right to step in and try to quash the beef, but I didn't know if his threats were enough to stop the madness. So just in case the message wasn't already crystal clear, I called #TeamDeanna together after school for an emergency meeting in the multipurpose room.

"Some of you had fun sticking it to the other team, but now it's time to call a truce," I told them. "We lost focus somewhere along the way, but let's not forget the purpose of what we initially set out to do, and that's show the Brookfield elite that they aren't the only ones who deserve accolades and honors like prom queen and king."

"Yeah, yeah…we remember…" Kristen said drily. She was still salty about not being able to exact even more revenge against Aubrey and her team for destroying our posters. I had never seen Kristen so unhinged. This new attitude was so unlike her, and I couldn't wait for prom night to arrive so that everyone could calm down and get back to normal.

"We've come too far to blow this now," Michael added. "So seriously, you guys, no more pranks and other shenanigans, because it would totally defeat the purpose if Deanna gets disqualified."

Everyone promised to be on their best behavior from there on out, but I couldn't be sure. Especially knowing what some of them were capable of.

"So are we still going to prom as a group?" I asked.

"Yeah, sure…"

"Why not?"

"We've all chipped in for the party bus, so we might as well…" To close out the meeting, I led a "Team Deanna" cheer, but there wasn't nearly as much enthusiasm as there was the very first time we did it. The core of the team's spirit had been deflated, and the wind had been taken out of many of their sails.

I stayed at school a little late to work on the Tyler Perry–Oscar Micheaux paper with Chad and Shelly. I still stood by the fact that they weren't the easiest two people to work with, so progress was slow, but good. So good, that I was cautiously optimistic that we would at least wind up with a B-plus. Not the best grade, but certainly not the worst, considering who I was working with.

When I finally made it home that evening, I walked into the living room and found my parents huddled together on the sofa.

Mom was crying her eyes out, and Dad had his arm around her, trying to comfort her. My first thought was that Grandpa Parker had suffered another heart attack, only fatal this time. I dropped my book bag in the doorway and approached them cautiously. "What's wrong?" I asked, which for some reason caused my mother to start bawling even harder.

Dad handed her a couple of Kleenex and told me, "You got a letter in the mail from a college today…"

My parents don't usually open my personal mail, but they'd obviously been so anxious to hear the verdict that they just couldn't help themselves.

And, uh-oh…if Mom was crying then it couldn't be good news. My hands shook as I read the letter Dad handed me.

Dear Ms. Parker,
We have reviewed your application for admission to Princeton University, and based on your exceptionally high grade point average and outstanding scores on your college admission exams, we are pleased to offer you a full scholarship to our university starting in the fall of this year…

"I GOT IN!" I jumped so high my head almost hit the ceiling. I had been accepted to one of the top universities in the entire world.

I was so over-the-moon happy, I ran from room to room screaming like a maniac for almost five minutes. When I finally calmed down, I went back into the living room and hugged my parents. "But wait, Deanna, that's not all that came today," Mom said, handing me a stack of letters that turned out to be from the other four colleges I'd applied to: Spelman, Northwestern University, Georgia Tech and Howard University. I read the letters one by one, and found out that they had all accepted me with full scholarships.

I breathed a huge sigh of relief. All of the hard work had paid off. Now the only thing left to do was choose which school I would be attending in the fall.

"Congratulations, Deanna, we're so proud of you," Dad said with a wide smile on his face. I saw the tears glistening in his eyes, but he was too tough to let them fall. It was okay with me, though. I still got the message loud and clear.

Mom dabbed at her eyes with a tissue and blew her nose. "You did it," she whispered in my ear and held me tight. "I never doubted that you would make it, and now you're on your way."

It had been a long, hard road. We had been through a lot individually and as a family, so it was a happy moment for all of us.

twelve

AUBREY GARRETT

MY custom-made prom dress designed by none other than the great Jules Jamison finally arrived via FedEx the day before prom. Unfortunately, over half of the hand-beaded jewels that were supposed to embellish the bodice were rattling around at the bottom of the garment bag.

The box the dress had shipped in was marked "Fragile! Handle With Care!" but the package was dented and battered, indicating that it had been severely manhandled on the way from New York to Texas.

I was so shocked by the horrible condition of my dress that my knees buckled and I almost fainted.

Thankfully, my mother caught me before I hit the floor. She helped me to the sofa and started fanning me with the latest copy of *Vogue* magazine.

"Oh, noooo…" I moaned, unable to believe that anyone's luck could be this bad.

"It's okay, Aubrey, don't worry. This is a setback, but it's not a total disaster," Mom tried to assure me. "Esther Knox is a wonderful seamstress, and I'm sure she can have all those jewels sewn back onto the dress in no time."

Esther Knox had been my mother's personal tailor for years, and she was very good at making alterations, but this was a couture gown we were talking about. Could a nearsighted sixty-four-year-old woman really have my dress in good, wearable condition before Saturday afternoon? I prayed that she could. That was all I could do at that point because I didn't have a backup dress, and there was no plan B. Prom was less than twenty-four hours away. It was literally a race against the clock.

DEANNA PARKER

It seemed like months had passed since the prom queen announcements were made instead of just two weeks. But prom weekend finally arrived. That Friday during seventh period, there was an assembly held in the auditorium where the faculty and prom committee talked to everyone who'd be attending the prom about the importance of making good decisions on the big night.

"Don't drink and drive," "don't use drugs" and "abstain from sex" were the main bullet points. In other words, "Don't do anything you know in your heart is wrong, which are things that we adults probably did on our own prom nights."

They also talked to us about the behaviors that were expected, and the ones that would not be tolerated. There was to be: no twerking, no gyrating on anyone else's body parts and absolutely no spiking the punch. "Offenders will be tossed out immediately, no questions asked!"

The next morning, I woke up bright and early, anxious to get started on the full day of beauty my Mom had scheduled for me at Empress Salon. In the span of a few hours, I hoped to go from shabby to chic with a facial, a French manicure and pedicure, hair and makeup.

It was my first time getting pampered and glammed up at a high-end Dallas salon, and I enjoyed every moment of the experience, but while sitting in the chair getting my hair curled, I came down with a serious case of pre-prom jitters. A thousand what-ifs raced through my mind all at once. What if Michael doesn't think I look pretty, and that inviting me to prom was a huge mistake? What if I, or someone else, accidentally spill punch on my dress? What if I don't have fun? What if I don't win prom queen, and end up letting my entire team down?

I took a few deep breaths and reminded myself that even if all those things happened, which was highly unlikely, I was still on my way to college, and still destined for greatness no matter what happened tonight.

"Voila!" Chauncey said after putting the finishing touches on my makeup. He spun my chair around to face the mirror, and I barely recognized the person staring back at me. The makeup was tasteful and subtle, and my shoulder-length hair had been cut in soft layers that framed my face. I was so happy with the results, I couldn't help but grin back at my reflection in the mirror. I wasn't even fully dressed yet, but I already looked and felt like a million bucks.

AUBREY GARRETT

Mrs. Esther Knox will eternally be on my Christmas card list because of the last-minute miracle she was able to perform on my prom dress. A few hours before prom, she returned the dress to me in such perfect condition, I would've thought the designer himself had done the work if I didn't know better.

With the dress issue out of the way, I now had to deal with prom-mom who was on a rampage, acting as if it were her special night instead of mine.

"Aubrey, stop all that tweeting and into the shower," she

said, snatching my cell phone right out of my hands. "Julian will be here before you know it!"

It always happened before every big event where I had to get dressed to the hilt. Mom hovers over me, instructing me on how to get dressed as if I had no clue what to do without her. And I should have known that prom night wouldn't be any different. We have a small salon area set up in the lower level of our house, so thankfully, I didn't have to go out to a crowded beauty salon and wait in line to get my hair and makeup done. My mother called her trusty glam squad over to help me get ready, but we butted heads on everything from how they should do my hair to what shades of lip gloss and eye shadow to use.

After months of worry and anticipation followed by a major mishap, it was finally time to wear my custom-made creation.

"You're not my little girl anymore, fooling around in my closet," Mom said, as she helped me slip my dress on over my head. "I'm so proud of the woman you're blossoming into."

"Well, I have you to thank for that, because you've been such a great role model," I told her, which seemed to make her happy.

Once I had the dress on, I twirled in the full-length mirror attached to my closet door, feeling like Cinderella on her way to the ball. The dress had turned out to be all that I had hoped it would be, and everything in between.

"Oh, my God, I've never seen you look more gorgeous!" my mother said, wiping tears away.

"Mom, why you crying?" I asked, hoping I wouldn't start crying myself and ruin my makeup.

"Because next you'll be graduating from high school, going off to college, and then getting married and having a family of your own…" Before I knew it, Mom dissolved into a tearful sobbing mess in front of my eyes. I hugged my mother close to me, not even caring if her tears stained my dress.

"Chad is out of the picture, so the marriage thing isn't happening for at least another ten to fifteen years," I assured her.

"And speaking of Chad…" She dabbed at her eyes with a tissue and blew her nose. "It's probably going to be hard for you to see him tonight, but put him out of your mind and just concentrate on enjoying yourself. He made his choice and is now what?"

"Null and void!" I said, using one of her favorite catch-phrases.

Mom gave me a fist bump. "You got that exactly right!" she said, beaming with pride.

I thought putting Chad out of my mind was going to be impossible, and then Julian arrived to pick me up in his father's silver Mercedes-Benz, looking like my knight in shining armor.

His tuxedo was black, and his shirt and the tiny flower in his breast pocket were the same shades of yellow as my dress. It was the exact same ensemble Chad would have worn if we'd gone to prom together, only Julian looked like an elegant gentleman in his, instead of an overgrown boy playing dress-up, like Chad.

A wide smile bloomed on Julian's face when he saw me all glammed up and ready to go. "You look like an angel transported straight from heaven," he told me. "And I'm so honored to have the prettiest girl in the world on my arm tonight." He kissed the back of my hand ever so gently, and then slipped a yellow gardenia corsage on my wrist.

Mom took a few pictures of Julian and me, and then we were off to the pre-prom party at Mia's house. Mia lived just a few minutes away, and when we arrived at her house, all of my other friends were already there with their dates. Some of the guys were wearing top hats and tailcoats, and I wasn't the least bit surprised that all of my girls looked fabulous.

Jessica looked regal in a backless purple satin gown. Kimberly looked radiant in a strapless fuchsia dress with rhinestones across the bodice, and Mia had embraced her inner princess with a white sequined ball gown and matching tiara.

There was no need to introduce Julian to my friends, because one thing about this group is that all of our parents were friends and knew one another from the social organizations they belonged to.

We spent a good fifteen minutes telling one another how great we all looked, and then started taking pictures in every way possible: individually, in couples, just the girls, then just the guys and then one big group picture.

With the picture-taking out of the way, we helped ourselves to yummy catered hors d'oeuvres. There were all kinds of tempura, sushi, spring rolls, fruit kabobs, finger sandwiches and pastries, all of which Julian kept shoveling into his mouth at an alarming rate of speed.

I understood that he was a big boy with a huge appetite, but the way he was double-dipping everything like a caveman who didn't know how to behave in public was embarrassing.

"Maybe you should slow down on the appetizers," I said diplomatically. "The limo is on its way, and we'll be heading to dinner in about twenty minutes."

"I know," Julian said with his mouth full, "but I haven't eaten anything since breakfast, and I'm starving!"

In the limo headed to the restaurant, Julian started rubbing his eyes and loosening his tie. He looked so itchy and uncomfortable, I leaned over and whispered, "What's the matter?" in his ear.

"It's my allergies," he said, as if he were in pain. "I think I ate something that I shouldn't have…"

As a kid, I remembered that Julian had had such severe asthma that he was forced to carry an inhaler with him at all times, but I didn't know that he had food allergies, too.

By the time we arrived at Jasper's Steakhouse, Julian had morphed from his normal handsome self into a hideous troll. All I could think as I looked at his red, lumpy and distorted face was *EWW!*

thirteen

DEANNA PARKER

All day I had been more excited than nervous, but nervousness completely won out when Michael showed up to take me to prom. He was on time, but I was still in the process of getting dressed, which made me even more panicky. I ditched my glasses and struggled for five minutes to put my contact lenses in. Once that was done, I ran around the room tossing things into my evening bag that were essential: breath mints, lip gloss, my cell phone and the pepper spray Dad had given me to use in case Michael got too fresh.

After touching up my makeup, I sprayed on a layer of perfume and slipped on the bronze strappy heels that I'd spent hours practicing how to walk in correctly.

Gripping the wooden railway for support, I headed downstairs to make my big reveal. Mom was waiting at the bottom of the stairs with a video camera rolling, and when she saw me, she made that sharp squealing sound that people usually make when they accidentally stub their toe.

"Oh, Dee Dee, you look gorgeous!" she said excitedly, and then fluffed my hair just a bit.

I fully expected for my Dad to be in the living room coincidentally cleaning his gun collection, but Michael and Dad were sitting on the sofa talking about the NBA playoffs like two old buddies. Michael immediately stood up when I entered the room, and the big smile that emerged on his face made me feel as if I had done something right.

"Hey, Deanna," he said, his voice quivering a bit. "You look just as breathtaking as I thought you would."

Dad shot Michael a hard look that read "Back off, buddy!" Then he turned to me, looking like a proud papa. "Daughter, you look marvelous tonight… Tyra Banks, eat your heart out!"

Instead of a corsage, Michael presented me with a bouquet of assorted flowers, which I thought was a nice touch since I'm not a big fan of corsages, anyway.

"What time should I have Deanna back home?" Michael asked my parents politely.

Mom smiled at his thoughtfulness, but Dad barked, "Have her home at midnight, and not a minute after!"

"Don't mind him," Mom interjected. "Two a.m. is reasonable, and if you need to stay out later, just call us and let us know."

Dad snarled and grunted to himself, but to my surprise and relief, he didn't say much else. Apparently he had come to grips with the fact that I had grown up and he couldn't shelter me forever. It was time to let me fly on my own, and trust that my prom night wouldn't turn out the same way my sister's did, simply because Erica and I were two completely different individuals.

Michael and I left my house arm in arm and walked out into a warm spring evening where the moon was already glowing in the sky. He escorted me to the sleek, black party bus that was idling in the middle of the street, and the sheer size of it was a shocker to me.

Renting a party bus had been Michael's idea, and I just assumed that he meant one of those cute little stubby buses that aren't much bigger than a van, but the actual party bus we ended up with was about seventy feet long, and was the exact same type of bus that superstars go out on tour in.

"Hello, young lady, watch your step," the bus driver said as Michael helped me climb onboard.

My mouth fell open when I saw that the inside looked like a nightclub on wheels with twirling neon lights, a large sitting area and the requisite stripper pole just in case you were into that sort of thing. There was a restroom onboard, a master bedroom with a humongous flat-screen television, and a refrigerator stocked with an assortment of nonalcoholic beverages like bottled water, Red Bull, juice and soda.

"Now this is what I call a party bus!" I said, giving Michael a fist bump.

"I'm glad you like it!" He grinned, looking pleased with himself.

I was thoroughly impressed and felt like a real VIP, even though the bus wasn't just for the two of us.

Since it would take too much time to make the numerous different stops to pick kids up from their respective homes, the plan was for us all to meet up at Pappadeaux Seafood Kitchen where we'd have dinner, and then all head to prom on the party bus from there.

On the way to the restaurant, Michael popped open a bottle of cold sparkling apple cider. He filled a red plastic cup with bubbly and handed it to me, and then filled one for himself.

Michael raised his cup for a toast. "To the best night of our lives!"

I tapped my cup against his. "Cheers!"

Prom was held at the exclusive Royal Crest Country Club. People arrived by every mode of transportation imaginable:

limousines, tricked-out SUVs, souped-up sports cars, tractor-trailer cabs, pickup trucks, old schools and even motorcycles.

Maybe I'm biased, but I think #TeamDeanna had the best prom entrance of the night. There were about forty of us in total, and we arrived to prom like true rock stars. Everyone outside the venue paused and stared at the colossal black bus with party lights across the top; the looks on their faces as we filed off the bus were priceless. People did double- and triple-takes, because as a whole; the so-called nerds, dorks, band geeks, slackers, freaks, loners, losers, outcasts, burnouts and theater geeks had all cleaned up extremely well, and we looked *good!*

I had already gotten tons of comments on my dress, and Kristen, April and Trish were all wearing different colors and variations of the same frilly party dress with a thigh-high split, which I thought was really cute.

"We look so hot, it should be illegal," I said to my girls as we strutted our stuff down the red carpet.

"I know, right?" April giggled, and we started clowning around, taking pictures of one another with our camera phones.

Inside, the prom committee had done an awesome job on the decorations.

The theme for the prom was "An Evening in Paradise" and the colors were red, black and silver. Balloons floated underfoot, and the ballroom was showered in pink mood lighting, which made it look like an enchanted Mediterranean paradise.

Ms. Franklin, the school secretary, stood behind a decorated table by the main entrance. She was all dolled up in a navy blue sequined dress, and had on more makeup than I had ever seen her wear. She greeted us with a cheerful "Welcome to prom!" and then gave us each a ballot to cast our votes for prom royalty.

I voted for Chad for prom king, but for some unknown reason, my legs felt like noodles when I checked the box next to my own name.

After casting our votes, Michael grabbed my hand and we headed straight to the dance floor.

The campaign was over, and it was out of my hands at that point. There was nothing left to do but relax, have fun and create beautiful prom memories.

fourteen

AUBREY GARRETT

I'd been looking forward to senior prom for years, and had envisioned that my night would be this storybook-perfect fairy-tale event, but that vision had evaporated and turned to dust by the time our stretch Hummer limousine finally made it to the Royal Crest Country Club.

Julian's food allergies had caused his lips, tongue and head to swell to twice their normal size, and he had knots on his face the size of golf balls.

"Are you sure you don't want to go get some medical attention?" I practically pleaded with Julian.

He smiled as best as he could, and said, "No, I should be okay in about an hour. I've waited so long for a date with you, nothing is going to ruin this night for me, not even allergies."

I rolled my eyes and sighed. Great. It was just my luck that my perfect dream date and potential boyfriend looked like an alien. I shuddered just thinking about what our prom pictures were going to look like.

The atmosphere was festive from the minute we walked in the door. I was anxious to get the party started, as we all were, but the first order of business was to cast our votes for prom royalty.

While waiting in line to receive my ballot, I checked out

what some of the other girls were wearing. I counted at least ten girls who were wearing the same strapless fuchsia dress with rhinestones across the bodice. In fact, it was the same dress that Kimberly was wearing, which made me feel so bad for my friend, but that's the chance you take when you buy a dress off the rack.

Other looks ranged from Hollywood glamour to hood-rat chic. The hood-rat chic category consisted of dresses that were too short, too tight, too tacky, too revealing or a combination of all the above. Several girls were riding that fine line between sexy and trashy, wearing risqué dresses that showed all their assets.

The girl standing in line in front of me was on point, though. I admired her black mermaid-style dress so much that I tapped her on the shoulder and said, "I love your dress!"

When the girl turned around, I saw that it was Judy Reeves, minus the dental braces and the acne.

"Thanks, Aubrey," she said with a wink. "You don't look so bad yourself!"

I'd only seen Judy once or twice from a distance since that disastrous meltdown she'd had at her own party, but tonight she looked so amazing I almost thought that it was a completely different person. Judy's hairstyle was trendy, her makeup was flawless and that dress she was wearing showed that Jessica Rabbit didn't have a thing on her.

"Wait, let me get a picture of two of the prom-queen nominees," Mia said, and snapped a picture as Judy and I stood side by side holding our voting ballots. Standing there with pen in hand, I couldn't help but notice that Judy had checked the box next to my name and even circled "Aubrey Garrett" for emphasis.

"You're voting for me?" I asked, incredulous.

"Sure, why not?" Judy said happily. "Maybe it's just me, but I think it's bad sportsmanship to vote for yourself."

That was news to me, because that was exactly what I had done. Manny Gomez got my vote for prom king instead of Chad, but I had definitely voted for myself.

I gave Judy a warm smile and said, "Thank you," thinking that she really wasn't so bad after all.

My plan was to stash Julian away at a table and leave him there until his face returned to normal, but he wasn't having it. That boy stuck to me like Velcro and barely let me out of his sight. I went out on the dance floor to party with my friends, and Julian was right there. I went to the restroom to make sure my hair and makeup were still intact, and when I came out Julian was right outside the door waiting for me.

Chad and I were at the same place at the same time, so it was inevitable that we would run into each other, and of course, Julian was right by my side when we did.

"What's good, Elephant Man?" Chad asked Julian with a laugh.

"Not much, just chilling with your ex-girlfriend and showing her the best time she's had in years," Julian replied, cool as a cucumber, and looking just as lumpy as one, too.

Julian showing me the best time I've had in years was far from the truth, but I kept my mouth shut because Chad didn't need to know otherwise.

I hated to admit it, but Chad looked rather spiffy in his charcoal-gray suit and black dress shirt.

It was a completely different tux from the one we had picked out for him to wear a few months ago, which was a good thing, because otherwise he and Julian would have looked like twins.

"So are you here by yourself, or did you bring a date?" I asked Chad.

"Me and a couple of the guys are hanging out, but I see you didn't waste any time replacing me with this knockoff scrub," Chad said, referring to Julian.

"Hey, I'm nobody's scrub," Julian said, getting in Chad's face. "And it's not my fault that you were too stupid to recognize what a good girl you had."

Chad's jaw clenched the way it does when he's ticked off. I stepped between the two of them because they had a history of getting into scuffles that quickly escalated to the point of trying to literally take each other's heads off.

While I stood there like a referee trying to diffuse the situation, Principal Ellerbee walked onto the stage at the front of the room with a microphone in his hand.

"All right everybody, the votes are in, and it's time for the coronation of the prom royalty. Will the nominees for king and queen please come to the stage?"

I breathed a sigh of relief and pushed Chad away from Julian, and toward the stage. It was finally time to find out if I would be presented with the crown that I had been clawing, scratching and fighting so hard for, for so long.

DEANNA PARKER

Judy Reeves had a certain glow about her that I've never seen before. Who knew that she actually had a killer body under all those grandma clothes she usually wore? I sure didn't. Seeing Judy on a day-to-day basis, you'd just assume it would take one heckuva fairy godmother to make her look special, but I was blown away by her transformation.

I couldn't put my finger on it, but there was something different about Aubrey, too. Ever since the day we'd been forced to call a truce in the principal's office, she had seemed like a changed person. Her aura was different, and she appeared to be kinder, gentler and a lot less bitchy.

But what let me really know that things weren't the same with Aubrey was when I walked up on stage and as soon as I got up there, she looked me over from head to toe and said, "My, don't you look fabulous tonight!" The compliment stunned me so much, all I could do was mutter, "Likewise…"

It was a weird moment, only because I never imagined that Aubrey and I could ever be so cordial to each other, and when she grabbed my hand as the principal prepared to announce the winners, I wondered who this person really was, and what she had done with the old Aubrey Garrett.

Fifteen

AUBREY GARRETT

The night had reached its most climactic moment.

I stood between Deanna and Judy and grabbed each of their hands, because their nervousness was making me nervous, and suddenly I was the most anxious I'd ever been in my entire life.

"The race for prom queen was the closest it has ever been in Brookfield school history," Principal Ellerbee said. "In fact it was so close that the winner won by one single vote..."

Everyone gasped in unison, and then the room got so quiet, I was sure that everyone could hear my heartbeat thumping in my chest.

"And this year's prom queen is none other than...AUBREY GARRETT!"

Glitter confetti fell down around us like snow, and my supporters went completely wild. They were all on their feet, jumping up and down like maniacs. I was happy that my team was so thrilled that we had won, but personally I was just relieved that it was all over.

Victory was mine, but it wasn't nearly as sweet as I'd thought it would be.

Up until the second my name was called, I had imagined that I would be overwhelmed with a sense of complete, unbridled joy. But when it actually happened, shame was the only emotion I felt.

During the campaign period, I exhibited some rather unladylike behavior, and had sunk to a level that I wasn't proud of. I had done some sneaky, backhanded things to win a crown that probably wasn't worth much more than a measly hundred bucks or so. Chad won prom king, so he was the one whose duty it was to coronate me with a huge glittery tiara, a scepter and a satin sash that said PROM QUEEN.

"Congratulations," Chad said, kissing me ever-so-sweetly on the cheek. It would have been a very special moment if everything had gone the way I'd planned it, but things had gone so far left, it was hard to stand there pretending that they were right. Chad's kiss had been just for show, and his congratulations seemed hollow and insincere.

Deanna was gracious enough to clap for me, and looked as though she was taking it all in stride, but one look at Judy's face and I could tell that she was devastated. Her nomination may have been a joke to some, but the possibility of being crowned prom queen had meant the world to her. It was a chance for her to finally be "seen" by the kids who never took the time to notice her before, unless they were making her the butt of some mean-spirited prank or joke.

All Judy wanted was to be accepted, admired and deemed worthy of friendship. She had come alive during the campaign. The nomination had given her hope, and she took the opportunity and seized it with both hands.

"Well, Aubrey, what do you have to say?" Principal Ellerbee asked, shoving the microphone in front of me. I tried to look out over the crowd, but the overhead lights were shining so brightly, all I could see were shadows.

"Thanks to everyone who voted for me, and even those

who didn't because this whole process has been a huge learning experience for me," I said. "I won by a single vote, but what you all don't know is that more than likely, it was Judy's vote for me that tipped the scale in my favor. You know, Judy really is a terrific person, and she deserves this more than I do. So, without further ado, I hereby forfeit this title and bestow it to Miss Judy Reeves!"

Judy's mouth dropped open and tears gushed from her eyes as I bestowed her with the sash, scepter and crown.

#TeamAubrey wasn't entirely happy with my decision. People started yelling out things like "WHAT?!" "No way!" and "This is a joke, right?"

A low chorus of boos started somewhere in the room, but someone in another section of the room started the slow clap, which eventually picked up speed. It was hard to tell if the applause was genuine or sarcastic, but it didn't matter to me. I had done the right thing at the right moment, and that was all that mattered.

"At this time, I ask the king and queen to take to the dance floor for the royal dance," Principal Ellerbee said.

Judy was giddy and radiant as she and Chad danced together for the king and queen dance. For the rest of the night, random people kept coming up to me commenting on what a good deed I'd done, including Chad.

"That was a great thing you did for Judy, and I am so proud of you for that," he told me. "It looks like Aubrey Garrett is finally growing up."

I laughed. "Yeah, I guess so, huh?"

"So does that mean you have room enough in your heart to forgive me for being a jerk these last few months?" he asked, giving me flirty, puppy-dog eyes.

I sighed and thought it over for a few seconds. "Sure, Chad, I can forgive you. I won't *forget,* but we can be friends, or at least cordial whenever we see each other."

"Friends? I was hoping we could get back to being more than that," Chad said, looking as though he wanted to kiss me.

I couldn't believe what I was hearing. What nerve! I knew that Chad would want me back sooner or later, but I had no idea it would be that soon. What did he think I was, some kind of toy that he could pick up and put down whenever the mood struck him?

The old Aubrey would have gotten ignorant and indignant, but I just said, "Yes, Chad, *just friends.* We've been tied at the hip and going back and forth with these games for too long. I'm over it, and I just want to do me for a while."

"Oh, so you're picking him over me?" Chad asked, turning to look at Julian, who was watching us from a respectful distance.

"No, I'm not picking Julian over you. I'm not picking anyone. For now, I want to fly solo and see how high I can soar on my own. Not as the girlfriend of Chad Campbell, or as the daughter of Steven and Jeannette Garrett. Just Aubrey... period."

"I understand, and I respect that," Chad said thoughtfully. "But can I at least get one dance with you tonight?"

All night long the DJ had played salsa, house music, techno, hip-hop, a little bit of country and a little bit of rock-and-roll, but at that moment he slowed the tempo down with a John Legend ballad.

With Julian standing in the wings watching and scratching at the hives on his face, Chad and I danced our very last dance at Brookfield High.

★ ★ ★

One of the biggest lessons that came from my whole prom experience is that perfection doesn't exist. You can aim for it and hope for it, but in the end, things are going to turn out how they were meant to turn out, so it's best to just relax and enjoy the ride.

Prom didn't turn out to be nearly as perfect as I had planned it, but at least I had one crazy story to tell my future kids and grandkids.

sixteen

DEANNA PARKER

I was robbed! That was the first thing that came to mind after hearing that Aubrey had won prom queen. No one likes to lose, even if it is by one single vote. But I got over it fairly quickly, because I agreed with Aubrey's decision. If any one of us actually deserved to win, it was Judy.

After the nominations came out, the entire school divided into two camps. It was either #TeamAubrey or #TeamDeanna. Few people even considered joining #TeamJudy, which was unfortunate because she ran her campaign with the skill and precision of a seasoned politician, but without all the trickery and negativity.

So in the end, justice is better than injustice. At least that's what I like to think, anyway.

Another thing that made the loss easier to accept was that I went from underdog whose chances of winning were considered very slim to a true contender. I may not have won the ultimate prize, but it was still a win in my book. I had been pushed to venture outside of my comfort zone and in the process, accidentally started a movement that I hoped would continue long after I had left Brookfield High. #TeamDeanna had been heard. Our presence had been felt, and no one was going to forget anytime soon that we had managed to change the fabric of Brookfield for the better.

Prom was a blast. Michael was the perfect date, and when he brought me home from an after-party at two the next morning, I was so glad that I hadn't skipped the whole prom experience as I had originally planned.

It's funny how life works. Just a few short weeks before, I couldn't wait to get out of high school and start my life. Now that I'd become friends with some really awesome people, I wished we had more time to spend together.

Finals week came right after prom, and graduation was the following week after that. I was named valedictorian of the graduating class, which was the ultimate consolation prize for me.

My speech as valedictorian was about resilience and inner toughness. The last paragraph was:

"As we stand here today on the cusp of adulthood, and at the threshold of our respective dates with destiny, my wish is that we all take with us the simple truth that we are all more alike than we are unalike. And whatever differences we may have are not so big that we can't see one another through the eyes of compassion, and not call one another any name but 'friend.' So friends, I give you all my heartfelt congratulations and wish you well as we leave Brookfield High, and venture out into this thing called life…and I challenge you all to go out and WIN!"

I ended the speech by reciting the poem "If—" by Rudyard Kipling. By the time I finished, all of my "friends" were on their feet, whooping it up as though we were at a pep rally instead of a graduation ceremony.

I took my seat on the dais along with the other distinguished guests of honor and looked out at my classmates. I hadn't grown up with any of these kids, but in that moment, I felt as if we all had known each other all of our lives.

AUBREY GARRETT

I couldn't help but be proud of Deanna in that moment. Her speech was inspiring and had me looking forward to what lay ahead of me, which was college.

I'm not an academic prodigy like Deanna, I admit that wholeheartedly, but contrary to popular belief, my mother didn't raise a dummy. Historically, my grades fluctuated between a B and C average, yet they were still good enough to get me into Rutgers University in New Jersey. Since fashion was in my blood, I planned to follow in Mom's footsteps and become the head buyer for a major department store such as Saks or Macy's.

I didn't get in Rutgers on a full scholarship or anything grand like that, but my parents were just so happy that I'd gotten accepted at a decent school that they didn't mind paying for my college education out of their own pockets. At least that's what they said at the time. Of course as the new and improved Aubrey Garrett, I'll get a job or two to help out with the cost.

I'd heard through the grapevine that Deanna had been accepted to Princeton, which is also in New Jersey, and just 20 miles from the campus I'll be attending. Who knows, maybe one of these days we'll run into each other at some bookstore or coffee shop off campus, and laugh about the time we ran against each other for prom queen. I'd like that. And I'd like it even more if we kept in touch and finally became the great friends I know we are capable of being.

★ ★ ★

When it comes to finishing high school, you get to take a few things with you, such as your yearbook, class ring, commencement cap and gown, and things like that, but most important of all are your memories.

Senior year will always have a special place in my heart, because I ended up growing in leaps and bounds at a point where I thought I already knew everything. The life lessons came fast and furious, but at the end of it all, I had a better understanding of what truly matters in life, and what never did.

★ ★ ★ ★ ★